Chapter 1 The Lady Whose Bag Has Been Robbed

Peter Wang felt sad and dejected as he walked out of the Human Resources office.

He found it so difficult to accept the result.? From where he came from, he was feared by all the gangs. They even called him "Mighty Soldier King". Here in the city, he couldn't even find a decent job because he lacked a college degree. Suddenly, his phone rang. Peter noticed and picked it up immediately.

"Peter, " said the voice from the other line. It was his girlfriend.? "It's over. I'm breaking up with you." "You've been gone for so long. I need a boyfriend, not a phone pal."

"Darling, pleaseâ€"" Peter tried to get her back. "I know I've been gone, but I'm back now. I'll always be with you now."

"Oh yeah? Well, what can you give me?" "A dishwasher working abroad earns much more money than you." "What exactly can you give me, huh?" she challenged, "Do you even have savings after working all these years? Have you found a single stable job since you got back? Will you be able to give me the things I want?"

"I can, I promise! I'll buy you the biggest house you will ever want! Darling, I'm really sorry I've been gone. I'm sorry that we're struggling. I'm having a hard time finding a job in the city, but it will be better soon, I promise. Things will get better, and when they doâ€""

"And how would you do that?", the girl interrupted. "How are things going to get better, Peter? Will you ever get to buy me a BMW car? Will you ever get to buy me a Louis Vuitton handbag? Ferragamo shoes? Chanel suits? Ha! You can't even afford to buy me a-hundred-square-meter house, for Christ's sake."

Peter was silent.

She sighed. "You don't need to say anything, Peter. I'm tired. I can't deal with this anymore. Goodbye, Peter, " she said as she hung up.

Peter held his hand-phone tightly, dumbfounded. Despite her muffled voice from the static of his old Nokia, her message was clear as day.

"AHHHH! Help! Somebody, help! Thief, thief! That thief stole my bag!" Peter heard someone scream from the other end of the street.

A lady in uniform was screaming in panic and desperation, running as fast as her high-heeled shoes would take her.

A man with dark sunglasses holding a Louis Vuitton handbag was fleeing from the scene towards a motorcycle.

"Go away! Right now!" He shouted to the onlookers as he jumped onto his vehicle.

As soon as he did, he crunched his brow, turned the handles and accelerated.

In shock, every person on the sidewalk squeezed themselves up to the wall as the motorcycle zoomed past them. Nobody dared block its way.

It's risky to be involved in robberies nowadays. Nobody wants to get hurt.

The lady in a suit watched the motorcycle drive away, helplessly.

The sight infuriated Peter.

As the motorcycle approached, he planted his feet firmly on the ground, pulled his left leg back, and with all his might, flung it into the raging vehicle in a strong forceful kick as soon as it passed in front of him.

The kick took the man by surprise. He couldn't believe what happened! His motorcycle tumbled sharply and it went spinning on the pavement. The impact threw him to the further end of the road and forced him to drop the stolen bag to the ground.

"Ahhhhh!"

The pedestrians held their hands to their mouths as they screamed.

Peter, indifferent to the commotion, walked to the side of the man, calmly picked up the bag, and handed it to the lady. "Here's your bag, ma'am."

"Th-thank you." The lady managed to say when she realized that he was talking to her. She was still stunned from the events that just happened.

Peter inspected the lady for half a second before diverting his gaze.

"Not at all, it's my pleasure."

Peter turned to leave.

The lady looked like a corporate professional. He imagined her in her air-conditioned office and exquisite jewelry.

'We come from two different worlds, ' he thought. 'It's useless to think about her.'

"Wait a second!" Peter felt a hand grasp his elbow from behind. "I'm Elaine Dai. What's your name? Iâ€¦ just want to thank you for your help, " she continued. "Can we have lunch together?"

She looked at him as she awaited his response.

Peter is at his mid-20's, standing 180 cm tall. His face has well-defined angles on his forehead, cheeks, and jawline. He's not the type that you

would notice in a crowd, but he's not bad-looking
either.

"You're welcome, really. It's no trouble at all. You
don't need to take me out for lunch. Thanks for the
offer, though. I have to go." Peter pulled his hand
away gently as he refused her invitation.

He was still thinking about his very recent breakup.
Less than an hour ago, the love of his life walked
away from him. Apart from that, he's broke and
unemployed. It was such a bad time to accept a lunch
invite.

Elaine stood perplexed at his immediate refusal.

For most people, Elaine is a sight to behold. She
had light skin and brown hair that emphasized her
bright almond eyes. She had men falling at her feet
and any of them would have accepted her lunch invite
in a heartbeat.

But Peter, he just refused her without hesitation.
'Have I lost my charm?' she thought sadly. 'He
didn't even tell me his name, ' she realized.

Peter was about to walk away when he heard a voice
from behind him.

"Stop!" It was the man from the motorcycle! He
pushed himself up and turned to Peter, holding a
sharp, silver blade.

He didn't have serious injuries despite his fall.
Like a rabid beast, he shot Peter a deadly stare.

'This should have been an easy robbery if he didn't
get in the way, ' the man thought. 'It's time to
give him a lesson.'

"Are you talking to me?" Peter turned to the man,
unthreatened.

Peter hesitated because the man was badly injured. He stood in disbelief at the challenge thrown at him.

"What are you planning to do?" asked Peter "STOP!" Elaine cried. "STOP OR I'LL CALL THE POLICE!" Elaine rushed in front of Peter, holding up her phone.

"Call the police?" the motorcycle driver asked manically. "Fuck the police! You'll both be dead by the time they get here!" The man started running towards Elaine, the sun shining brightly against his knife. The people in the street stood frozen in the background.

Elaine turned pale. She trembled. She didn't know what to do! Growing up comfortably in the city, she thought these things could only happen in the movies!

Peter gasped. 'What the hell? This man must be crazy if he could stab someone in broad daylight! It seems he hasn't learned his lesson!'

The man was about to stab Elaine. But Peter reacted faster.

Thank you for reading. Please leave your valuable review. It will help us provide you with more interesting novels. More top billionaire romance novels await you at moboreader.net

Chapter 2 The Girl He Met In The Bar
On reflex, Peter managed to grab the attacker's weapon hand and slap him with his free hand.

The man failed to dodge, getting his face bloody and teeth knocked out.

In his rage, Peter charged and started to throw the man punch after punch until his face was red and swollen all over.

PA PA PA PA PA!

Peter punched and kicked with all his strength.

He thought about everything that happened today â€"his breakup, his failure to find a job â€"and put them all in his fists. He felt no remorse for the troublemaker.

"You're lucky this time. The next time you cause trouble again, I swear I'll kill you. Go!" Peter said, dismissing the young man.

Realizing his defeat, the man retreated holding on to his battered face. He didn't even dare grab his motorcycle as he ran away. He shot Peter a vengeful look. 'You'll pay for this, ' he thought.

Peter ignored him. If he had the balls to come take revenge, Peter would show no mercy!

Peter felt good about the skirmish. It was a much-needed release of all the tension he felt for the day. As he was about to leave, he heard Elaine falling down from behind him.

Peter quickly turned to keep her from falling.

"Are you OK?" Peter asked as he held her. He felt his heart beat faster when he felt her skin against his. Her beauty was tempting.

"My foot is sprained." Elaine replied, feeling embarrassed. Her face turned hot as she felt his touch.

In slow, careful steps, Peter held Elaine as they walked to a nearby restaurant.

Peter couldn't help but feel a little lighter with Elaine's gentle touch and sweet scent.

Meanwhile, Elaine's face grew hotter and redder with their proximity.

The people in the restaurant shot curious glances at the sight of the couple entering, especially with Elaine's uniform. Their eyes followed the new guests as they walked to find a table.

Peter helped Elaine to her seat, took his own, and breathed a big sigh of relief.

He surely enjoyed the fight, but inside, he knew that it did get a little out of hand. The adrenaline felt good, but it wasn't enough to erase the pain and frustration inside him.

"Please give me a bowl of your most expensive noodles, with additional meat." Peter said to the waiter.

HAHA.

The people around them started exchanging smirks and mocking glances.

They felt bad for Elaine thinking that her cheapskate boyfriend took her on a date to this low-end restaurant, while she was clearly a woman of class.

"Sorry I couldn't take you somewhere nicer. I've been having trouble finding a job. I'm kind of running out of money." Peter confessed, ignoring the murmurs. He really had no money and he didn't pretend to be a rich man.

"It's OK. I'll pay," Elaine said, growing more and more curious about Peter.

He could have taken advantage of her while they were walking if he wanted to. She would have been too weak to fight back. Still, he didn't. Also, he was genuine and honest about his situation.

She preferred this kind of man over rich hypocrites.

Suddenly, she had an idea.? "You mentioned you were having trouble finding a job? You're fast and strong, and our company needs a bodyguard. Why don't you try applying in our company?"

"What? Really? Sure, of course!" Peter replied excitedly.

Peter had been trying to find a job the whole week. He never knew how difficult it was to find one until he experienced it himself. He even considered taking a job in the construction site â€"moving bricks and carrying cement â€"just because it was the only job he could find where they didn't need an extensive educational background.

Naturally, it was impossible for him to not be excited about the opportunity Elaine mentioned. He would choose security work over construction, any day, except that even security guards were required to have college degrees. This immediately disqualified Peter, to his disappointment.

"Alright, then. Find me at the Personal Section of Silverland Group on the tenth floor, at ten o'clock, sharp. Tell the receptionist you have an appointment with me. I'll be the one to make arrangements. Don't be late."

Elaine was afraid he would refuse her again the way he did when she invited him to get dinner. Now that he agreed, Elaine made sure he wouldn't back out.

"Okay, I won't. Thank you! Thank you so much!" Peter became even more excited as the idea sunk in. He knew that this was a really great opportunity.

Although Peter has only been back to A city for a week, he has already heard of the reputation of Silverland Group.

They were one the of ten biggest companies and best employers in the city; even security guards were well-paid.

It was difficult to land a security job, though. Apart from having a college degree, a recommendation from company management was a requirement. It would be a true honor to be part of Silverland Group's security roster.

They exchanged contact information after the meal before going their separate ways. ?"Don't be late, okay?", Elaine reminded. ?"I won't!" he promised.

Peter looked for a place to celebrate the highlight of his job hunt.

He decided to go to a bar called Sunny. Guests flowed in as the crowd of young people danced to the heavy metal music in the background.

The women in the bar wore clothes that revealed long legs, ample bosoms, sexy backs, and shapely bodies. The air was steamy, in more ways than one.

College students and corporate employees frequented the place.

The carefree youngsters, sophisticated professionals, and enchanting women made Sunny a great go-to whether you're looking for a place to chill, or to let loose.

Beer in hand, Peter watched the attractive girls on the dance floor, from a seat at the corner. He felt good. This was the first time he got to relax since he arrived at the city.

"Hey, is this seat taken?" He heard a cool voice ask. ??Turning to ask the speaker to find a seat somewhere else, he froze as he found an exceptionally beautiful girl looking back at him.

She's probably around twenty-three or twenty-four. She didn't look like she was wearing makeup, but she still looked extremely beautiful with her clean, sharp eyebrows, full lips and pretty nose.

Her black mesh dress was modest, compared to all the other girls in the bar.

It didn't show much skin, but it didn't fail to show off her perfect figure, Small waist, and long legs, either.

Elaine, to Peter, was a goddess. While her beauty was definitely breathtaking, it would still be possible to get her attention with enough effort. This girl, though, was a fairy: completely and surely unattainable.

It made him wonder what she's doing in this stuffy bar.

Without waiting for him to respond, the girl took the empty seat from across the table, grabbed the nearest beer, and began to drink. She paid no notice of Peter's shock.

He found it difficult to reconcile the sight of the drunkard in front of him, with the dainty fairy he imagined her to be.

Also, the price of the beer was thirty-eight dollars!

He felt extremely distressed.

One bottle...

Two bottles...

Three bottles...

Four bottles... 'When is this girl gonna stop?!'

As if on cue, the girl carelessly put down her last bottle of beer, dropped her head on her arms, rested them on the table, and began to cry. Peter sat, dumbstruck.

Chapter 3 The Girl With An Angelic Body, But An Evil
Heart
"What the fuck!"

Peter rarely cussed, but at this moment, he couldn't
help himself.

"Hey, hey, hey. Listen to me, lady. If you're gonna
cry, take it somewhere else. People here are gonna
think I did something to you!"

He could already feel the suspicious glances of the
people around them.

A girl this beautiful would easily be targeted by
douchebags who wanted to score, as soon as she
entered the bar.

Peter groaned.

"Shut up! I'm going to cry as much as I want, you
stinky men. You're all BASTARDS! Good-for-nothing
assholes!"

Hysterically, the girl stood, grabbed Peter's
shoulders and started trying to tear at his clothes,
beating his chest, shouting and crying.

Peter felt even more embarrassed with the scene the
girl was causing. And yet, he couldn't simply shove
her away as that would even make him look worse! He
felt so helpless to do anything.

If only there was an easy, decent way to just knock
her unconscious.

"Hey, STOP! You're right. All men are bad. We're all JERKS. Now, can you stop crying? Calm down. Sit, let's drink and talk about it. Maybe I can help you, "

Peter managed to say despite the annoyance he felt. 'This girl is nut. What did I ever do to her?' he thought.

"NO!" she said in defiance. "You're just like all of them! You're all assholes!" She screamed as she started to pull at his clothes more intensely; she almost tore off his jacket.

Peter was at a loss on what to do. In his attempt to scout for someone who could help, He caught sight of a bare-armed burly man covered in tattoos, followed by a band of equally-fearsome hooligans with dyed hair. It was clear that they were gangsters.

Their posture showed no fear. Clearly, they had established their dominance in this part of town.

"Hey, asshole. Get your hands off my sister! You dare touch her, huh? You DARE TOUCH HER, you son of a bitch? You're asking for DEATH!"

The bare-armed man said as he walked towards him, eyes burning with rage, fists clenched tight.

'Are you blind?!' Peter thought. 'Can't you see that your sister is the one holding me? Who the fuck is this ugly pighead? It's impossible for you and this beautiful girl to be related!'

Before Peter could say a word, the girl suddenly made a move that stunned everyone.

Abruptly, she stopped crying, grabbed hold of an empty bottle on the table, and smashed it on the bare-armed man's head.

"Sister? Who the fuck are you calling sister? I would be damned to be related to someone as ugly as you! Do you think you can just take advantage of me like that? Eat blood, motherfucker!"

She said as the bottle hit the man again. The impact was enough to cause pain, but not injury.

"You fucking bitch! How dare you hit me! You're dead meat! Skin this girl and chop this guy's balls off! You'll both be wishing you were dead once we're done with you."

The bare-armed man ordered his men while feeling at his beaten head.

"You bitch dare to insult me. You are going to DIE." In a drunken rage, the girl held the bottle in her hand tighter, ready to fight.

Peter grabbed her and pulled her behind him. He grabbed one bottle on each hand and prepared as they approached.

PLA!

With one swift movement, he smashed the bottle in his left hand against the bare-armed man's head. The bottle broke, and the man's skull along with it.

PLA!

The bottle in his right hand hit the second man squarely on the face, blood spurting everywhere. With a thud, he fell on the ground.

Without stopping, Peter lifted his leg and delivered kicks in succession, as more men approached.

CRACK, POW, PLA! One by one, six or seven men fell to the ground, screaming with pain.

A small crowd started to gather around the scene, while some people decided to quietly leave the bar in fear of getting involved and putting themselves in danger. For a while, the bar was in chaos.

"WOW! Nice shot! Punch him in the face! Beat them to death! Give these bastards what they deserve!"

The girl didn't seem at all distressed about the situation. She even seemed rather amused and greatly entertained.

"What, are you crazy?? We have to run!" Peter cried as he pulled her in, hurriedly making their way out of the bar

As the bar's security personnel were fast approaching them. Had they not made their exit, they would have been caught! Although Peter didn't care much about being involved in messy situations, he decided that it was best to avoid trouble.

"Why are we going? I haven't had enough yet! Let me go!" The girl stubbornly struggled to escape his grip.

Losing his patience, Peter grabbed the girl, covered her mouth and fled, taking advantage of the chaos. 'She is really not afraid to get herself in trouble, ' Peter thought. 'This girl is giving me a headache.'

Peter kept running until he found a corner that was not visible from the bar. His frustration crept up to him. 'Why do these things have to happen just when I'm already happy and relaxed?'

He decided that he never wanted to see this girl again, and he would do his best to make sure of that.

"Gosh, I am so tired and my feet are killing me! I haven't had that much fun in ages! ? Oh by the way, handsome. I'm Bella Song. What's your name WeChat number?" Bella asked Peter.

All she wanted that night was to drink away her sorrows. Who would have thought something as exciting as this would happen? Now she felt so much better.

Bella felt drawn to Peter because, despite his strong and masculine facade, he had a kind aura and gentle demeanor. Compared to all the other people in the bar, he looked like the most honest of them all.

She never would have expected that someone who seemed to be as good-natured as him could actually throw punches the way he did.

Peter proceeded to hail a cab at the sidewalk, ignoring Bella's question. As soon as he got one, he grabbed Bella and shoved her into the taxi. ? "Name or phone number is not necessary. I want this to be the last time I'll see you. Clear? Bye bye."

"You bastard!" Bella said before the taxi door closed in front of her. Pissed, she stopped the cab and got off, determined to give the asshole a piece of her mind. By the time she managed to climb down, though, he was already gone.

'How dare you treat me like this. You'll be sorry the next time I see you, ' Bella thought sitting angrily as her cab drove away.

Thank you for reading. Please leave your valuable review. It will help us provide you with more interesting novels. More top billionaire romance novels await you at moboreader.net

Chapter 4 You Are Not Strong Enough
Peter took a shower as soon as he got home. He had a very long and eventful day, and he immediately fell asleep as soon as he hit his pillow.

At 9:45 am the next morning, Peter arrived at Silverland Group, clean-shaven and ready for his appointment.

Greeting the beautiful receptionist and jotting his name down to log-in, he then proceeded to the Human Resources office on the 10th floor and knocked gently.

"Come in, please." Peter opened the door and walked in with the beautiful female voice.

He found Elaine on her desk, organizing a bunch of files in front of her.

The office was a little bit stuffy, so the coat she wore the day was hung at a rack beside her table. She wore a white checkered skirt with the top buttons unfastened. Peter couldn't help but noticing her well-defined cleavage that were slightly visible through her open collar.

Peter found his heart beating faster again, so he quickly decided to look away, diverting his gaze to the nameplate on her table:

"Elaine Dai, President for Human Resource"

Peter was surprised. He didn't expect Elaine to hold such a high position.

She was not just an ordinary working professional, she was one of the top dogs in this multi-million dollar company! Surely she was earning a lot of money! Peter assumed that she was an entry-level HR staff, at best.

"I'm so glad to see you here, Peter, " She said smiling as she finished, setting aside the folders in front of her. She stood and handed him a set of cleanly bound documents. "I've arranged it for you. Fill the application forms up and then I'll walk you to the Security Department."

Peter thanked her and started writing down his details. When he finished, Elaine personally escorted him to the Security office.

Peter could see the other employees exchange jealous and curious glances at the sight of their beautiful HR president personally escorting a new applicant.

Elaine was known to be one of the most beautiful employees in the company. She always looked approachable, but it wasn't easy to get close to her.

It was known that several CEOs from other companies were refused when they tried to ask her out.

Outside of her professional duties, this was the first time they saw her pay much attention to a guy.

'This guy must be really special, ' the employees thought.

The security office staff did not do a very good job hiding their surprise when Elaine walked into their office accompanying a new applicant. To them, Elaine was a goddess: impossible to get close to. They barely even see her around.

She introduced Peter and left, turning him over to their care.

Soon later, Peter received the news that he was accepted into the company as a security guard. His area of assignment: the reception hall.

For this, he would be working with Jack, his senior.

Jack was about 30 years old, his face aged with experience.

"Hey, buddy, I heard Miss Dai took you here in person. You must have a really strong backer from the higher-ups. I might need your help in the future." Jack said as he approached to shake his new partner's hand.

"Nah. I don't know anyone up there. I just happen to be Miss Dai's friend." Peter immediately clarified.

Rumors about "connections" he might have with management might cause trouble

â€"not just for Peter, but also for Elaine â€"so Peter thought it was best to avoid them.

He decided that he would keep a low profile.

"Haa, don't you shit with me. You guys don't look like ''friends'. You guys look like you're in a very happy relationship! Hahaha" Jack kept teasing, Testing Peter's patience. Peter wanted nothing more but for his senior to stop talking.

Ignoring Jack's further remarks, Peter proceeded to the reception hall, taking in his surroundings. The two receptionists got his attention.

'Wow, ' he thought, 'even the receptionists here are very beautiful and fashionable.' They wore a white shirt paired with a black vest as their uniform. The rest of their outfit was mostly covered by the desk in front of them.

"Hey, newbie, come here." A voice interrupted his thoughts.

Peter rushed over as soon as he realized where the voice was coming from. "Sir, what's the matter?"

It was Eric Zhen, Peter's new supervisor, the man Elaine introduced when they entered the Security Office. Peter thought it's best to be on the man's good side.

"Come with me so I can orient you about how we do things in the company." Eric said sharply, going to the Security Office.

Peter followed him without a word.

Jack followed quietly.

The Security Office of Silverland Group turns out to be bigger than a conference room. There were sofas for security staff to rest on, and a lot of exercise equipment that they could use.

"Hey newbie, what's your name again?" Eric asked, scrunching his eyebrows.

"Peter, sir. Peter Wang." He reluctantly replied. He had a bad feeling about what was going to happen next.

"OK, Peter, good." Suddenly, Eric let out a thunderous laugh. "I just wanted to ask if there's anything between you and Miss Dai! So what is it, eh? Are you together?"

"We're just friends." Peter answered.

"Is that so?" Eric raised one eyebrow, clearly unconvinced. Peter's answer wasn't what he expected. He apparently received orders from his own superior to check in on these two's relationship status.

"Yes." Peter nodded.

"Good, very good!" Eric was disappointed and angry. Now that Peter could not tell the truth by common inquiry, it was better to teach him a lesson by force.

"Okay. Now let me give you a taste of how we do things here as a security staff. First, you have to be strong. Second, you have to handle stress well. Right now, I want you to show me if you're capable enough for this job."

With that, Eric clenched his fists and got ready to fight. His bones cracked as he did his stretches.

People in the room started to take notice. They felt nervous for Peter, knowing that Eric was a fearsome fighter.

He used to be assigned as a Special Forces agent in the military where he got extensive training. It was known that he could beat up seasoned soldiers by the number. Peter stood no chance.

This "orientation" would surely not end well. People in the room wanted this to excite their nerve.

"Mr. Zhen, " Jack suddenly said. "Peter is new to the team and he's clearly no match for you. May I have the honor to take your place, instead?"

Underneath a goofy and laid-back facade, Jack was highly perceptive and he wanted to make sure no one would be hurt. Eric was angry with Peter and the fight would leave Peter seriously injured.

"Are you trying to say something? I'm your supervisor and I don't like being interrupted." Asserting his authority, Eric thew Jack a heavy punch.

This took Jack by surprise, making him unable to dodge. He fell on the ground with his mouth bleeding.

Eric didn't hold back with that punch.

Peter looked at Jack with gratitude, and at Eric with outrage.

He did not expect Jack to be hurt because he stood up for him. After all, Jack said those words with so much respect. Had he known, he surely would have been able to do something to prevent it from happening the way it did.

"Hey, newbie. Ready?" Eric asked Peter, ignoring the fallen Jack.

"I AM READY." Peter said, eager for revenge. He told Eric his name but he kept calling him "newbie" to humiliate him.

"Fine." Eric snorted. Swiftly, he grabbed Peter's neck and shot his knee up to hit his abdomen.

Peter clenched his teeth. It looked like Eric underestimated him thinking that the simple move would be enough to beat him. It was clear that the man sized Peter up totally.

Within a millisecond of seeing his opponent's leg flex, Peter moved his body to avoid the incoming kick and smoothly sidestepped to bring himself behind Eric. Peter locked the man's two arms from the back, making it impossible for him to throw more punches.

With incredible strength, Peter pulled Eric back, making him lose his balance. Establishing a good advantage, Peter delivered a strong knee up against his back.

BANG! Eric screamed in pain as he started to fall on the ground. Mid-air, Peter elbowed him squarely on the face, accelerating his fall.

Eric finally fell, unable to stand up again.

Short and clean. That was a good fight.

Thank you for reading. Please leave your valuable review. It will help us provide you with more interesting novels. More top billionaire romance novels await you at moboreader.net

Chapter 5 The Bad Brothers
Sounds of heavy breaths filled the room that now grew very quiet.

Eyes wide open, the security guards in the area didn't expect what happened.

"Mr. Zhen, forgive me of forgetting your name. You're right, though. You do need a strong body to qualify as a good leader, " Peter said cooly.

Eric tried to get up but failed. He felt like he
wanted to spit out blood. He yelled at the guards in
the room, "What are you doing, you stupid pigs! Beat
the crap out of this guy! I'll back you up if
anything happens! I'm the boss here! Follow my
orders, or leave!"

Eric would not let his authority be questioned like
that, especially in front of his men.

The guards hesitated. They didn't enjoy being called
insulting names either.

They knew they'd only get beaten up as the guy was
clearly stronger than Eric. But Eric was their
leader; they knew they had to do as they were told.

Before he could enforce his orders, Peter decided to
finish him off with one big kick. Peter kicked Eric
so hard so fast that Eric immediately blacked out.

He already beat the crap out of Eric. He didn't mind
adding one more solid blow. He did not want to fight
all the guards. It was enough to have friction with
Eric, but he couldn't risk being on the bad side of
all the other guards.

"Call 120!"

"Take him to the hospital!"

The guards were smart enough not to fight Peter.
They focused instead on attending to Eric and
carrying him out. Peter and Jack were left alone in
the room.

"Jack, are you OK?" Peter asked Jack.

"I'm good." Jack shook his head, with a frightened
gaze at Peter, his hand clutching his chest. He
didn't expect Peter to be such a strong fighter.

"Ok, then. Let's get to work." Peter smiled as if
nothing happened.

Jack grinned. "Hey, buddy. I like your attitude, but you offended Eric. I'd bet good money you won't be allowed to stay anymore. He's the cousin of the Head of Security, Bob Zhen. I'm sure he won't let you off the hook.

Bob is much tougher than Eric. He has really strong connections with some big guy, he'll be a difficult person to be up against. I'd be calling Miss Dai right about now if I were you."

Jack suggested, genuinely concerned about Peter's predicament.

"What? Nah." Peter waved away the suggestion. "Why bother Miss Dai with such a small issue? Plus, I don't believe the Silverland Group would fire me for an incident as petty as this."

'Besides, what would I tell her? That I beat the team leader to death in less than 2 minutes at work? Haha, nothing good will ever come from that.' Asking for Elaine's help was the last thing Peter wanted to do in this situation.

In the reception hall, Peter went about his day as he would normally.

The two receptionists saw Eric being carried out by the other security guards earlier that day, and after hearing what happened, started to admire Peter secretly for what he had done.

Apparently, Eric had been harassing them with crude jokes and indecent proposals, for the longest time. It drove them crazy but they couldn't say anything because of his position in the company.

They felt as if what Peter did was a stand against him for all the abuse he has caused them, and they appreciated it very much.

"Hey girls. Is everything okay? Do I have something on my face?" Peter asked when he noticed their quick glances.

'Hmm, do I look handsome today? Is spring coming? Why have I been encountering so many pretty girls who seem to pay me special attention?' he thought.

He met Elaine and that moody fairy yesterday, and now these two attractive girls seemed to fancy him as well.

The girls just giggled when he came over to ask them what was wrong with the way he looked, the girl on the left even looking down shyly, hiding her flushed cheeks. The girl on the right was a little bolder. She leaned forward and put her chin on her bent fist, flashing him a very seductive look.

"Peter, you are so handsome. How about grabbing dinner with me tonight?"

"What? Really?" Peter hurriedly felt his pockets. "I don't think I have enough money. Do I have to pay the bill?"

'What the fuck? What a douchebag!'

Jack thought, overhearing the conversation. 'Why not just go out with me, pretty lady? I have money. I'll get you whatever you want to eat.'

"Hahahahaha!"

The girl burst out laughing. "Oh Peter, you are so silly! Relax, you don't have to pay the bill.

I'm Shelly Huang. And this is my friend, Lisa Ye." Shelly said pointing at her friend. "Nice to meet you."

"Hi, " Peter said with a smile. "My name is Peter Wang. Peter actually means 'stone' in Greek, and..." Peter's introduction was cut short with a yell coming from across the room.

"HEY, PRETTY BOY. What are you doing? This is office hour, not flirting hour. Who gave you permission to fool around? Come here!"

A 6-foot tall burly man of thirty towered over him with a glare that could have made an average man scared shitless.

Shelly and Lisa exchanged worried looks. Even Jack turned pale.

"Uhh, Peter, this is Bob Zhen, Head of Security." Shelly managed to say. "Mr. Zhen is..."

"No one asked you to speak, lady! Who do you think you are? I'll have a word with your manager!"

Shelly trembled.

Peter's eyes narrowed. 'Is this Silverland Group, or the back alleys? This feels more like a gang than a company to me!' Behind their backs, people called Eric "Bitch" and Bob "Fuck". Peter now saw how accurate these names were.

"You must be Peter Wang. I've heard a LOT about you. I heard you were the BEST â€"the best at disrespecting authority and flirting on the job on the first day at work, that is, " Bob said sarcastically. "Listen, boy, " he said with his face only a few inches away from Peter's. "I don't care where you came from, or who you think you are. You're fired.

Also, we called the police. You hurt people and you are going to pay. They should be here to arrest you soon." Bob said, pointing his finger directly at Peter.

"But.. he started it. He attacked me first. He said it was to test my physical fitness and ability to adapt to stressful situations." Peter said quietly.

"Holy shit! Eric won't do that, you little liar. You started the fight and you hurt him on purpose.

That's the story, and that's what the police will believe."

'Little liar?' Peter thought.

"That's a lie and you know it. Eric started the fight. He tried to punch me first. What I did was self-defense."

"Mr. Zhen." Jack stepped forward and said, "I can testify to what Peter said."

"What did you just say?" Bob shouted at Jack. "Testify? Who cares what you say, Jack? Who you think you are?" "I said, " Jack said, emphasizing his every word, "I.. can.. TESTIFYâ€"" ??"You disrespectful piece of â€"-" Bob roared, and with all his might, threw Jack a big, heavy punch."

Chapter 6 The Mysterious Enchantress
Jack prepared himself as he saw the punch coming towards him. Bob was fast and strong, and Jack knew he wasn't skilled enough to doge it the way Peter could. He couldn't even defeat Eric. Surely, he was no match for Bob.

Peter had other plans, though. He would not allow this bully to get his way. With quick precision, he slapped Bob's hand away from his friend, and delivered a swift counter attack.

Bob didn't see that coming. In his years in this company, no one had ever stood up against him before.

Peter's kick landed on his Belly. He felt a sharp pain, and with a thud, his heavy body landed on the floor.

The room fell silent. No one could believe what they were seeing.

"How...how dare you!" Bob said through gritted teeth. "You...you'll be sorry.." Bob was infuriated. Such humiliation! The Head of Security was beaten up by a newbie!

In his rage, Bob got up and steadied himself, ready to put Peter in his place. Suddenly, the sound of sirens started to fill the air as two police cars arrived at the building entrance. Six policemen started to approach.

Upon seeing them, Bob immediately calmed himself down. "Officer Zhang, thanks for coming. This guy hit my brother and got him wounded! Arrest him immediately!"

The officer gave Bob a knowing nod before approaching Peter. "Come with us, son. We'll have word with you at the station."

Peter looked at Bob and the policeman. It was obvious they knew each other. "Sir, it wasn't my fault!" Peter defended. "They set me up!"

"Hey, son. Are you resisting arrest?" Officer Zhang said coldly.

"Resisting arrest?" Peter laughed. "I'd be glad to come with you. But first, show me your warrant."

Officer Zhang froze. It was unusual for ordinary men to stay calm and think clearly under the stress of being surrounded by the police.

He collected himself right away. "I apologize for my error in speaking, Mr. Wang, " Officer Zhang started. "What I meant to say was that we received reports about you assaulting Mr. Eric Zhen. Please come with us; we would need your cooperation in the investigation."

"No! I'm not going, " Peter said defiantly. He was not a fool! He knew it was a trap. Once he got to the police station, he wouldn't be able to go out without getting a good beating.

"Are you refusing to cooperate, Mr. Wang?" Officer Zhang was about to lose his patience.

"That wasn't what I was saying, officer." Peter explained. "I would actually be very happy to cooperate. I would like to request that it be done here, though. I'm sorry, but I'm afraid I can't go with you to the precinct."

"Here, this might help, " he said as he handed over his phone and played a video.

Both Bob and the policeman were stunned after watching. It was a very clear recording of the fight!

The video was irrefutable evidence of Peter's account!

Officer Zhang handed Peter back his phone and left without another word. He had no reason to stay any longer.

"You have balls! But go feeling proud of yourself. You might feel like you won, but let me remind you that you're fired!"

Bob was furious that Peter foiled his plans, but it didn't matter! No matter what, he was Head of the Security Department and he could do anything he wanted, including terminate his employment!

"You're firing me? Why exactly are you firing me, huh? Give me a reason!" Peter shot, also furious at the obvious powerplay.

"Reason? Hah! You're kidding, right?" Bob roared with laughter. "I am the Head of the Security Department, Peter. I can do ANYTHING I WANT and I do NOT need a fucking reason to do them. Understand? You want a reason? I'll give you a fucking reason. You're fired because I SAY SO."

Peter was at a loss for words. This was outrageous! No one should be allowed to fire anyone without a legitimate reason! Seeing that there was nothing he could do to stop it, he was determined to give Bob one good beating before he stepped out of Silverland Group's doors for the final time.

His thoughts were interrupted by a voice that echoed through the room. ??"Hey! All of you! What are you all doing here? It's office hours! Work or go home! You're not paid to slack around!"

The speaker was clearly an authority figure.

Every face in the room turned pale, except Peter who had no idea who was talking.

Shelly and Lisa looked so afraid that they almost buried their heads under their desks.

Bob, who looked so powerful and intimidating just a few seconds ago, almost looked like he wanted to cower for shelter.

The sight puzzled Peter so much. His curiosity about the identity of the speaker peaked.

'Who was that? People seem to be more afraid of her than they are of Bob!' Peter thought.

When he finally found the source of the echoing voice, Peter's mouth fell open.

She was so beautiful!

The black suit she wore accentuated her perfect body.

With her strong demeanor, she was surely a Senior Officer in the company!

Everyone seemed to be on their toes the moment she entered the building.

No one dared to look her in the eye. Every head was down and every mouth was silent.

My god! What an enchantress! 'I don't recall her looking like this last night. Who is this woman? Is she her twin or something?'

Peter got lost in his thoughts.

"Mr. Zhen, I heard something about your so-called 'authority' to fire employees without a reason. Tell me, since when were you the boss of Silverland Group? Did you get a promotion I didn't hear of?"

The woman looked very cold. Her glance fell on Peter as she was scanning the room, but she gave no sign of recognition.

"I'm sorry, Ma'am, that wasn't what I meant. Please understand, that wasn't what I was implying." Peter couldn't believe what he was hearing. Was there actually fear in Bob's voice? Peter kept his mouth shut. One wrong move and his dismissal might actually push through. No one would be able to help him if that happened now.

"You'd better be sure that wasn't what you were implying. I don't want to hear you say that again, or you will be the first to be fired without a valid reason. Is that clear?" ??Bob nodded in full submission. "Well, what are you all looking at? Is this a show?" she shouted at everyone in the room. "Go back to work!"

That was harsh.

"Yes, Ma'am. Right away, Ma'am." Bob didn't dare say anything else. Humiliated, he quietly made his exit.

'Serves him right, ' Peter thought. 'What a pussy. He pretends to be all tough to the people under him, but he's like a scaredy cat to the higher-ups.' Peter grew very curious about that mysterious woman.

She was probably the President or Executive Vice President of the company to be able to talk to Bob like that.

The woman exited as smoothly as she entered, barely throwing a glance at Peter. As she was about to enter the elevator, though, she suddenly looked as if she remembered something. Out of the blue, she pointed a finger at Peter.

"New guy, Come to my office in ten minutes. Be late and you're fired."

Thank you for reading. Please leave your valuable review. It will help us provide you with more interesting novels. More top billionaire romance novels await you at moboreader.net

Chapter 7 Spineless
Not waiting for a response, the woman entered the elevator and left.

Peter was stunned.

'Are security guards really treated this way? I get threatened to be fired casually!' thought Peter.

"Who was that woman? She was so arrogant!" Peter asked Shelley before she covered his mouth hurriedly to stop him.

"Shush, Peter! It's dangerous to talk about Miss Song like that. Do you even care about your career? Leave me out of it if you want to ruin yours. I happen to like my job here." Shelly looked as if she was about to cry.

Bella had a notorious reputation. As the President of Silverland Group, she was highly objective and calculating in all her decisions. She valued results and efficiency above all, which allowed her to be highly impartial. On her bad days, she could be found reprimanding anyone who happened to cross her path, sometimes even firing them with no reason at all.

Senior company executives and general staff alike were all wise enough to be careful around her on these occasions. It was very risky to talk about her badly, even in private. The consequences could be dire.

"Just be sure to be careful, Peter. Remember to stay calm when you meet Miss Song. Don't speak unless spoken to, and never interrupt her. Be sure to not annoy her, else, that's a sure bye-bye." Shelly whispered

As Lisa nodded in agreement. "It's true. Miss Song doesn't need a reason to fire anybody."

"I'm sorry, Peter. I can't help you out here, man." Jack sighed.

Peter shifted uncomfortably. 'It's just a woman. What's the worse that could happen? You should calm down like me, rather than be nervous. Besides, so what if she fires me? This isn't a very nice place anyway. I'll just be a punching bag here if I stay. There's probably something out there better for me.' Peter tried to convince himself.

'Damn it! I've killed so many people in the battlefield and now I'm afraid of a woman in an office? What is wrong with you, Peter? Worst case scenario, we go back to the construction site. That isn't the worst!'

The elevator doors opened. Peter puffed up his chest. straightened himself out, and started to walk as calmly as he could manage.

The 38th floor was where upper management held office, including the CEO.

Peter's eyes grew wide as he walked around.

One side of it was filled with beautiful women in uniform darting back and forth with swift but dainty steps, holding documents.

The silk black uniform made them all look so sexy!

'Well, I'm about to be fired, anyway. Might as well enjoy this while it lasts.'

The women gave him quick reproachful looks as they went about their business. It was obvious they didn't enjoy being checked out by an ordinary security guard.

It wasn't unusual for them to be checked out by guys who happenned to visit their floor, but Peter's gaze made them feel quite uncomfortable.

A secretary courteously greeted Peter as he entered the President's office.

He glanced at her name tag and greeted her. "Hey, Clair! My name is Peter Wang. Miss Song asked me to come to her office and I can't be late! Hurry, let me in!"

'Wow the nerve of this guy, giving me orders! Even the President wouldn't talk to me like that.'

Clair gave him a blank look.

'I've met so many people of different statures. This faceless, nameless security guard is unbelievable. I wonder what stupid he did to get Miss Song's attention?'

Despite her inner thoughts, Clair mustered a courteous smile. "Good day, Mr. Wang. Please wait, I'll inform Miss Song you're here."

"Hurry up! I can't be late!"

Clair nearly fell over. 'What an annoying security bastard!'

Peter felt satisfied.

A lot of people in the office looked at themselves from a pedestal. They seemed to feel like they were better than others, and Peter decided to give it a try in return. It felt fantastic!

Frankly, Peter was disappointed to encounter so much hassle on his first day of work, but he felt better after standing up for himself and his friends.

Judging from Shelly's and the others' tone, it's probably a really bad thing to be called to the President's office. He's almost sure he's going to be fired. There's nothing he could possibly do to make things worse.

After what seemed like a very long time, Clair walked out of Bella's office and gestured Peter to come in. Peter ran his fingers through his hair in an attempt to make them less unruly, then started to enter.

Bella was on her big mahogany table, her black suit placed against her majestic leather chair. She gave Peter a cold look and scanned him from head to toe.

He felt very uncomfortable. 'Still asserting your dominance until now, Miss President? What do you even get out of it?' Peter thought.

Utterly tired from a whole day of being sized up, Peter decided to just speak his mind. "Miss Song, I'm still very puzzled. Why did you call me to your office?"

Peter did his best to sound respectful despite the tension.

"I heard you beat up Eric, your group leader, and got him sent to the hospital. Then, you provoked Bob, the Head of Security. All these, on your first day. You're quite bold, Mr. Wang." Bella replied coldly.

'Yeah, you bet I did. And I can do the same thing to you if I get out of control. How do you plan to deal with me?' Peter thought. He decided to shift to a more humble tone.

"I deeply apologize for what happened, Miss Song. I promise I will not let that happen again, especially during work hours."

'Agh, Peter, you spineless pussy, ' he thought to himself. 'I shouldn't even be apologizing for having done the right thing, but this woman is heartless and probably won't listen to my reason. This is the best way to keep the job.'

"Hmm, why are you apologizing? I don't see anything you did wrong." She said calmly.

"What? No, what I did was very, very wrong!" 'Spineless pussy.'

Bang!

Bella stood up dropping her hands loudly on the table.

"Who said you did something wrong? What you did was right! Those arrogant bastards got what they deserved.

In my opinion, you were too soft. I heard Eric has just returned to work. You should have beaten him up harder so he'd be bedridden for three months or so."

Peter was speechless. Was this a test?

He couldn't believe what he was hearing! This woman was something unpredictable! What President would wish her staff were beaten down and incapacitated for three whole months?

Finally being able to recollect himself, Peter managed to reply. "I.. actually agree with you, Miss Song. Thank you. Next time, I'll do my best to make that five months."

He thought it would be best to just keep agreeing with this woman.

Bella didn't speak, but instead, kept staring at Peter.

One minute...

Two minutes...

Three minutes...

Peter grew impatient. Did I say something wrong?' He remembered that old saying "To be in the king's company is tantamount to living with a tiger". It couldn't be truer right now. He was at the edge of his seat, and he had no idea what would happen next.

Four minutes later, Bella let out a burst of laughter.

"Hahahahahahaha! Oh god! I can't help it! This is so funny! Hahahahaha! You see, handsome? I told you you couldn't escape me. You show up in front of me on your own, see? Hahahahahahaha!"

Chapter 8 Beat Up The Bastard
'Her again?!'

Peter couldn't believe what was happening.

"Woah! It's so nice to see you again! I actually had a dream about you on the night that we met. I always knew you were special, but I didn't expect you to be the CEO of this company! It suits you with your charm and elegance."

'Perhaps if I sweet-talk her, I'll get on her good side.' He might have forgotten the fact that he told her he never wanted to see her again.

"Hahaha, really, now?" She seemed flattered. It was working.

"Really, darling, " Peter assured her.

"Hmmm, interesting. I seem to remember things differently. In my vague memory, you said something like never wanting to see me again? And, hmm. Correct me if I'm wrong butâ€¦ I kind of remember you refused to give me your number, " Bella said sheepishly.

"I was having a really rough day, to be honest, " Peter replied desperately trying to salvage the situation. How could he have known she was the President of his then-future employer? "Plus, I was very tipsy so didn't think much of it. I'm sorry if I said anything harsh."

"Hmmâ€¦ Okay. Now that you said you were sorry and that you were really drunk that night, I will accept your apology, " Bella said with a cute pout.

"Aww, thank you so much, darling. You're beautiful on the outside and on the inside." Seeing that Bella was not angry anymore, Peter started to shift the topic back to work. "Now that we're friends, my darling angel, I'm wondering if we can talk about additional compensation, and maybe a promotion. What do you think?"

Suddenly, Bella's expression changed. The sweet playful girl was gone and the big boss was back. "You shall address me as Miss Song, Mr. Wang."

'What the fuck?'

Peter couldn't believe it. All the flattery was useless!

"I will not take orders from a mere security guard about who I will promote and how much I will pay my employees. Get out! You're fired!" Bella said, loudly slamming her hands on her desk as she stood up.

'Shit!'

Peter felt very frustrated. In a snap, Bella felt like a totally different person!

He said what she wanted to hear, but she still went bananas out of nowhere!

"Well screw you! You're a bullshit CEO. I don't even want to work here anymore!" Peter yelled and started running towards Bella.

"What are you going to do with me?" Bella asked, both alarmed and mildly excited, as she backed up slowly, slumping down her chair.

"What am I going to do? I'm going to do you." Pressing against her, he seized her arms and pushed her to the office desk. With one swift movement, he swung his hand towards her ass.

PAK!

The sound echoed in the big office. Bella's body shook. She felt pain all over. It felt painful but she bore the slappings without a sound.

"How dare you bite the hand that feeds you. You'll regret this, you bitch!" Remembering the power play and injustice he encountered all throughout the day,

Peter felt his rage rise from inside him and slapped harder and harder.

Pak! Pak! Pak!

Sounds of flesh hitting flesh continued to fill the room.

Peter went on and on until he felt like it was enough.

He had a huge feeling of embarrassment as soon as he calmed down. He might have slapped her too heavily, but she deserved it after what she did. He had rescued her in the bar but now she was giving him a hard time in the job he landed.

Bella was on the desk, lying down on her stomach, with her buttocks raised. She was red from anger, glaring at him.

Her body's position… Her face… Her eyes…

"Miss Song, I deeply apologize for what happened. I will now leave and be sure that you never see me again." Eaten by guilt, Peter decided to exit and concede to Bella's decision to fire him.

He was about to reach for the door when he heard Bella speak. "Leave that door, or I will call the police to arrest you for molesting me, the moment you do. My office is under heavy security and surveillance and I have every piece of evidence against you, "

Said Bella as she slowly got herself to stand up despite the pangs of pain.

'God, this bastard doesn't know how to act properly, ' she thought.

"What do you want from me?: Peter asked, puzzled at the recent turn of events. Still, he lost his temper and he did what he did. He just had to accept the consequences.

"Go and work now! You are not allowed to quit the job without my permission. You are not allowed to leave Silverland Group, and you will be on-call, whenever I want!" Bella said calmly and indifferently.

"Iâ€¦ thought I was fired." Peter could not understand what she wanted to do.

"I know. I take it back."

"Fine. What if someone else fires me?" 'This woman must be a masochist, ' Peter thought. Had he known, he would have started slapping her the moment he entered the room.

"No one is allowed to fire you, except me."

'What the hell?'

Giving up trying to understand the situation, Peter conceded and left.

Bella sat in relief after dismissing Peter but found herself quickly standing up again. Her buttocks hurt like crazy! "Fuck!" she said irritably. 'That was embarrassing, ' she thought, 'He's so strong, and his slaps were so painful! But at least he's not totally useless. I guess I'll be able to push through with my plan. I felt guilty for using you then, but now we're even.'

Peter took out one big sigh of relief the moment he stepped out of the President's office.

'There's a solution to everything, ' Peter was not worried about his future anymore. He now had a job that could pay the billsâ€¦

Peter forced a smile as he greeted the secretary on his way out, and proceeded back to the hall.

Upon his arrival, anger started to well up from inside him again.

A short bald man was talking loudly at Shelly, pointing his finger at her face closely. At one point, he even slapped her!

Shelley shrunk and tears started to run down her face. Poor girl!

Lisa, on the other hand, looked nothing better. Her face was red and swollen from crying.

Jack was nowhere to be seen.

'Who does this man think he is, making a scene in this company? He must be a real asshole to even bully these two sweethearts.'

"Hey! Stop what you're doing!" Peter shouted as he ran and tackled the man, giving him a good beating.

"I was gone two minutes and suddenly you bastards come in and make trouble? Does bullying our receptionists make you feel more manly?

You look like such a dignified man in your suit, but underneath it all, you're just a sick bastard. Get out of this building!"

Peter started to beat the man up and kicked him out of the hall

After thirty seconds of anger.

Shelly and Lisa exchanged worried looks. They appreciated what he did but there seemed to be a little problem.

"Uhh€¦ Peter?" Shelly hesitated. "That's Mr. Kang. He's our supervisor."

Chapter 9 Anger Over The Affair

Suddenly, a burst of excited laughter sounded, "Hahaha! You can't deny what you've done because I have you on record. What do you have to say for yourself?"

The two brothers, Bob and Eric, appeared in the hall. Bob had a cell phone in his hand, and he was recording Peter. Looking pleased, he said, "Do you think you're the only one who secretly records videos? You didn't expect this, didn't you? I'd like to see how you can get away with assault this time."

Then, Eric spoke up angrily, "I've told you before that, if you hit me, you'll pay for it! And now that you've offended our brother, you have no choice but to go straight to jail and be taught a lesson.

As a matter of fact, I can tell you that, in addition to your punishment, I will not let go of these two women who are related to you. Not only am I going to kick them out of Silverland Group, but I'm also going to find someone to gang rape them and make them suffer for the rest of their lives. This is the price you have to pay for offending me!"

Eric's hate for Peter was evidently far greater than Bob's at the time. Even as Peter's superior, Eric had been beaten by Peter and was sent to the hospital immediately after. That was Peter's first day of work. Eric had been beaten so badly that he had to be carried out on a stretcher. That humiliating scene was seen by so many people that it had easily become an unforgettable moment of his life.

Eric could imagine that the news would soon be spread throughout the company, making him the butt of many jokes.

Peter's eyes slightly narrowed as he saw the two men appear. And, of course, he immediately realized that all of this had been planned by the brothers. Their ultimate aim was to get back at him.

The bald man's behavior was pathetic and ridiculous. He had been used by the two men without him knowing it.

"One of you bastards deserves to die, and the other deserves to be beaten. Both of you are really brothers. I can see the resemblance of your stupidity and viciousness. If I'm going to jail soon, I'm going to beat you both up before I do, all for the people you've bullied!" Peter sneered and started rushing at them like an unstoppable tornado.

He believed that everyone had a bottom-line that they could never touch, and that when that principle was violated, they would react with surprising force.

No matter how much Bob and Eric would threaten him, or even hurt him, Peter could let them off. But since they had the audacity to attack Shelly and Lisa, he would not let them get away with it. Not only that, but they had also said such shameless words and made such hateful threats. Damn it!

Seeing Peter rush forward, Eric's eyes flashed with fear. Subconsciously, he hid behind Bob.

And Bob, he reacted otherwise. He had been wanting to beat Peter up, so when he saw Peter come toward them, he felt excited and pumped up. He hadn't gotten the chance to hit Peter before, so now, he felt that this was a godsend for him to fight back.

Bob was not as cowardly as his cousin Eric. He used to be a top special forces soldier, and his fighting skills were far more superior than Eric's.

"Drop dead, you asshole!" Bob let out a roar and, at the same time, professionally threw out a punch, which gathered a great deal of wind toward Peter.

The punch he threw was so powerful that it seemed to have had an immense amount of force with it.

Peter rolled his eyes as he shaped his right hand like an eagle's claw. Suddenly, he grasped Bob by the wrist and pulled him forward.

This action made Bob unstable, causing him to be driven forward. For the first time in his life, shock was strewn across Bob's eyes.

He had no idea that Peter could easily grab his large fist just like that. He couldn't believe it. He had just punched hard enough to turn over a cow, but he wasn't even able to bring Peter down.

Peter did not give Bob any time to think. The moment Bob leaned forward, Peter's right knee curled up and hit Bob's abdomen.

A loud thud was heard. Before anyone could react, Bob was found collapsed on the ground. His blood flowed in streams.

Without giving Bob a chance to get up, Peter stomped on him again and treated him like a dead dog.

"It seems that your physical condition is not good. You're not qualified to be a security chief. How could you possibly qualify for that position with your poor health and poor fighting skills?"

Peter's voice was full of sarcasm.

Bob's face turned red. He was afraid and ashamed at the same time. He had never thought that he would ever be trampled on the ground by Peter!

They had only gone for one round, yet he had completely lost the bout so soon.

Eric the idiot was hiding in the back, completely scared. His mind went utterly blank.

Peter had beaten his cousin, who he had thought was so strong, with one stroke. How strong Peter was!

Eric was so weak with fear that he could barely stand. The thought that he had offended such a powerful man made him tremble with fear. He even nearly fainted the next second.

Peter was not in a hurry to speak, so he stepped on Bob and tortured him for a while. When he realized that Eric's fear had reached a critical point, he looked at Eric coldly.

"Down on your knees! Now!" he shouted.

Thump!

Hearing Peter's voice, Eric, who was extremely frightened, shivered and fell to his knees without hesitation.

He thought that Peter looked terrifying, especially with his cold eyes, which seemed to have no emotion. He had no doubt that Peter would rush to him at any moment and tear him to pieces.

Eric was so afraid of Peter that he was scared out of his wits. He was so pale that he dared not move or even breathe aloud.

"Do you remember what you said just now? You said that you were going to fire them and that you were going to have them gang-raped, remember?" Peter's voice was cold and emotionless. Every sentence he spoke sliced like a frigid shard of ice.

"No, I didn't! I swear I didn't!" Eric quickly shook his head in denial and started shaking violently. He was so afraid of Peter that he thought he was a devil. Eric had no courage to bear the demon's wrath.

"No? You mean you didn't say those horrible things?" Peter narrowed his eyes chillingly, then raised his hand, and slapped Eric several times. ''Are you implying that my ears are not working well? Or that I'm getting old so I heard it wrong? Or I'm deaf? Delusional?"

"No, no, that's not what I meant! I swear I didn't mean it! Please! I was wrong. I admit that I did... I did say those words... " Eric's brain buzzed with each slap, and he felt that the sky and the earth was dimming before his eyes. He would rather pass out than face Peter the devil. On the verge of tears, he had to quickly change his response.

"Are you sure you did?" Peter raised his hand again and slapped Eric several more times. "How can you say such mean things? I'm going to kill you, you son of a bitch!"

No matter what he said, he was wrong. No matter what he said, he would get beaten. Eric felt that he would rather die than endure such torture. Was the damn answer yes or no?

Peter gave Eric a good beating before stopping. Then, he pointed to Bob, who was at his feet, and told Eric, "Now, it's your turn to hit him!"

"How dare you!'' Bob was furious. "Peter Wang, how insidious you are! Your attempt to separate us brothers in this way will never succeed!"

"Am I really insidious? Okay, let's try and see if it works." Peter smiled cunningly and looked at Eric. "Are you going to hit Bob or not? If you refuse, you're the one who's gonna end up miserable. Make up your mind quickly, Sir, my patience is limited."

The terrible threat worked. Poor Eric shook his fist and said, "Of course, of course, I'll hit him!" Eric gritted his teeth and jumped at Bob. He had no choice. His hard punch made Bob cry with pain.

"How dare you! How dare you fucking hit me?" Bob was furious. "You son of a bitch! You didn't even have the courage to fight back. You would rather murder your own brother! I've taken care of you all these years, and you fucking dared beat me. You are such a heartless man who repays kindness with enmity!"

Bob shouted angrily and pulled Eric to the ground. The two men started to wrestle violently.

"How can you blame me when you saw that I was forced to do this? Besides, I didn't punch you that hard. It was like there was no effort at all. How could you hit me back so hard? Are you trying to get back at me? I'll kill you, you bastard!"

"You are such a heartless man who repays kindness with enmity! I will kill you now."

The two brothers began to complain to each other at first, and gradually, they began to quarrel. When the argument got more heated, it turned into a fight. They hit each other harder and harder each time, and soon, they were all black and blue, out of breath. But even so, they were still so angry that they couldn't stop fighting, not for a while. They were still punching each other.

Shelly and Lisa were so stunned that they couldn't make any sound. It had never occurred to them that things would turn out this way, that these two bad guys would be defeated so easily, and that they would still be killing each other.

Just then, the bald man who had been thrown out of the door by Peter came in with an angry look on his face. He was trying to settle accounts with Peter when he saw the two brothers beating each other. He was shocked. He had no idea what was going on.

While he was in a trance, Peter suddenly grabbed him and threw him at the two fighting brothers. It all happened so suddenly that no one had any time to react.

Bob and Eric, in particular, had been badly beaten up by Peter, and they had also been fighting with each other for some time, so they were now bruised and wounded. At that moment, Peter took the opportunity to throw the bald man into their fight, which would surely make things worse. The brothers, blinded by their anger, did not even think about how it had happened, let alone who was to blame. They just wanted to vent their anger, so they grabbed the bald man and started beating him up.

By this time, the fight between the two brothers had completely evolved into a scuffle between the three. The three men were beating each other up so badly that their screams followed one after another. At this point, the scene seemed ridiculous.

Peter had already taken out his mobile phone and recorded it as if he were shooting a Hollywood blockbuster. He, as the victor, was admiring the absurdity and stupidity of these shameless men.

"Hello, 911? There are several people fighting here, and it is becoming very violent. They are all covered in blood. I hope you can send a medical team here. It's urgent. You guys have to move a little bit faster. If you guys are late, they might bleed to death." Peter watched the miserable scene of the three scuffling men for a while until he felt his anger had dissipated. Then, he stopped filming and called 911 for help. In fact, what he had said on the phone left the operator speechless.

The operator wondered in silence. He thought it strange that the caller did not immediately call the police when he saw the fight, and he even called 911 with a calm demeanor. Despite the confusion, the medical center did not treat news of injuries as a joke, so it dutifully set out to rescue the injured.

Ten minutes later, the ambulance crew rushed in and carried the three weak men away.

The hall, which had been filled with noise because of the three men's cries of pain, was suddenly quiet. Peter felt a lot more relaxed.

"I'm sorry I've caused you all this trouble. You've just been slapped in the face by that bald man. Does it still hurt?" Peter looked to Shelly and Lisa while asking them with concern.

"We're all right. Thank you." Shelly became scared when she saw Peter beating up the three bad guys, but she was relieved when she saw Peter's concerned eyes. She realized that Peter was a good man.

"Thank you, Peter." Lisa thanked Peter immediately, but her expression was a bit off.

Peter noticed that she seemed to have something more to say, so he asked, "What's the matter, Lisa? If you need me to teach them a few more lessons, I'll go to the hospital and beat them up again." Peter was going to leave as he spoke, pretending he was going to the hospital to beat people up.

He was really sorry that he had brought these two girls in trouble. If it hadn't been for his guilt, he wouldn't have been so angry, beating up the bastards at work.

"No, I'm really okay." Lisa grabbed Peter nervously. After what she had just seen and heard, she believed that Peter would do what he said and would rush to the hospital at once.

Shelly was so scared that she grabbed Peter by the other arm. She was afraid that he was going to do it. The three men were already dying, so if he hit them again, they might really die. Of course, the scums deserved to die, but there was no need for a nice guy like Peter to commit a crime for them.

Shelly and Lisa were so grateful to Peter that they didn't want to put him in any danger.

"Now that you two are all right, I can rest assured. I'll treat you to lunch to calm you down." Peter was relieved to hear that all was well with the two girls.

"Well, all right."

Both of the girls agreed. They seemed to have made up their minds and went straight to the front desk to pick up their things.

Wondering why they did it, Peter asked, "What are you doing? Why are you packing up?"

"Because we've been fired. That bald man is our leader, Director Kang. We'll never get away with it when he gets back. But it doesn't matter. Even if we get fired, we can still look for jobs in other companies. I'm so smart, beautiful, and talented that I'm sure I can find another one soon enough, "

Shelly said with a sigh, but she quickly regained her confidence. She believed in her own abilities and that there was always a way out. She, then, consoled Lisa, who was depressed beside her, "Lisa, don't worry. We're still young, so we still have a lot of time to learn and find new things for ourselves. We have a bright future ahead of us."

Lisa was encouraged, so she nodded. She felt that her gloomy mood about losing her job had improved a lot and that everything would be all right.

"You both got fired?" Peter was shocked. He couldn't believe it. "That's impossible. I don't think you two need to pack up and leave. I'm going to talk to the president of our company right now, and she would certainly agree that you both shouldn't get fired for it. I promise you that as long as I work here, you will not be fired. Trust me."

As Peter spoke, he headed for the elevator to get on Bella's floor. If Shelly and Lisa would be sacked because he had punched someone, he'd be guilty of it for the rest of his life.

"Wait a minute." Shelly stopped Peter and asked, somewhat doubtfully, "Peter, didn't you get fired, too?"

She thought that Peter had been fired because he had been called to the President's Office, which meant that he had to have made an unforgivable mistake. As a matter of fact, according to her previous experience, anyone called into the office by the president would be scolded and ended up being miserably fired.

"Fired? Why do you think I got fired?" Peter was a little upset. When he saw the expressions on Shelly's and Lisa's faces, he realized that they both thought he had been fired. It felt as if they would have liked him to be fired, so he was puzzled.

"It's so strange that you didn't get fired. Why didn't you get fired? That's strange, " muttered Shelly, which made Peter even more confused and a little defensive.

Peter, then, suddenly looked up, stood up straight, combed his hair with his right hand, and acted confident. "It does makes sense, " he bragged, "I am handsome and strong, so I belong to a good company. There's no way I'm going to get fired."

Shelly couldn't believe it, of course, so she made a skeptical face toward the narcissistic Peter. She had a feeling that there might be some affair between Peter and the president. "Peter, please tell me honestly. Did you know Miss Song before? Are you two lovers?"

"I'll tell you a secret. You must not tell anyone. Bella, the President, has fallen in love with me, and we love each other so much that she won't say no to anything I say. She can give up everything for me and forgive all of my mistakes. So you can take my word that you will not get fired. In fact, I will go and get her to agree to it right away."

Peter had to brag to comfort the two girls. He realized that if Bella knew what he was saying, that would be the end of him. He made it seem like what he had said was real that he felt sorry for Bella.

But he didn't think it would matter because Bella wouldn't hear it. But he was clearly wrong.

"Are you sure you're telling the truth?" Just as Peter finished boasting, a voice came up from behind him, and it clearly belonged to Bella.

Chapter 10 Meeting The Parents
Shelly and Lisa lowered their heads with their mouths closed tightly to hold back from chuckling out loud. Since they were already fired, they didn't fear Bella as much as they did before.

Shit!

In shock, Peter nearly fell down.

He turned around only to find that Bella was behind him wearing a stern face.

"Oh, Miss Song... I was... I was just praising your beauty." Peter was cheeky enough to have quickly changed his words to flattery.

Bella snorted and took no more notice of him. She looked right at the other two and said, "Don't you know that it's working hours? Go back to work! If you gossip during work again, I will send you both home."

"Yes, President!" "Yes, President!" The two replied immediately with immense joy and rushed to their work hastily. They were not fools. What Bella had said meant that they were not fired.

As for Peter, well... Good luck to him.

"Get your ass over here!" After having scolded Shelly and Lisa, Bella turned to Peter and coldly ordered him. With the tapping of her black stilettos, Bella walked out like a queen.

Peter's face twitched bitterly. He had no choice but to follow her.

They reached a stylish red Hummer soon. Bella leaned on the car leisurely with single hand holding the front part, turning round and squinting at Peter.

"You said I was at your beck and call, right? If you asked me to kneel down, I would dare not stand. That's what you said, no? So, now, should your humble servant kneel down to show respects?"

A luxurious car and a gorgeous woman should have probably exhilarated Peter and driven him crazy under other circumstances. But now, the only thing he wanted to do was to run away.

"Oh, that... You must have misheard me. Right, you definitely must have misheard me." Peter desperately put up a struggle to deny it.

"Hmph!" Bella snorted and said, "It's okay. There is a chance to make up for what you've done. If your performance is good enough to satisfy me tonight, I'll just let it go. How is that?"

Peter mumbled in hesitation, "Miss... Miss Song, I'm not an easy boy."

"What do you mean?" Bella was a little confused with his words.

"Didn't you just say that you wanted to see my performance tonight?" Blushing, he continued, "Even though I am quite confident with my ability, this would be my first time. I have never had a girlfriend yet... "

What the fuck?!

Bella got so angry that she slammed her high heels onto Peter and said, "Shut up, you asshole! What are you thinking about? Do you think a toad like you has a chance with a swan like me? In your dreams!"

What an asshole! How could he assume that?

"What? What performance were you talking about then?" Confused, Peter asked as soon as he had dodged the kick.

"Pretending to be my boyfriend in front of my parents, " Bella replied impatiently.

"No!" Peter refused since he was in quite a bad mood now.

"Men would rather prefer death over humiliation. You are playing with me, my body, and my feelings. I will never do it, no matter how much money you give me, because I'm a man with dignity. By the way, how much can you offer?"

Bella became a little worried upon hearing the first part of his statement. If Peter would be stubborn and refuse to help her, her whole plan would be in vain. Hearing the whole remarks, she was both relieved and contemptuous.

"If you do well, I'll give you 5, 000!"

"5, 000?" His mouth went agape at what he had heard.

"Fine. 10, 000!" Bella frowned. Was he going to demand an exorbitant price?

"10, 000?" Peter opened his mouth even wider.

Bella was a little annoyed, so she said, "Tell you what, don't push your luck. If you abuse it too much, I will go to the police station and show them the video."

"Please don't..." Quickly, Peter grabbed her hand to stop her, and then he said, "I mean, 5, 000 is already more than what I had expected. God knows how you misunderstood me and even offered me 10, 000. Well, I must accept it if you insist. Would you pay by cash or PayPal?"

Bella was stunned at the response of this ballsy guy.

"I'll pay you after you behave well tonight."

"But, at least, you should give me some downpayment, right?"

This guy was driving her crazy, so Bella immediately transferred 5, 000 through her PayPal account. Without wasting any more time, she made Peter get into the Hummer before they both left the Silverland Group.

After receiving a great sum of money into his account, Peter smiled with joy, and then, he sneakily glanced at Bella.

He had seen beautiful women drive Hummers before, but this was the first time he had seen one in Golden City. Although slender and delicate, Bella was driving such a huge thing, which didn't look compatible at all, like beauty and beast in real life.

But she was quite skillful in driving. As the Hummer ran fast along the road, the growling of the engine complemented Bella's beautiful appearance, adding on to her confidence and charisma.

"Have you seen enough?" Suddenly, Bella turned slightly and asked enchantingly with a smile.

"Of course not, you are so beautiful. It would never be enough." Peter shivered, immediately looking away after taking a last glance at her chest.

Just a second ago, she was an ice-cold tigress, but now, she seemed like a sexy and charming seductress. What a capricious woman! He'd better behave himself.

Bella paid no more attention to him and concentrated on driving. After half an hour, they showed up in Sawgrass Mansion.

Sawgrass Mansion was a high-end shopping center which featured luxury brands. Bella first took Peter to a salon to get a haircut. After that, they proceeded to the designer shops to pick out some clothes.

Peter knew that these were only going to be used for the dinner tonight, so he made the most out of it without any embarrassment.

Under the disdainful looks of the saleswomen, Peter selected two expensive suits and had Bella pay for them.

The saleswomen were astonished. They had never seen a boy toy this proud and shameless. This bastard really had gotten himself some dumb luck.

At around 6:00 PM, the both of them had finished getting ready, and then, Bella and Peter headed straight for dinner.

Norman Restaurant, a fancy French restaurant. The guests here were either distinguished celebrities, swanky nouveau riches, or spoiled kids.

Peter wore a business suit while Bella was in a black cheongsam. As soon as they had stepped in the venue, they caught all of the attention of everyone in the restaurant.

Peter had an imposing appearance. He stood tall and straight like a javelin, full of masculine charm.

Dressed in a black embroidered cheongsam, Bella put her hair in an elegant updo, looking like a graceful empress.

They looked like the perfect couple.

Bella held Peter's arm closely with her loving eyes staring straight at him all of the time as if he was the only man in the world.

Peter was feeling quite nervous and shy, for he had never done this meeting the parents kind of thing before, not even when he was the soldier king. Pretending to be someone's boyfriend or not, it was indeed a first for him. He was starting to get anxious. This situation seemed worse than when he was in the battlefield.

"You'd better act naturally. Don't you get us into trouble. One more thing, you are my boyfriend. Stop keeping such a distance from me. Look at you. Does it look like you're dating me? Now, get close, and put your arm around my waist."

Bella was unsatisfied with Peter's actions, so she scolded him in a low voice when nobody was looking at them. She didn't mind it, and she was a woman. But why was it bothering Peter, who was a man?

They stopped in front of a VIP room. Bella took Peter's arm and wrapped it around her waist before she opened the door and went inside.

There were three people in the room, two men and a woman.

The elder couple had to be Bella's parents, for Bella bore some resemblance to the elder man.

Another handsome, young man, who was around 27 or 28 years old, was inside the room. His clothes and his watch were all famous brands; all of the things he was wearing were worth at least a million. He seemed like a wealthy chap at first sight.

The young man was dressed decently, but the expression and look on his face made people uncomfortable.

The moment Bella appeared, his first glance was to her breasts and then to her face. There was a hint of lust deep in his eyes.

But when his glance shifted to Peter, there was only viciousness and gloom. Even though it was just a glimpse, Peter didn't miss it.

Damn it. Peter knew he had fallen into Bella's trap again, and this dinner wouldn't be an easy task.

Chapter 11 Alfred Gao

"Bella, finally, you're here. Why did you bring an outsider? Don't you know that this is a family gathering? Who is this man?"

When the middle-aged woman saw Bella, she stood up happily, but her smiling face faded the moment she saw Peter.

"Dad, this is my boyfriend, Peter Wang." Bella didn't pay any attention to the woman, but she directly addressed the older man, introducing Peter to him. Then, she asked Peter to take a seat.

"Rex, look at your daughter. Even if I am just a stepmother who had nothing to do with her upbringing, she should not be this rude to me. How could she bring an outsider knowing that this is a family gathering? What kind of boyfriend did she bring? What would Alfred think about this? What a joke!"

Jane Wang pointed at Bella, looking furious.

"Bella, you're just making a fool out of yourself. When did you get yourself a boyfriend? Why didn't you tell me? Have you forgotten that you have a fiancé?"

Rex Song also frowned, seemingly a little displeased.

"I've been busy lately, and I haven't had the time to tell you, " Bella said casually.

Rex looked at his daughter Bella, and wanted to say something, but eventually he decided to shut his mouth.

The young man never spoke a word, only keeping a smile on his face. It was only the chillness in his eyes, which was unintentionally showed from time to time, that exposed his true feelings, that he was not as calm and composed as he looked.

"Nice to meet you, Uncle Rex and Aunt Jane." Although Peter was feeling bewildered, he still mustered up his courage to greet them.

Rex just ignored Peter's greeting. He did not even take a look at him.

On the other hand, Jane jumped up right away to scold him.

"Aunt Jane? Who is your Aunt Jane? We are having a family gathering here. Who are you and what are you doing here? Get out of here. Get out now !"

Smack!

Before Peter could say anything, Bella slammed her hand on the table and sprang to her feet. "That's none of your business. He's my boyfriend, so I will go if he leaves! What's more, since you said that this is a family gathering, then what's this person doing here? Why can he come here but my boyfriend cannot?"

Bella said, pointing at Alfred Gao.

Feeling the need to, Alfred stood up and spoke,
"Aunt Jane, Bella, what is the point of arguing at
this nice place? Come on, since we're already here,
let's just sit down and enjoy the meal together."

He was polite and well-mannered, and after saying
that, he asked the waitress to take their orders.

It was a French restaurant, so most of the
waitresses were foreigners.

He spoke fluently in French to the servers. With his
perfect grasp of the French language, coupled with
his gentlemanly demeanor, Alfred Gao, a handsome
gentleman, would make any man feel ashamed of
himself.

Rex watched him interact with the foreign waitresses
and nodded with approval in his eyes. He was
thinking how Alfred was indeed a skillful and
competent man. If Bella could marry him, he would be
happy about it.

In the meantime, Jane's heart was pounding with
admiration, even her anger started to vanish. She
glanced at Peter, with a look of contempt in her
eyes, and thought, 'How dare he compete with Mr. Gao
for Bella! Doesn't he even know what he looks like?'

Bella's face turned white, as if someone had just
slapped her face.

If Peter were her real boyfriend, it would be okay
because he would just have to suck it up and deal
with the situation. But Peter was not. Once Peter
would feel humiliated and wronged by comparison, she
was afraid that he would just get up and leave.

She knew how stubborn Peter was, so even Bella
herself might not be able to stop him once he
decided to leave.

Thinking of this, Bella glanced at Peter stealthily and immediately regretted looking at him as what she saw almost made her fly into a rage.

Peter was staring and ogling at the foreign waitress without blinking his eyes, even almost drooling.

'Bastard. Even though this is a high-end French restaurant with well-groomed and beautiful foreign waitresses, can't he manage to behave himself?'

After Alfred ordered his meal, he frowned and looked at Peter, sneering at him with his eyes. He told the waitress in fluent French, "I'll order these first. Please go to my friend and see if he wants anything else."

Alfred wanted to make Peter feel a little uncomfortable. If a man would get embarrassed like that, he would not be able to stand the shame, so he would most likely leave in disgrace. Alfred was taking so much time in ordering, simply because he was trying to make time for Peter to excuse himself and leave.

But Peter was not moving a finger as if he had no intentions to get out of the place. In this case, Alfred would just make a fool out of him.

Maybe Peter could speak a little English, but he most certainly would not be able to speak any French at all. That would be impossible.

The beautiful waitress frowned and went to Peter's side shortly. Then, she asked him in French if he needed anything more.

She had also noticed that Peter had been staring at her, which annoyed her, of course. They were in a high-end French restaurant. People who came here were all well-educated, so no customer would stare at her like that. But how could he?

It was just her professionalism and proper work ethics that were keeping her from flipping out on

him. When the beautiful waitress walked toward
Peter, the smile on her face disappeared, and her
attitude toward Peter was totally different from
what she had shown Alfred.

As Bella watched the waitress walk toward Peter, she
immediately felt uneasy. Even she, president of
Silverland Group, did not know much French, so how
could Peter, a mere security guard, know French?

With this, she hated Alfred Gao even more. It was
obvious what he was trying to do, and it was
despicable.

Peter saw the beautiful waitress coming, and he
suddenly became serious. Then, he blurted out in
fluent French, "Beautiful lady, please pardon me for
my rudeness. I didn't mean to stare, but I saw a
stain on your skirt and I've been looking for an
opportunity to tell you about it, but you've been
busy and I never had the chance to."

Hearing Peter speak French so fluently, it was not
only Bella who was shocked, but also Alfred, Rex,
and Jane.

Stunned, the waitress, then, looked at her skirt.
After that, she lowered her head in shame and
panicked. "I'm sorry, sir. I've misunderstood you."

No one else could hear the accent in the way Peter
spoke, but she, a French girl, could. His French had
a strong royal accent, and his pronunciation was
more authentic than that of most French commoners.
Such a person definitely had a superb identity and
background.

The waitress even felt a little upset and annoyed by
the stain on her skirt. She had even hoped that
Peter had been looking at her, not at the stain.

"It's nothing." Peter waved his hand politely and
began to order.

'This guy must have happened to know French by luck,' Jane thought. Seeing this, her face turned red, full of remorse.

A streak of gloom flashed through Alfred's eyes but soon disappeared.

Only the eyes of Rex lit up for a while, but he did not say anything, either.

Bella was completely dumbfounded. If they weren't in a family gathering, she would want to ask Peter who he was right then and there.

With his strong fighting skills and ability to speak French, how could such a man work as a security guard in Silverland Group? Did he have a hidden agenda?

The meal was soon served, and they began to enjoy the exquisite food.

In the meantime, the beautiful waitress kept winking at Peter, trying to seduce him, implying something somehow.

Looking at this scene irritated Bella. She could do nothing but just glare at Peter. Fortunately, he was behaving very well. He was just having his food with his head down, and that kept Bella from losing her temper.

Looking at Peter, who was only concerned with eating and drinking, Alfred thought of another way to humiliate him.

"I would like to introduce myself. I am Alfred Gao, chairman of Alfred Group. Where do you work, my friend?" He raised his glass to greet Peter.

"Alfred Group?" Peter, who was quietly eating and drinking, finally raised his head for the first time, his eyes full of surprise.

When Alfred saw Peter's expression, he was secretly satisfied and proud of himself. Although Alfred Group was not as prominent as Silverland Group, it was not far off and it was also well-known in Golden City.

The most important thing was that, Alfred Group, was Alfred Gao's own company. Anyone would know that only by hearing the name. So, Alfred thought that he had intimidated Peter with this.

Chapter 12 One Million Dollars
"I've never heard of it before." Peter ducked his head to eat after spouting that sentence.

Alfred almost froze with shock when he heard the words that came out from Peter's mouth.

Alfred felt like he had punched a soft pillow. His blow was supposed to be powerful, yet it seemed pretty useless after what Peter had said. "How about you? What do you do, bro?" Alfred was by no means going to reconcile with his defeat.

"What do I do?" Peter repeated. He was startled for a second, and then he said, "I have a normal job. I'm a security guard."

Bella felt a chill down her spine with what Peter had said. She hurriedly put her hand over Peter's mouth to stop him. "Oh dear, see how careless you are. You've got some crumbs on your face. Let me clean them for you."

Bella gently wiped the crumbs off with her little hand as she nervously tried to make up an excuse.

She was burning with rage inside, but she was trying to hold it in.

'You bastard!' She cursed him in her mind, 'How can you tell the truth? Now everybody knows you are a fake, you idiot.' Such a clichéd romance plot like a CEO falling in love with a security guard was only applicable in chic-lit books. Nobody would believe them!

However, it was already too late when she covered Peter's mouth.

Alfred was dazed for a while, and then he broke into a laugh. "Security guard? Interesting, " he paused and then continued, "I'll give you one million bucks if you get out of here right now. What do you say?"

A million?

'Shit!' Bella had a bad feeling about it.

"Really?" Peter asked, his eyes beaming at the amount of money mentioned.

"Yeah. I'm serious, " Alfred said as he nodded.

Peter showed him his bank account details on his phone without any hesitation. "Transfer it to me now. I'll get out of this room as soon as the money arrives!"

Bella ground her teeth in anger. If she had a gun in her hand, she would definitely shoot him in no time! Son of a bitch! How could he betray her for money!

However, Alfred was still laughing. To him, a million was just a drop in the ocean.

Once Peter had received the money, he rose up from his seat and got out of the room immediately, without looking back. Bella wanted to stop him, but she failed to.

Alfred burst into laughter again. "Did you see what kind of man he was, Bella?" he asked and continued, "He's not the right person for you. Whether he's your real boyfriend or not, he's not reliable."

"Yes, Bella. Alfred is right. I don't think he's reliable, either. Look at Alfred. He really loves you, " Jane agreed.

Bella's face turned pale. The sparkle in her eyes dimmed, and a cold, hard knot tightened in her chest.

Her purpose of bringing Peter to see her parents today was to let them give up the idea of fixing her up with Alfred. But now, everything had turned the other way around. Peter had betrayed her for a million!

Strangely, Bella felt mortified and inexplicably sad. She had gotten too mad that she might end up literally killing him.

"I gotta go now. I still have something else to do. Enjoy your meals." Bella had no mood to stay since Peter had left. She stood up and intended to leave after she saying those words drily.

Jane wanted to stop her by grabbing her arm, but she let Bella go when she saw Alfred's eyes.

Alfred knew that it was useless to force her to stay. He believed that she would be his and only his in a matter of time.

Bella quickly walked to the door of the room. Just as she had opened the door and was about to step out, a man walked into the room.The two people collided with each other. She raised her head and froze on the spot. The man was none other than Peter! That bastard!

She stared at his face disappointingly. The anger that she was holding in suddenly ignited within her again. She really wanted to slaughter him into pieces right now!

However, at that moment, Peter held her arms with both his hands. "Sweetie, are you all right? Did I hurt you just now?" he asked anxiously, "Oh my god! You look ghastly, my dear. Who made you this mad? Where are you going? Have you finished eating?"

The sudden hug and all these questions disarmed Bella a little, but she still gave him a scornful glare.

"Didn't you just leave with the money? Why did you come back?"

"You're still here. How can I leave without you?" Peter feigned surprise. "That idiot promised to give me a million if I left the room. I was thinking of going to the restroom anyway, so I agreed. And why not? It's one million!"

He didn't leave her after all...

Bella couldn't help but laugh. Peter's explanation made her feel warm.

However, Alfred was driven crazy. He finally realized that he was fooled by Peter.

"I will remember you! Let's wait and see!" Alfred said furiously. He pulled a long face as he looked at the two people holding each other, and then he left immediately. A surge of envy was evident in his eyes when he left.

He would definitely beat Peter up if he were not a security guard and if they were not in a high-end restaurant.

"You, the two of you..." Jane stuttered, pointing at Peter and Bella. She was too mad to say anything. Angrily, she hurried off after Alfred.

Rex left the room unhurriedly after taking a glance at Peter with interest.

"Can you let me go?" Bella said coldly when all of the people were out of their sight.

"Sorry, I almost forgot." Peter loosened his hands unwillingly. It felt good... holding her. How he wished he could hold her longer.

"Let's go." Since everybody had left, Bella didn't want to stay any there, either.

"But those dishes hadn't been touched, yet."

"Then, enjoy them yourself."

"Fine, never mind then. But can I, at least, pack them up?"

"Oh, come on!"

With the neon lights shining brightly against the nightscape of Golden City, the beautiful scene was a sight to see.

The fiery, red Hummer was like a tank dominating the road, causing countless of people to stare. As the cold wind blew in from the window, Bella felt both her heart and body refreshed.

However, when she saw the aggrieved and depressed expression on Peter's face, her good mood suddenly dissipated.

"Do you have anything to say? Just spit it out. Don't show me that face."

"Fine, then. I'll say it since you asked. Miss Song, how did you like my performance tonight?"

"Not bad." Bella frowned. She seemed to know what Peter had wanted to say.

Sure enough!

"Then, when can I get the other 5, 000?" Peter asked.

"Screw you!"

Bella spluttered sharply. She slammed her foot on the gas pedal, speeding up, faster and faster.

Peter was frustrated. He was already certain that the 5, 000 was nothing more than words.

Along the road, Bella was rigid with anger. The car sped up steeply, non-stop. Looking at Bella's cold face, Peter just sat quietly. He didn't dare say a word, for he feared that this bitch would get them in a disastrous accident if he made her even more unhappy.

In the end, Bella drove Peter to the beach. After getting off the car, she took her shoes off immediately and walked on the sand barefoot.

She looked very relaxed while walking along the beach, especially with the sea breeze brushing against her face and the waves crashing on the shore. The cool and invigorating wind seemed to be blowing away all of her frustrations.

Peter didn't disturb her, for he knew that she was not in a good mood. He followed her quietly. He looked at her curvy back and her free-flowing dress, and suddenly, he noticed how beautiful and charming she was at that moment.

A moment later, Bella sat down on the sand with her hands over her knees and started to cry.

This moment, she looked more like an ordinary, helpless lady than a cold, bitchy CEO.

Peter sat down next to her quietly, still not saying a word. He felt a surge of empathy, thinking that it was not easy to be a rigid CEO. All the people saw was the superficial side of her, the powerful and glorified version of her, but who knew that she could be sad and helpless, too?

Bella sobbed for a while. Suddenly, she raised her head and hugged Peter. She closed her eyes and said, "Kiss me."

Her words caught him off guard. What should he do? Should he kiss her or should he kiss her? Maybe, he should kiss her? Ugh, why did God always put him in such difficult situations?

Looking at her charming nose, appealing cheekbones, her flaming lips... Peter's brain went totally blank. He closed his eyes involuntarily and bowed his head slowly.

Suddenly, a few snickers brought them back to their senses before Peter's lips had reached Bella's, destroying the beautiful moment completely.

"Whoa, bro. Thanks for the free live performance. Hey lady, since you look lonely and desperate, how about we spend the night with you?"

"Dude, she's hot. She really turns me on. We'll have fun tonight."

Some strange voices came out from the dark. Then, several men with glossy faces appeared, walking in their direction.

Chapter 13 Opponents Always Meet

These guys were wearing earrings, had cigarettes between their lips, and adorned tattoos on their bodies. There was a kind of evilness in their eyes, and they looked like a group of ruffians.

'Damn it! Who are these people? How dare they come out and make troubles at such a critical moment!'

Peter was about to kiss Bella, but the moment was interrupted by these guys. He immediately boiled over with rage, and he couldn't control his temper at all.

"Break their necks!" Bella was even more furious. She was not afraid of them, so she uttered such words.

She was confident in Peter's fighting skills. Bob was completely defeated by him, let alone these low-class ruffians.

"Okay!" Peter grinned and then raised his head.

At that moment, he unexpectedly saw a familiar face. But he was seeing not one but two familiar faces.

One was the bare-armed man whose head was cracked by Peter in the bar when the latter made efforts to save Bella. The other was the bag snatcher who was badly beaten by Peter when he robbed Elaine a few days ago.

"You?"

"It's you!"

The two men also saw Peter at once, and their eyes flashed with immense anger.

When these two guys saw Peter, they completely forgot about the beautiful Bella; instead, they rushed toward Peter furiously.

"It's the guy who beat me up that night. Teach him a lesson for me!"

"That bastard! He got himself involved in my business and messed it up. He also made me lose a motorcycle. Brothers, let's make that guy suffer and kill him!"

All clenching their fists, the two guys screamed so loud, adrenaline pumping through their veins. Hearing their words, the other young men hesitated only for a second. Then, they also showed their eagerness and rushed toward Peter.

A dozen guys instantly darted toward Peter in a rage. The scene was quite frightening, especially since it was one against many.

With his mouth twitching, Peter took two steps back and said, "Brothers, you've mistaken me for someone else. Do you believe me?"

"Of course not!" The bare-armed man was the first who dashed toward Peter. Raising his huge fist, he did not hesitate to hit him.

"Please, believe me. I'm telling the truth. Brother, we are all civilized people. Let's not do this, okay?"

Upon saying that, Peter jumped aside and dodged his opponent's attack, and the bare-armed man received a sudden kick in his ass.

With the surprise hit, the bare-armed man was thrown forward to the ground. He screamed so loud and tried to get up but couldn't.

"I told you not to be so rude, but you didn't listen to me. So it's not my fault, " Peter mumbled, dodging a kick and giving a punch to the person in front of him at the same time.

Bam!

A young man was hit in the nose. The bridge of his nose immediately cracked and broke with blood dripping on his face. This guy was thrown backwards with great strength and, then he fell down embarrassed to the ground.

"The bridge of your nose is so fragile; it can't even bear a punch from me. How weak!"

The young man wanted to curse Peter, but he could only do so in his mind. 'Shit! Is the bridge of your nose as hard as my fist? I'll punch you in return.'

Moving on angrily, Peter produced two more kicks, one for each of the two men who tried to attack him. The two young men screamed. They were thrown away, with hands over their bellies.

"What the hell! This guy has some skills. Brothers, let's take our weapons out."

Seeing that the situation was not good, the other six or seven young men stopped in their tracks immediately and pulled out their weapons.

In an instant, all of these men had weapons in their hands.

There were flick knives, fruit knives, short steel tubes, iron wrenches, and so on. One of the guys even brought a sledgehammer. In short, they took out whatever on them.

On seeing this, Bella couldn't help but worry about Peter.

If the thugs were bare-handed, she wouldn't worry about him, but now, things were different. The men had weapons now. What if Peter would get hurt real bad?

Bella didn't know why she suddenly became so concerned about Peter.

Focused on the battle he was in, Peter had no clue what Bella was thinking about in that particular moment. Looking at the various weapons, he jumped up at once, with his mouth twitching.

"What are you guys doing? What are you trying to do? How dare you take out your knives and hammers in broad daylight? Are you guys outlaws?"

"What nonsense are you saying! It's dark now, not broad daylight. You're such a fool!" Seeing Peter's arrogance, a young man couldn't help but curse at him furiously. Afterwards, summoned by the young man who spoke, his comrades rushed toward Peter aggressively.

"You, all of youâ€¦ Don't make me do it. You're not the only ones who have weapons. I do, too!" Peter gnashed teeth in hatred as if he had made up his mind because he had been forced to.

Frightened by his imposing manner, the young men instantly stopped in amazement. They all froze, wondering what Peter's next move would be.

Bella breathed a sigh of relief. The fighting spirit in her eyes was restored.

However, Peter's next act almost made them gauge their eyes out.

Suddenly, he took off his shoes and carried them respectively in his left and right hands.

"Are those your weapons?" One of the young men felt a little confused.

"Yes. What's wrong? Are you scared?" With a satisfied expression, Peter raised the shiny leather shoes in both his hands. "I'm warning you all. My shoes are as ruthless as your knives and swords. They won't spare anyone. I'm afraid I'll hurt you."

"Shit! We got fooled!"

"Go ahead! Slice him up!"

The patience of this group of young men had already gone with the absurdity that Peter had been showing them.

'A pair of leather shoes as his ultimate weapon? This bastard is insulting our IQ and scorning our dignity!'

In an instant, several young men eagerly rushed close to Peter. They were about to hit him with various weapons — knives, sticks, hammers, and so on.

Peter smiled. Twisting his body from side to side to align his spine, he waved his shoes and threw them out with a confusing posture.

Bam, bam, bam, bam!

With a few smacking sounds, four young men were hit by the soles of the shoes. They all felt a burning pain in their faces, and then, they fell to the ground with dizziness. Blood gushed out of their mouths with some of their teeth mixed in it. What a miserable sight!

"I told you guys that my shoes would spare no one, but you didn't believe me, " Peter mumbled, looking towards the last three people standing.

Two of them were holding a knife and a stick respectively; they wanted to attack Peter, but they were also hesitating. The other one was hiding far behind them. He couldn't dare rush forward.

That coward was the bag snatcher. He was cleverer than the bare-armed man. He had just shouted some aggressive and threatening words, but he didn't act upon them.

He knew that Peter's strength was too much. Even if they would be able to defeat him, the first person who would rush up to him would be beaten up for sure.

But to his surprise, in just a few moments, all of
his friends got thrown down by Peter.

Knowing that it was almost impossible to escape, the
bag snatcher took a glance at Bella who was near
him. Then, he gritted his teeth and ran toward her
at full speed.

What was that bag-snatching douceface trying to do?

Thank you for reading. Please leave your valuable
review. It will help us provide you with more
interesting novels. More top billionaire romance
novels await you at moboreader.net

Chapter 14 Alfred's Revenge
Peter saw what the clumsy bag-snatcher was trying to
do, but he was confident that the robber would reap
what he had sown, and therefore, Peter did not stop
him.

Bella seemed like a delicate, pretty girl who could
not do any harm to others, but she had the
capability to fight. It was a piece of cake for
Bella to beat up that clumsy bag-snatcher.

The robber ran over to Bella and shouted at the same
time, "Bastard, you've got guts? Now, kneel down
before me. Otherwise, I'll mar this woman's face!"

"Ahh! ! !"

The robber curled into a ball as he felt the wincing
pain coming from his lower body before he had even
finished his words.

His face was distorted due to the agony he was
feeling.

Bella had lifted her right knee, hitting the
robber's crotch brutally.

"You said you were going to mar my face?" Bella squinted at the robber, and suddenly, she pulled his hair to drag him down to the ground. Then, she grabbed two cobblestones and hit him with them.

The robber was in so much pain that he opened his mouth wide and screamed out loud.

If he could turn back the clock, he would rather deal with Peter than this insane woman.

The people around them, including Peter, were surprised at what had just happened.

Violent and ferocious!

It was better to stay far away from this tough beauty.

Peter even felt chills upon witnessing the stunt that Bella had conducted.

He now felt lucky that he had not kissed her. If he had dared kiss her, who knew what could happen... He feared the consequences.

Bella's attack to the crotch was a lesson for Peter, indeed. No man would be able to survive that intense impact.

"Miss Song, what should we do with these two men?" Peter asked with a low voice after seeing Bella stop.

Bella squinted at the two men. They knelt down instantly, out of fear, before Bella made any sound.

"Sir, madame, I'm sorry!"

"Sir, madame, I will never dare do that again!"

"We were wrong!"

"Please show us your mercy and let us go!"

"We are sorry for trying to harm you couple!"

"We are guilty!"

The two men begged for mercy with tears as they slapped their own faces.

They were slapping themselves with much force. The sound of the smacks could be heard by everyone. Soon, their face were swollen like balls.

They did not want to result to this at all, but they had no choice. Peter and Bella were just too strong for them. The thugs would hit themselves rather than get beaten up by Peter and Bella.

But honestly, they would prefer to get hit by Peter because they would still be able to procreate. If they were hit by Bella, on the other hand... their ability to procreate would be close to none.

Peter felt a little bit compassionate when he saw these two hitting themselves so roughly. However, when Peter heard the men call them a couple, he felt no compassion anymore, wanting to zip their mouths immediately.

They were not a couple at all! If Bella got angry because of this, Peter would then suffer.

"Let's go!" Bella blushed when the two men called Peter and her a couple, but she decided to let go of it. She glanced at Peter and went directly to her Hummer. Peter followed her immediately.

"Peter, who are you exactly?" Bella did not drive straight home, but she parked her car on the roadside and asked.

This question had been puzzling her the whole night.

Peter was not any commoner for sure because he had great fighting skills and could even speak fluent French.

"Who am I? I'm an ordinary security guard. Why did you ask? Are you feeling all right?" Peter wanted to joke over it.

"Will you ever hurt me?" Bella did not continue that topic but, instead, asked another question.

"No, I won't, " Peter answered with a serious face. He knew that only a firm answer could make Bella feel at ease.

"Let's get married, " Bella said as she leaned her body toward Peter.

Peter was too shocked to follow what Bella was saying.

But he had almost lost control as he was being seduced by the gorgeous Bella. He concentrated and focused very hard on trying to stay calm.

"Miss Song, I just remembered that I still have things to do. I have to leave now. See you later!" Peter pushed Bella away slightly sniffing the perfume on her. He, then, opened the car door and hastily went away.

Bella saw Peter running away. She was not angry with what he did, but she was confused with her own heart. She could not help asking herself, "Bella, Bella, do you like him? Do you love him? He has offended Alfred for you. How many other people will he need to offend for you?"

--

Peter just kept running until he could not see the red Hummer anymore. He finally felt relieved.

Bella seemed unusual tonight. He was afraid that he would not be able to control himself and go third base with her. If so, there would be a huge trouble.

"Handsome, you are sweating so bad. How about coming in and taking a shower to cool down?" Peter ran to a bathhouse without noticing. The voice suddenly sounded, and it was too late for Peter to react before he was dragged in.

Now that he had already gone inside, Peter decided not to go out immediately. He had just made more than a million tonight, so he could handle the cost.

Peter looked over the women with heavy make-up and declared, "I just want to take a bath. I don't need any other service."

"Set your mind at rest, handsome! There's no such special service here even if you want it, " the woman said that in an affectionate and sweet way.

"That's fine."

Peter reserved a private room and took a cold shower. He then lay down on the bed cozily. Suddenly, the door opened with the aroma of a woman's perfume soon after Peter lay down.

"I've said that I don't need any service..." Peter did not finish his words because he realized that the perfume was poisonous!

He held his breath immediately without any hesitation and soon put on his pants despite the strange woman in the room.

"The cops are here! It's a raid! Get out now!" At that time, someone was shouting, and it became chaotic outside.

Peter felt an unusual atmosphere. He had no time to put on his top, so he dashed toward the window with his clothes in his hand.

"You cannot go!" The woman ran to Peter, wanting to seize him.

Peter kicked the woman down coldly and broke the window glass without a second thought. He got out in no time and ran as fast as he could.

Wham!

The moment Peter had gotten out, the policemen broke down the door and went inside the room.

"Shit! Chase that man now!" The police officer saw that only a woman was in the room and that Peter was nowhere to be found. He cursed angrily and led the other police to look for Peter.

However, they all were stopped in their tracks.

They were on the third floor and did not dare jump.

--

Alfred was drinking with a few young ladies and young men in a luxurious room of Alfred Club.

These young men were in expensive clothes, adorned with jewelry. It was easy to tell that they were born with silver spoons in their mouths.

Alfred was in the middle. Apparently, he was the leader of these young men.

Alfred was chatting with his fellows while glancing at his phone from time to time. He was waiting for something, obviously.

Peter was just nobody, so Alfred made arrangements to fuck Peter up. Tonight, he would utterly discredit Peter's reputation, making him a nobody to Bella.

At that moment, the phone alerted. Alfred picked up the phone with a bleak smile on his face.

Thank you for reading. Please leave your valuable review. It will help us provide you with more interesting novels. More top billionaire romance novels await you at moboreader.net

Chapter 15 Robbery
"Boss, weâ€¦ failed the missionâ€¦" The man said trembling over the phone.

"I know you will make it. That's great. Wait... What did you say? You failed the mission? You did what?!" Alfred hadn't expected that they would fail the mission. His joy was replaced by rage within a second. When he jumped to his feet, all eyes in the room turned to him.

"We didn't expect him to be so vigilant. He doesn't seem poisoned at all! He even managed to jump from the third floor and escape!"

"You worthless piece of garbage!" Alfred boomed. "I paid good money for this mission, and you all pissed me over! Pray that I'll never see you again!"

He yelled, ending the conversation.

Alfred was so furious he didn't want to talk to any of his men.

'You're lucky this time, Peter Wang, but trust me that your happy days are running out soon.' Alfred swore as he stormed out of the hall.

--

Peter kept running until he was very far away from the small bathing place, and then he hailed a cab to get a ride home.

'I know you did this, Alfred. But you know I should thank you for keeping my life interesting.' Lost in his thoughts, Peter devised a plan to defeat Alfred.

Peter was new to the city. He didn't have friends yet, but he managed to make a few enemies. Alfred was one of them. Alfred was a very powerful man because of his connections to the local police. This was also why it was easy for Peter to trace the incident back to him.

Exhausted from the day's happenings, Peter entered his home and immediately fell into a deep slumber.

--

Peter hummed a tune as he rode an old electric vehicle to work, the next day. The skies were beautiful and sunny.

Around him, he saw people shifting past each other â€"some of them in a hurry, some rather lost in their own thoughts. Peter felt happy just seeing so much life around him. Plus, there were a lot of beautiful women too!

Suddenly, an accident occurred!

While in the middle of a fun tune in his head, Peter heard loud gasps from the surrounding crowd. A middle-aged woman passing in front of his vehicle suddenly fell to the ground!

'Fuck!

Is this a modus operandi for a robbery?'

Peter was very confused.

'You've got to be kidding me! I'm riding a used electric bicycle and my clothes are not expensive! I look like a loser! I don't look rich at all! Of all the people she'd try to rob, why me?' This woman must be crazy to try to rob Peter. He had nothing valuable on him!

Seeing that the woman hadn't done anything to validate his suspicions, Peter felt like there was something very, very wrong. Looking closer, Peter realized that she was actually in pain.

Peter's expression changed. 'She needs help!' He immediately got off his vehicle and started massaging her chest with his hands.

'Shit, she's having a heart attack!'

"You idiot! What are you doing? Let my mom go!"

Said a girl from behind him. In her panic, she threw him a kick

Which Peter caught before it could hit him. 'Wow, these are smooth, strong and white legs, ' he couldn't help observing. At the same time, he felt offended.

He was only trying to help, why did this girl immediately think he was up to no good? 'This is why a lot of people would rather just stand on the side than step up and help.'

Although the woman's legs were beautiful, it wasn't a good time to dwell on it. Concentrating on the middle-aged woman, Peter continued massaging her chest.

She was seriously ill! If Peter didn't act quickly, she might have already lost her life!

Audrey looked at Peter wide-eyed. She didn't expect the idiot to be quick enough to catch her leg.

Now she couldn't move and it was very annoying. She also saw what he was doing to her mom, and that drove her into a rage.

"You maniac! What are you doing to my mom? I'm going to kill you, I swear!" In her anger, Audrey failed to notice her mom's pale face, and the reason why her mom was allowing Peter to continue what he was doing.

Clearly, her prejudice came before her senses.

Audrey and her mom were shopping before she had to buy a drink to quench her thirst. The moment she got back, the sight of her mom on the floor and Peter touching her chest was the first thing she saw.

'PERVERT!' Audrey marched towards him wanting to throw her drink at him.

Also angry, Peter pushed Audrey away as he caught her leg, causing her to painfully fall to the ground as well.

"Have you lost your mind, little girl? Can't you see I'm trying to save your mom's life? Look at her! She looks awful!

Despite your anxiety, how could you even think I'd take advantage of your mom in the middle of the road? It's a public fucking place, I'm not an idiot!"

Audrey was a beautiful girl of 18 years with long, black hair that swayed gently in the breeze.

Her T-shirt and denim shorts flattered her figure.

She was the type of girl Peter would normally hit on. He would do whatever he can to find a way to talk to her and get her WeChat number. With Audrey, though, his first emotion was clearly that of anger.

"Use your head, lady! Don't be stupid!"

Peter finished, as he turned to his vehicle to leave.

"Wait!" The middle-aged woman called out. "Thank you for your help, young man. You saved my life."

"My daughter is a spoiled brat. I'm sorry for what she did to you. Please understand."

The woman glared at her daughter, walked to Peter, and gave him a bow of appreciation. Peter felt odd seeing an older woman show him respect.

Audrey gave Peter a piercing look.

She refused to accept her misgiving, being spoiled from childhood. She hated being blamed for anything, and what Peter said infuriated her.

"Please, ma'am, you don't have to do that. I accept your apology." Peter said quickly walking to the middle-aged woman to help her stand straight from her bow. "It seems that you've been ill for years. Please go to the hospital so it won't get worse."

"Go to the hospital?" The middle-aged woman shook her head. "I've seen many doctors already, no one could cure my disease.

Speaking of which, what you did to me just now was a traditional Chinese medical massage, correct?"

Peter nodded. "I actually feel so much better. Do you think you can treat my disease?"

The woman was positive that Peter could help her with what she was feeling. The relief she felt now was something she had never felt before with all the advice and procedures given by other medical professionals.

"Uh... Yes, ma'am, I think I can treat you, butâ€¦" Peter hesitated.

"But what? Don't worry. Money is not a problem. If you can cure my mother, you can get as much as you want." Audrey cut him off, excited when she heard that Peter could possibly cure her mother. Despite being spoiled and selfish, her mother meant a lot to her. She would give anything to see her healed.

Thank you for reading. Please leave your valuable review. It will help us provide you with more

Chapter 16 The Dinner Incident

"Audrey, stop!" The woman scolded her daughter. "Please don't mind my daughter. Again, she is very spoiled. But don't worry, we have some savings. We will surely pay you back for your services once you cure me."

The woman was honest about their financial situation and was polite enough to call the money as the therapy payment.

This chronic disease had troubled her for so long. She always suffered so much when she had attacks. Even medicine couldn't relieve her much.

When Peter said that he could cure her, she felt very excited and worried that he might be offended because of her daughter.

"Ma'am, you misunderstood me, " said Peter, "I'm not worried about the money. Your disease is not something that can be easily cured. Treatment takes time, and there is no way to speed it up."

The woman felt embarrassed for assuming that money was the issue right away. "I'm willing to go through treatment no matter how long it takes, young man. By the way, how long would it be?"

She asked nervously. Could it be another 3 years? 5 years? Could she handle it if it lasted for that long?

"That depends, ma'am. If things go well, it could be around a week. Otherwise, it could take as long as a month." Peter replied, a worried look across his face.

Audrey was stupefied

As she stopped herself from grabbing her drink and throwing the bottle at Peter again.

'One week or a month? That's nothing! How is that a long time? Even a fever takes a couple of days, and it's reasonable that my mom's chronic disease would take longer!

This bastard must be bragging. He's doing it on purpose!'

The longer Audrey looked at Peter, the more annoyed she became.

"Really?" the middle-aged woman asked. "Please, sir. Can you please check up on me when you are available?" The woman was on cloud nine. She almost wanted him to do the first checkup, then and there.

"I'm not available during the day because I have work. After work is ideal for me. How about this: I'll visit you this evening, after work."

The woman had been nothing but courteous and appreciative. Peter couldn't find it in himself to refuse her.

"Okay, " she replied. Although a little disappointed with the wait, she knew that it would be futile to negotiate a sooner schedule. They exchanged private numbers and went their separate ways.

The events that morning delayed Peter's travel by half an hour, causing him to be late at work.

With Bob in the hospital, though, no one was there to reprimand him, so that was good.

Peter parked his motorcycle next to a white BMW in the basement parking lot, and hurriedly got dressed for work.

"Hey, bro. Want a cigarette?" He was on his way to playfully tease Shelly and Lisa after arriving at the reception hall when Jack asked.

Seeing what Peter had done, Jack's admiration for Peter shot overwhelmingly high so he wanted to stay on his good side.

On his first day of work, Peter beat the security manager and sent him to the hospital. A regular employee would have been fired had he done the same thing, but Peter still worked freely with no consequence whatsoever. He could bet his life that Peter had a really strong connection with someone powerful in Silverland Group. So today, he bought a pack of premium cigarettes specifically to please Peter.

"Hey, Jack. I don't think we're allowed to smoke during work hours. Besides, aren't you supposed to be working, lazybones? Good luck getting your salary if we fail Miss Song and Silverland Group."

Peter said, offended with Jack's offer.

Jack was stunned.

'Me? How am I the lazy one when you're already half an hour late? How am I the one neglecting my duty? Besides, why did you take my cigarette pack and put it in your pocket if you didn't want to smoke?'

"Smoking is bad for you, don't you know? I'm confiscating it to keep you safe because we're colleagues and good friends. You're welcome, "

Peter preached, making him look like such a good guy in contrast to Jack. What a cheeky fellow who hustled Jack's cigarettes in a reasonable excuse!

Jack fumed with anger. If Peter hadn't had powerful background and if he hadn't been so strong, Jack would have punched him on the face.

Shelly and Lisa were both stifling their laughter.

'Peter is so dreamy.'

Peter didn't see neither Elaine nor Bella throughout
the day. It seemed as though they had forgotten he
existed.

Finally, a calm day for Peter. He spent it on work,
amusing Shelly and Lisa and teaching Jack his
lesson.

"Wait for us after work, Peter. We want to treat you
to dinner!" Shelly told him sweetly as their shift
was about to end. Jack felt very envious.

"Sure! I'd also say yes for other invitations. If
you know what I mean, " Peter said slyly. He'd never
refuse such a good offer.

"Mm, naughty." Shelly blushed and looked at Peter
shyly. As for Lisa, she almost hid under the table.

As Peter was entering the parking lot, he noticed
that the BMW parked beside his motorcycle was
struggling to get out of the parking space.

The driver seemed to be having a hard time
manoeuvring with his motorcycle there.

Through the slightly tinted windows, Peter realized
that inside it was Clair, Bella's secretary. Peter
smirked. Instead of removing his motorcycle, he
stood back, crossed his arms, and watched her
struggle to get out of the parking space.

Clair was losing her patience. 'Whose damn
motorcycle is this? It occupies half of the space
and it's parked too close to my car!'

Other drivers may find the feat pretty simple to do,
but as a new driver, it was an unwelcome obstacle
for Clair.

She went forward and backward several times, each
attempt failing. 'AGGGH!' she said in her

frustration. As she was about to get off the car to remove the motorcycle out of the way herself, she saw a guy walking towards her from the corner of her eye.

When she realized who he was, she got even more furious.

"What are you laughing at? Piss off or I swear I'll run you over!" Clair yelled at Peter, rolling her eyes angrily.

Peter called her bluff. Instead of standing aside, he walked right behind her car. "Really, now? Here, I'm standing still. Do you think you can hit me?"

Clair was infuriated. How dare this bastard mock her and her driving skills!

"Asshole!" Out of anger Clair got off her car and kicked over Peter's old motorcycle. Then she backed her car and cursed, "Wait there if you have guts! I'll kill you!"

"What the fuck?" Peter jumped back, dismayed. "Why did you do that? My motorcycle was parked correctly! You need to pay for that or whatever. This isn't over!"

He shouted as he ran to his motorcycle to inspect if there was significant damage.

"I wondered who the asshole owner of the motorcycle was. Had I known it was you, I would have given it more kicks!" Clair replied.

Clair smirked, gloating. Snorting condescendingly, she zoomed away with her BMW, leaving Peter behind.

"Hey! Stop!" Peter jumped on his motorcycle and started to go after her.

Nobody knew how many times his vehicle had been resold. There was no way he'd be able to catch up to a BMW. Clair was already gone by the time he got out of the parking lot.

"This isn't over, I swear, " Peter murmured, disappointed.

"You're crazy, Peter!" Shelly and Lisa said in disbelief. "You said you were driving, but we didn't expect you meant thisâ€¦ thing." They remarked, looking at his shabby motorcycle.

"Yeah, isn't it cool? It cost me 250! It's energy saving and congestion-free!" Peter spoke as if he didn't have an old motorcycle, but a Lamborghini. He was very proud.

"Uhh..."

Shelly and Lisa exchanged glances, unable to comment anything.

"Well if you don't want to ride my motorcycle, then fine. I guess I'll go now." he said losing his patience. He felt disappointed that they looked down on his motorcycle.

"No, wait, of course, we'll ride."

Shelly immediately said, climbing behind Peter. Lisa hesitated but decided to sit behind Shelly as well.

The vehicle felt like it was only meant for two riders. Three made it feel very crowded. Even though the two girls were slim, they struggled to fit.

Shelly already had almost her full upper body resting on Peter's back, which made her blush despite her usual sass.

"Hold tight." Peter smiled, feeling her body heat on his back.

"Ouch!" Shelly cried, holding on to Peter tightly.

The sight of Peter carrying two girls in his
motorcycle sparked envy in every person they passed,
Especially the ones who drove cars. They would have
wanted to run him over and invite the two beautiful
girls into their cars.

With Shelly navigating, Peter sped through the
highway and smoothy maneuvered around the cars in
traffic. They arrived at a posh and expensive-
looking restaurant.

"Woah. You don't have to treat me to somewhere that
expensive, Shelly. I'd be happy with some grilled
food at the side of the road." Peter frowned,
intimidated at the sight.

The girls were very young. Peter was sure they
didn't have too much money on them yet.

If they dined here, he was sure they'd spend 1, 000
at a minimum. If they went to the sidewalk vendors,
instead, 100 would already be more than enough for
the three of them.

Shelly appreciated Peter's concern for their money.
As she was about to say something in response, she
was cut off by an offensive remark.

"Stop pretending to be rich, beggar. You don't
belong here! Shame on you! I hate people like you!"

A beer-bellied, middle-aged man with a face too
wrinkled for his age, appeared in front of them.
Following him was an overdressed, but plain-looking
woman.

He sneered at Peter and diverted his gaze to Shelly
and Lisa, smiling. "Hello, pretty ladies. May I have
the honor of joining you for dinner? Feel free to
order anything you like. I can surely afford it."

Thank you for reading. Please leave your valuable
review. It will help us provide you with more

interesting novels. More top billionaire romance
novels await you at moboreader.net

Chapter 17 Be Proven Wrong
The middle-aged man waved the key of the Mercedes-
Benz on his hands as if to show off his wealth.

Peter frowned and said nothing. He was too lazy to
pay any attention to such an annoying person.

"I am busy, " Shelly told the middle-aged man. Her
good mood was destroyed for the most part.

If not for her good personality and fear of
offending people, she would have rushed up to beat
him.

'I invited Peter over for dinner, and that's none of
your business. Why can't you just stop talking?'
thought Shelly. It made Shelly unhappy when the
middle-aged man said that Peter had no money but was
only pretending to be rich.

Shelly was the one who had asked Peter out, so the
middle-aged man said these things ignorant of her
feelings.

"Little girl, think about it. My name is Wayne
Huang. Though I'm not on the Forbes list of
billionaires, I flatter myself as a millionaire. Be
with me, and I'll give you thirty or fifty thousand
a month."

Wayne was not angered by Shelly's cold attitude, and
even asked her to be one of his lovers.

After saying that, he turned to Peter and said in a
scornful voice, "If I am not mistaken, he drove you
in that battered motorcycle. Such a poor man... He
can drive nothing but that cheap motorcycle his
whole life. You won't have any future with this guy.

I advise you to leave him as soon as possible. He's a good-for-nothing, dirt-poor wimp."

Shelly stared angrily at Wayne as if she was shooting bullets through her eyes, even Lisa couldn't help but get angry at this man.

Peter was even more depressed. He had never said a word from the start, yet he was being attacked by the aggressive language, even though he was innocent.

At this time, Peter had to opened his mouth. He looked at the woman beside Wayne Huang and said, "Ma'am, don't you mind that he flirts with other girls in front of you like this?"

Snort!

When Wayne Huang heard Peter's words, his smile became more contemptuous. Then, he said, "Cowards are cowards. They can only turn to women.

She's not my wife. Even if she were, she would not dare discipline me."

Wayne Huang saw Peter's skeptical face, so he pointed to the woman and asked her, "Would you dare discipline me if I flirt with those two women?"

"I wouldn't dare. They're even lucky that you like them." Turning to Peter, she said, "Wayne and I are just ordinary friends. I don't have any right to put him in his place."

Although the woman seemed very uncomfortable, probably wanting to kick the shameless Wayne Huang, she had to say those words against her conscience.

She was just a chick whom Wayne Huang was sleeping with. If she offended Wayne Huang, she would be abandoned by him. That's not what she wanted.

Shelly and Lisa were dumbfounded.

Although they did not pay any special attention to Wayne Huang earlier, they still saw that the two were very intimate with each other when they got out of the Mercedes-Benz.

The two girls had always been disgusted with people like Wayne Huang.

Peter smirked. It was the first time that he had ever encountered a woman who humbled herself like this.

"See, I'm right. For the trouble of bringing these two beautiful women to me, take this thousand and get out of my way. Now, they are mine."

Wayne Huang haughtily said as he pulled out a thousand from his bag and slammed the bills in front of Peter.

Peter took the money and put it in his pocket. He bowed his head to Wayne Huang and went far away.

Shelly and Lisa didn't know what had just happened.

The Peter that they knew would not bow his head and allow himself to be humiliated.

But now...

Only for a thousand... Peter sold them off?

When Wayne Huang saw that Peter had bowed his head and left, he began to laugh wildly. "You see that? That's a coward! Would you still like to be with him? A wimp like that, who can only be bought for a thousand, is worth nothing. I can give you several thousands every day."

Wayne Huang gloated. But suddenly, he saw Peter coming back with his hand behind his back. He felt a little humiliated, so he shouted at Peter, "Haven't you already left? What are you doing back here? Go away! Now!"

Wayne Huang's voice stopped abruptly.

Peter suddenly raised the hand behind his back. He was actually holding a brick!

"You... What do you want to do?"

Wayne Huang's face turned pale.

Peter grinned and said, "Isn't it obvious? I want to hit you!"

Just after that, he raised the brick and smashed down on Wayne Huang's head.

With a loud bang, the brick broke into two halves, and Wayne Huang's head dripped with blood.

As soon as Peter threw the remnants of the brick in his hand, he grabbed Wayne Huang's collar with one hand and slapped him in the face with the other.

Slap! "Fuck you! I have endured your words for a long time. Is it that great to be rich? How dare you wave your wealth in front of me!"

Slap!

"You have women around you, and you dared disrespect them? You're really asking for a beating, aren't you?"

Slap! "So what if I drive that battered motorcycle? Does that have anything to do with you?" Slap! "What if I am a coward? What do you care?"

Slap! "That woman can't handle you, right? Then, I will!"

Slap! "Scumbag!"

Slap! "You monster!" Slap! "Fucking bastard!"

Slap! "You asshole!" Slap! "Arrogant doucheface!" Slap! "Son of a bitch!"

Peter cursed at him with every slap that he served.
In an instant, more than a dozen red palm marks were
on his face which put Wayne Huang in so much pain.

His face had bloated, so he could not speak. Both
his cheeks were very swollen and red. Not only that,
but his mouth was drenched with blood. If he opened
his mouth, blood would surely come out.

Shelly and Lisa breathed a sigh of relief. They both
knew that Peter would come through and not let
anyone step on him. However, when they saw Wayne
Huang's bloody face, they felt a little scared.

Peter had hit him so hard. What if the police came?

The woman who was with Wayne Huang was in shock.

Although she felt very happy because Wayne Huang
deserved to be beaten, she could not show it.

"Wayne, are you okay? You, you bastard... Go to
hell! I'll call the police and have them arrest you
for hitting Wayne!

The woman yelled and pulled out her cell phone as
she had decided to call the police.

"No! Don't you dare!"

Peter shouted. Then, he knocked off the woman's
mobile phone, grabbed Shelly and Lisa, and ran.
"Come on, girls! What are youwaiting for?"

In the dumbfounded eyes of the crowd, the three
quickly got on the battered motorcycle and
disappeared without a trace.

Far from the restaurant, the three stopped at a
barbecue stall.

Under the envious and jealous gaze of the diners,
Peter took Shelly and Lisa to find a place to sit
down, and then he took out a thousand, slapped them

on the table, and proudly said, "Whatever you want to eat, whatever you want to drink, order it. I have the money."

The diners around were startled. A few of the guys who had some lascivious thoughts about Shelly and Lisa immediately dispelled the idea.

Peter drove a battered motorcycle, he had two beautiful women with him, and he had thrown a thousand at a barbecue stall. Obviously, he was a nouveau riche.

They hated this kind of flashy men who acted arrogant in front of ordinary people.

Shelly and Lisa rolled their eyes at Peter.

Peter was disgraceful. He was using Wayne Huang's money to pretend that he was rich.

If Wayne Huang had known that not only he was beaten by Peter, but Peter had also pretended to be rich with the one thousand Wayne Huang gave, it would give Wayne Huang a heart attack.

When the boss of the barbecue stall saw the money, he laughed happily. He not only provided them with good service, but also showed high work efficiency. Not long, all the dishes that were ordered by the three were put on the table.

While eating and drinking, Peter joked around with Shelly and Lisa. With only a slight joke that came out of Peter's mouth, the two girls chuckled, blushing. They knew that Peter was teasing with them, and they teased back.

When the diners around saw them having a great time, they envied Peter and admired him greatly at the same time. No wonder he was able to be with two beautiful women. Besides being rich, his charisma was also overwhelming.

Time slipped away with Peter's jokes, so it was already 9:00 PM before they knew it. Although Shelly and Lisa still wanted to have one more round of drinks with Peter, they still had to go to work early tomorrow. Reluctantly, they bade their goodbyes to Peter.

Peter settled the bill and gave a hundred to the owner with a smile. He was about to leave, but suddenly around five or six young people at the next table stood up to surround him.

Seeing this scene, Peter couldn't help but narrow his eyes.

Could't they help it at last?

Chapter 18 Someone Is Killing
Peter had actually been paying attention to these guys for a long time. Ever since they showed up, they kept on peeking sideways at him every now and then. Obviously, they weren't here to eat; instead, they were here for him.

On top of all that, although they had disguised themselves as ordinary hooligans, Peter could easily tell that they were not just some street gangsters. He could sense that these guys were far more dangerous than they looked. Most likely, they were guys that had killed before.

"Hey sexy lady, how much for a night?" A young man, who looked like the leader of the group, drunkenly asked. His attention had been locked on Shelly and Lisa this whole time as if he was going to swallow them up.

The guys behind him were laughing loudly, all of
them surrounding Peter and the two girls, whether
intentionally or unintentionally.

Lisa was a well-behaved girl. She had never been in
such a tricky situation before. She was so scared
that her face turned pale; she hid behind Peter
immediately.

Shelly was much braver than Lisa. It was probably
because Peter was with them. She didn't show any
signs of being frightened at all.

"You asshole, take your money and go the fuck home
to your mommy!" With dauntless courage and Peter's
presence, Shelly screamed, grabbed an empty bottle
from the table, and slammed it on the young man's
head.

They had only wanted to have a nice, quiet dinner
with Peter, but things had just been going awry.
They had already drawn two bunches of thugs in one
night.

Unfortunately, Shelly looked stronger than she
actually was. Indeed, she was very fast but not fast
enough to hit the young man's head.

Blocking the hit from Shelly, the young man whipped
his hand through the air and flicked Shelly's soft
and fair hand aside. The bottle flew away from them
and dropped on the ground, shattering to pieces.

"What a hot chick! I love hot chicks. This should be
fun, " The young man said as he licked his lips in
thirst. Instead of getting mad at Shelly, he became
more impudent.

Shelly ground her teeth and pouted. She could feel
her cheeks flush with anger. However, she could not
do anything but to turn to Peter.

With a scornful face, the young man suddenly laughed
when he saw Shelly turn to Peter for help. He yelled

at Peter, "Hey, little boy. I'm interested in these two girls, so you'd better get out of here right now, or I'll kick your ass."

Peter hesitated for a second, and then he turned away without saying a word.

His reaction made the young man's jaw drop. That wasn't what he had expected. In an ideal situation, Peter should have been mad at him, therefore giving him a chance to hit Peter. After all, he had disrespected the girls in public.

To walk away from the circle, Peter told the guys blocking his way, "Excuse me, bro."

"Excuse me?" The young guys were dazed at first, but then they broke into a laugh. They were here for Peter. How could they let him go?

The group of thugs didn't expect that the man that Mr. Gao had asked them to deal with was a coward. Since they found out that he was a wimp, they came up with a plan to humiliate him, instead.

One of the young guys smirked, lifted one of his legs, and rested it on the stool next to him. He, then, pointed at the gap between his legs and said, "Go under and crawl through like a dog. Then, I'll let you leave."

"Yeah, yeah, go under, or we won't allow you to leave!"

"Damn it, why hadn't I thought of that? I have to record it with my phone. Who knows? It might go viral."

The rest of the men were laughing hysterically. One of them even spat on the floor, pointed at the glob of saliva, and said, "In addition to crawling through, you have to lick that and clean it like a dog!"

"Yes! Lick the floor clean!"

"Hahaha!"

The laughs and noises these young guys made had attracted many people's attention. Some of them observed from far away, waiting to see what was going to happen next.

Looking at Peter and his friends who were surrounded by the hoodlums, they felt very sorry for the girls.

However, the spectators didn't feel sorry for Peter. They thought that he was so cheeky and ostentatious to have brought two hot girls to dinner. He deserved this bad luck.

The owner of the barbecue stall was scared, so he hid himself, avoiding the situation. He had no guts to stop the farce. All he could do was pick up his mobile phone and call the police.

"Bo.. boss. This is not right. Please let me off, okay?" Peter bit his teeth and begged. He looked extremely frightened.

"Bullshit! Kneel down quick and lick it. Now!" One of the young men rolled his eyes and jumped up immediately. He faced Peter and patted one of his hands on poor Peter's face, wanting to slap him.

Ouch!

All of a sudden, Peter screamed and ducked to the side. As he did so, he stretched out his right leg quickly and gave the young rascal a wild kick in the ankle.

Inertia, coupled with Peter's kick, made the young rascal fall to the floor facedown. He uttered a piercing scream after his nose banged on the floor. Coincidentally, the moment he opened his mouth to scream, the spit on the floor happened to have gotten into his mouth.

All of the onlookers were surprised at the sight of it. They couldn't help but feel sick; some of them even began vomiting.

The companions of the young rascal were all in a daze, too.

Their friend hadn't even touched Peter, yet. Why did Peter scream? Also, how did their friend suddenly crash to the ground? It was all so weird.

Peter was evidently too fast, so they didn't see him kicking their friend's ankle.

"Hey bro, why were you so careless? This was your fault. I didn't do anything. You can't blame me for it."

Peter was still pretending to be scared. He yelled innocently and acted flustered at the same time. In a panic, he accidentally knocked down a table, which made all the leftovers fly to the other young men.

"Fuck you. You are asking for it!"

"I will kill you!"

Looking at all the greasy stains on their bodies, the young men became furious. They yelled blindly and rushed at Peter.

"Ahhh, help! They want to kill us! Somebody, call the police!" At the sight of the angry men, Peter screamed again and again in fear. Out of self-defense, he grabbed some bamboo skewers on the table and began to throw away.

Whoosh! Whoosh! Whoosh!

Whether it was coincidence or not, the bamboo skewers that Peter had thrown happened to pierce three of the men's faces. What's worse, each of them had several skewers on their faces.

These bamboo skewers were knife-edged, so they were very sharp. As a result, the faces of these men were violently marred by the bamboo skewers.

They put their faces into their hands and kept screaming. However, the blood from their faces could be seen dripping through their fingers.

In the blink of an eye, four men out of six had already been attacked. The remaining two men seemed to have noticed that there was something wrong. Peter was not a wimp at all.

At this moment, Peter started shouting again, "Oh now, why are you all falling to the ground? Oh! And what's wrong with your faces? Why are there so many holes on them? Ahhh! They're bleeding, too."

The three men who had been punctured by the bamboo skewers stared at Peter's innocent expression and flew into a rage. They would rush to him and smash him into pieces if it were not for the continual bleeding on their faces.

"You do have it in you, kid. We were barking at the wrong tree, " One of the remaining two men gloomily said with clouded faces. They suddenly turned sober and became serious.

They locked their eyes at Peter. The feelings of hate and the desire to kill him all rose to the surface.

Even though the people around didn't know that the young men had intentions of killing Peter, they still feel uncomfortable and, therefore, decided to stay away from the situation.

It looked like the two men were very dangerous and unstoppable like mad dogs.

Upon seeing that there were only two men left, Peter turned from seemingly weak boy into a strong, confident man as if he didn't know that these men wanted to kill him.

He stretched out his finger and pointed at them, shouting aggressively, "I'm telling you, I know kung fu. You'd better run right now if you are smart. Otherwise, I won't go easy on you!"

"Oh, really? Then, I will teach you a le--" Before the young man finished speaking, Peter had already lifted the stool beside him and slammed it down to the man's head. He was so fast that the man had no time to react.

With a bang, the young man rolled his eyes and flopped heavily onto the ground, passing out before he was able to scream out.

And now, there was only one man standing.

The man glared at Peter angrily, but his legs were trembling.

That son of a bitch had been pretending to be weak all this time!

The speed of Peter lifting the stool was so fast that he only saw what had happened afterward. He didn't even have time to react.

"Do you want to teach me a lesson, too?" Peter looked at the last young man and smirked.

Chapter 19 The Jerk
"No. No more!" The man hastily shook his head. He was not a fool to get beaten up, given that he was no match for Peter.

Peter glowered at the man and shouted, "Then, get out of my sight now!"

"I will. I'm leaving!" In fear, the man was about to scoot away. However, it was already too late. With sirens wailing, three police cars appeared on site.

The police cars stopped on the roadside in an orderly fashion. Then, dozens of fully armed policemen got out of the vehicles and surrounded Peter and the others.

"Arrest them all, and bring them to me!" The head of the police did not even hesitate for a second and commanded to arrest Peter and the two girls without any intentions to figure out the truth.

Shelly and Lisa went pale upon seeing so many policemen gathering here. Their legs could not help but shake out of fear.

They were just ordinary women with normal lives, and they had never seen anything as frightening as this scene before.

Peter knew this had something to do with Alfred. The policemen did not even ask about what had happened. They just wanted to arrest them even without evidence.

Shelly and Lisa were about to be taken in handcuffs. When Peter saw that, he went to the head policeman and said, "Sir, these two woman have nothing to do with what happened just now. They are innocent and should not be treated this way."

"Who do you think you are? You are just a nobody! Your words count for nothing! We suspect them to be prostitutes. We have to take them to the police station, " the head policeman shouted as he glowered at Peter.

Prostitutes?

Peter was trying really hard not to punch the cop in front of him because he knew that the consequences would be very serious if he did, given the circumstance they were in.

Peter calmly said, "These are only allegations, not facts. Besides, you don't have any evidence. Even if you still take them away, there's no need for handcuffs."

Peter put on a loud, authoritative voice.

The policeman was furious because he felt that he had just been challenged by Peter. However, the people around the scene were watching them, and they all heard what Peter had said, so the policeman had to suppress his anger.

The public opinion was quite powerful these days. If he would lash out, his brutality might get posted on the internet and go viral, and then he would be doomed.

"Fine. No need for handcuffs. Just take them away, " The policeman said angrily, and then he went into a police car.

Peter, Shelly, and Lisa were all brought into the same car somehow. The others were taken to another two cars.

The policemen took Peter and the two girls and left the scene.

Peter looked furious in the car while

Shelly and Lisa were sitting beside him, leaning their bodies against him, trembling in fear.

The two women did not know what was going to happen after they arrived at the police station.

If they were accused for prostitution, even though it was not the truth, they would no longer be able to go back home because that would tarnish their names for a lifetime.

"Don't worry. You have done nothing wrong. The policemen should set you free, "

Peter comforted the two women upon seeing their pitiful facial expressions.

"Shut up!" Peter was interrupted by a shout from the passenger side. "You should take care of yourself, not others."

The policeman turned his head and smirked, "You two, I have seen women like you before. You look like regular office employees, but I know that you're prostitutes. You'd better admit that, so you won't suffer from the interrogation."

"We are not prostitutes! We are just receptionists. We really are not prostitutes."

"We've done nothing to violate any laws. You must be mistaken."

Shelly and Lisa trembled as they sat on the backseat of the car. They tried to clear their names with trembling voices because they could not bear the false accusations.

"Since you won't admit it, we can interrogate you later in the police station. We know how to let criminals admit their crimes."

The head of police believed in his accusation. There seemed to be no way to change his mind. He, then, faced the road and did not make any sound anymore.

The two girls' minds went blank. They did not know what else to do. They felt like they were entering a black hole, unsure of what would be waiting for them.

Their faces went pale, their lips were trembling, and they were in a total desperation.

Peter was so angry that he wanted to kill that devil.

He did not understand how a jerk like that could become a police.

Policemen should not have this kind of bullshit in their team. It was an insult to the police to have that kind of jerk in the system.

However, Peter knew that he had to endure all this. He would not assault the police, especially if it was not necessary for him to do so.

Peter did not argue with the policeman. Instead, he just kept comforting the two ladies.

He knew that it was useless to argue. It would do nothing good for him.

About twenty minutes later, they arrived at the southern branch of the police station of Golden City. When Peter and the two ladies were asked to get out of the car, he noticed that the other six people in the other two cars did not alight.

Peter had already figured out what was happening, but he still asked, "Sir, since we are being accused of affray, why didn't the others come along? You only arrested us, right?"

"Shut your mouth up! How dare you teach me how to deal with crimes?" The head policeman got angry, so he roughly kicked Peter on his buttocks.

Peter could have dodged that kick, but he did not. He let out a little shrill and fell down to the ground, even scratching his left arm in the ground to bleed a little.

"How could you hit me?" Peter shouted angrily.

"Hit you? I just wanted to!" The head policeman felt offended by Peter's questions. He wanted to beat

Peter to death. The other policemen saw this and stopped him in a hurry.

"Kid, you just had a taste of what we're going to do to you later!" The head policeman shouted as if he wanted Peter dead.

He was the one who was instructed by Alfred to arrest Peter in the bathhouse. However, he failed to seize Peter last night.

He got upset upon thinking of what had happened last night. His failure to capture Peter had angered Alfred. In addition to that, Peter had been challenging him. The policeman's fury was directed toward Peter.

Peter was soon taken to an interrogation room, and the ladies were taken to another.

--

Within the residential area of the municipal complex, in the big living room, a family of three was sitting on the sofa watching TV.

However, their attention was not on the TV but to the two phones on the tea table.

The elder woman in the family was Grace Feng, who had been rescued by Peter this morning. The younger woman in the room was her daughter, Audrey.

The man in the room was the father of Audrey, James Xie.

James was a handsome middle-aged man with distinct features. He had an upright temperament. One could tell that he was somebody who held a high position.

Grace glanced at the phone from time to time, a little bit anxious.

James saw that and said, "Grace, I think that the doctor will not come today. Let's go to bed and wait for him tomorrow, okay?"

James was furious. Some people had dared deceive him and fooled his wife. If he was not worried about Grace not being able to handle the blow, he really wanted to tell her that she had been tricked and that the so-called doctor would never show up.

Grace understood what James was trying to say. She shook her head and said, "No. I'm confident with my gut feeling, and I know a talent when I see one. That young man is not a fraud. He must be busy with his work and is not off duty, yet."

She continued, "What kind of company does Peter work in? He's putting in too many hours. It is already late, yet he is still at work."

Audrey had lost her patience, so she said, "Mom, it is already ten in the evening. Doesn't he have the basic courtesy of calling since he's late? I'm calling him!"

Audrey said that as she took out her phone and dialed Peter's number.

Chapter 20 Extort Confessions
Just as Peter got inside the interrogation room, he heard his phone rang.

As he took a look at his phone, he was suddenly reminded of his promise to treat the lady this evening.

"Peter, where are you? Why haven't you showed up, yet? Won't you come to treat my mom anymore?" Audrey asked the questions angrily.

"Uhm... I'm now at the police station, so I might not make it today..." Peter had not finished talking yet when the policeman came in and shouted at him, "You are not allowed to use your phone! Don't you know that you are a criminal now? Now, hang up!"

The man said that as he tried to grab Peter's phone.

Peter dodged the police's hit and said, "Oh, how could you beat people up? Sir, I'm the victim. I came here to assist you in your investigation. I'm not the suspect, nor a criminal. Even if I'm a criminal, I still have the right to call for an attorney to defend for me before any court decision would be made."

"Smartass!" The policeman burst into laughter, "You know how to hire an attorney? Give your phone to me. Otherwise, I will let you have a taste of what I can do. You want to hire an attorney. What a joke!"

"How can you act like this? Oh my god, what are you going to do with me?" Peter acted as if he was afraid. He made his voice tremble, saying, "Don't you know that there are CCTV cameras everywhere here? Sir, I bet that you don't want to be recorded extorting confessions."

As Peter said that, he hung up the phone call and pressed on the voice recording button.

He had to keep his phone on him because he wanted to call Bella for help when he would get the chance.

Peter had no other choice. He was in Golden City and he knew no one else, except Bella. If Bella would not help him, he would have to deal with the situation on his own.

"CCTV cameras? Hahaha!" The policeman teased when the door of the interrogation room was suddenly opened, and another three policemen came in.

"Have you shut off all the cameras?"

"Don't worry, Captain Niu. I have turned off all the cameras and the monitors in the control room. I've also sent our colleagues there home. Do what you want to do. No one would know what's happening here."

A policeman with small eyes and receding hairline said that with a big grin.

Apparently, it was not their first time to shut off the monitors. Who knew how many innocent people were wrongly accused here!

Peter was so furious at the moment. He was starting to get even more worried about the two ladies.

They did not have Peter by their side, so they would most likely own up to crimes they did not commit, under the extortion of the police.

"Kid, since you won't admit your crime, let me beat you up!" Captain Niu took out his baton and went toward Peter with a big grin on his face.

As he did so, he pressed a button on the baton, and sparks from it flew, making crackling noises.

The three other policemen all stood still with exited yet cold expressions on their faces. It seemed like they were used to seeing this scene.

--

Audrey heard the conversation in the phone. She thought for a while and told Grace, "Mom, that guy is in the police station. He was arrested!"

"Hmph!" Grace looked at James and said angrily, "Since when did the police have the right to prohibit others from hiring an attorney?"

James was also angry with what he had heard through the phone. It was like a slap on his face.

"I don't care about the details, but I want to know where he is now. I have to see him. I will let things go if Peter had really committed a crime. But if these people were doing him wrong, I will not forgive them!"

Grace said those words coldly. Although she seemed weak, her words stood a firm stance.

In the interrogation room

"Sir, you do know that you are violating the law, right?" Peter squinted as he said that.

"Violating the law? I am the law here!" Captain Niu laughed for a while, and suddenly, he stuck the baton to Peter.

With this, Peter became extremely angry. He quickly moved his hands to free them from the handcuffs. Then, he kicked the man.

The captain did not expect Peter to be able to free himself and fight back so fast. In the next second, he felt a huge pain coming from his stomach. He had been kicked away, so he fell, making himself land on the three policemen.

The three policemen were only watching from the sidelines. They did not expect that Captain Niu would be kicked away and fall down on them. They did not have time to react before Niu's body landed on them.

"Ahhh!" At that time, Peter screamed out and stomped his right feet to give him energy. He dashed fiercely and quickly toward the four men like a tiger chasing its prey.

The four men did not know what was going to happen. Peter's scream had confused them since they were the ones who got hurt.

Peter positioned himself near them and punched them aggressively.

"Punch!"

"Ouch, it hurts!"

"Punch!"

"I did nothing wrong!"

"Punch!"

"Oh my god, the policemen are hitting me!"

Peter screamed out every time he hit them with his fists. It sounded like he was the one getting severely hurt.

The four policemen almost burst into tears.

This was getting out of hand.

Peter beat the four men up for a while before stopping. He, then, took out his phone and was about to call Bella.

But he heard a voice from the outside, so he stopped dialing.

Then, he took some dust from the ground and smeared them on his face to make him look dirty. He also picked up the baton, turned it on, and stuck it to the hands of the captain.

The door of the interrogation room suddenly opened right after Peter did all that. A crowd of people rushed in with anger.

What James saw was that a policeman was poking Peter with the baton. That made him burst into flames!

His face was so bleak out of anger. If he had a gun, he might have shot those bastards.

Peter glanced at the people who barged in and saw Grace and Audrey. He was a little surprised, but he let out a cry of pain, and laid his body down to the ground.

Richard, the head policeman, was so afraid; he was sweating everywhere. He felt like he wanted to die right then and there.

These bastards were ruining his official career!

The four cops still had not come to their senses. However, they saw their leader standing behind James, with his head lowered. They figured that James must be somebody important.

They glowered at Peter and almost burst into tears.

This was too much!

"Sir, please help us out!"

"Sir, this guy would not confess to his crime. He even beat us!"

"Sir, we were wronged. What you're seeing is a set-up! He was the one who put the baton into my hand!"

They all begged for mercy, looking pitiful and scared. Everyone in that room was confused.

"So unfair!" Peter cried out weakly. Earlier, he had put on the handcuffs discreetly. Now, he held his hands up and said, "I was in handcuffs. How could I beat them up? And I'm not a fool. Why would I give them the baton to attack me?"

Shit!

Captain Niu could not believe his eyes as he saw Peter in handcuffs again. Now, it was impossible to save themselves from the situation.

Peter spoke again, "I was totally wronged. I did nothing bad! What I did was just self-defense. I was with my colleagues having dinner when a couple of bastards came over to assault my colleagues. I could not bear seeing that, so I stood up for them. Then, the guys humiliated me by forcing me to lick the floor and crawl between their legs."

"I'm a man. How could I do what they were forcing me to do? I fought back, of course. Then, when the policemen came, I thought everything would be okay, but instead, I'm being forced to confess a crime I did not commit. I thought they would uphold justice for us. I didn't expect what would happen next..."

Peter told everybody the truth. Then, he continued, "If you do not believe in me, you can ask those bastards over there. They had treated me like this, so I'm really afraid that my colleagues were being treated worse. Could you send anyone there to make sure they're okay?"

Richard heard what Peter said and sent his fellows to look for the two ladies immediately. The four policemen in the room did not even had the chance to speak.

They all went pale, seemingly faint.

Thank you for reading. Please leave your valuable review. It will help us provide you with more interesting novels. More top billionaire romance novels await you at moboreader.net

Chapter 21 Hit Them To Death
A few moments later, Shelly and Lisa were brought to the interrogation room where Peter was.

Upon seeing them, he felt relieved to know that they were okay.

Richard, the director of the police station wiped off the bead sweats that formed on his forehead. He stared at the three cops beside him and ordered, "Bring the other guys here. Right now!"

As the head of the police station, he had to act like he was on top of the whole situation, no matter what. But, deep inside, he wished that Peter had done something wrong.

Somehow, it seemed that the cops didn't hear his orders. They didn't make any move, only standing still in their spots.

"Didn't you hear me? Bring them here! Now!" Richard couldn't help but shout. He was so angry that his whole body trembled.

"Well... Uhm, sir, I have set them free..." Captain Niu gritted his teeth and answered. Then, he pointed at Shelly and Lisa and said, "These girls are part-time prostitutes. They had intentionally seduced those guys, which made the guy that girls are with jealous. It was them who had made the incident happen. Since those guys were innocent, I set them free."

One could say that the captain was smart. He was able to make up a story on the spot. Although it was a shoddy excuse, it still made sense anyway.

"That's not true! I was wronged." Peter jumped up immediately, looking extremely aggrieved.

"You are all policemen! You represent the justice system! How can you treat me with prejudice? Fine, I can understand if you only do me wrong, but what about those two girls? How can you do that to them? They are girls with decent office jobs, yet you call them prostitutes and ruin their reputations. So, you're saying that they are prostitutes and that I fought with those guys because I was jealous? Do you have any evidence?"

"Evidence?" Captain Niu was stunned when he heard this. Suddenly, he laughed grimly and said, "Well, you said that you were merely trying to defend yourself. Do you have any evidence?"

He was not a fool. He knew that Peter didn't have any evidence, so he countered Peter with a question, too.

If he admitted that he had no evidence, then he would definitely lose this argument. He might even be put into jail.

Cops could not arrest anyone without any evidence.

Captain Niu flashed a hideous and mischievous smile at Peter. He believed that Peter didn't have any evidence, either.

"Yes, I do!" And with that answer, Captain Niu was greatly shocked.

Peter quickly took his phone out of his pocket and opened a video. He said, "This video is an evidence. You can watch the video. It can prove that I was wronged and that it was all self-defense."

The video helped bring the truth to light. It showed that the six guys had deliberately started the provocation and attacked Peter as a group. Then, Peter was taken into the interrogation room. The recording of the video only stopped when Audrey had called Peter earlier.

After finishing the video, Captain Niu and the other cops got so frightened that their faces went completely pale. They couldn't deny the truth any longer.

They couldn't understand how Peter was able to record the video under that chaotic circumstance.

However, when Captain Niu saw a big hole on Peter's shirt, he understood everything.

After finishing the video, the expressions on the faces of James, Richard, and Grace looked terrible.

Richard got so angry that he was visibly trembling. If James was unwilling to let the incident go, his official career might be done for.

"I have the video, and I also have the voice recording. How about we listen to it together?" Peter didn't wait for their responses and played the voice recording.

He was a nice person, but he wasn't an angel. If he had the chance, he would've beaten them up to death.

But he was recording the whole farce, so he couldn't do what he had wanted to. Otherwise, his effort to record everything would be in vain.

Upon hearing this, the three cops were shocked, frozen. But not long after, it seemed like they had remembered something because their faces showed that they were completely pissed off.

At first, they didn't understand why Peter had been screaming a lot when he was beating them up. But now, they understood everything.

After they finished sorting things out in the police station, Peter went out of it with the two girls. It was already half past eleven in the evening. Those three cops were going to get punished for sure, but Peter didn't care about them at all. He believed that their boss would never let them off.

Also, Peter had found out what James's status was. He was the mayor of Golden City, the second in command of the city!

"Peter, I'm sorry. I didn't expect that this sort of thing would happen. If I had called you earlier, I would never have let you suffer from that, "

Grace apologized to him even though she had nothing to do with the incident. However, her husband was the mayor of the city. She was afraid that Peter would hate them and refuse to treat her disease, and since

Peter was the only one capable of treating her disease, Grace needed him badly. So, she was worried that Peter wouldn't want to have anything to do with her.

Peter was smart. He knew what Grace was worried about. Therefore, he smiled at her and said, "Auntie, don't worry. You had nothing to do with what happened. Instead, I need to thank for your help. I wouldn't know how to deal with the situation if you hadn't showed up.

Speaking of this, Peter thought a bit and said, "Here is the thing. Auntie, I need to send these two girls home first. If it's convenient for you, I will go to your house later and treat your disease. But if it's not convenient for you, I will see you tomorrow, instead. What do you think?"

"It's okay. I'll wait for you at my home tonight!" Grace replied immediately, relieved. Meanwhile, she felt a little embarrassed since it seemed like she was rushing him.

James observed Peter's behaviors the whole time, and he felt greatly surprised by him. Generally speaking, if people would hear that he was a mayor, they would either become nervous or ask for a favor from him.

But Peter was different. He was shocked when he heard that James was a mayor. However, he didn't dwell too much on it. For him, James was just a common person, too.

Shelly and Lisa had gone through so many things tonight. Besides, there was a mayor beside them, so

they got so nervous that they hid behind Peter and
said nothing.

Deep inside, they adored Peter even more.

Peter was freaking awesome! He was not only good at
fighting, but he also had connections with the
mayor.

Maybe Peter was from a rich and powerful family! The
reason why he was a security guard was because he
wanted to experience living a normal person's life.
That had to be the case!

These thoughts went running through the two girls'
minds.

After Audrey went out of the police station, she
stared at Peter coldly and said nothing.

'How disgusting! You promised to see my mom and
treat her disease, but you completely forgot about
it just because of two women!' Audrey cursed him
deep inside.

When she saw the two women holding his arms on both
sides, she hated him even more. For Audrey, Peter
was a shameless rascal and a cheat!

After sending Shelly and Lisa home, Peter went to
James's home and began his treatment on Grace.

It took about one hour for Peter to do the massage.
When it was finished, it was almost one o'clock in
the morning.

"Auntie, don't worry too much. Now that I have had a
good understanding of your condition, your disease
will be cured after three massage sessions. Okay.
That's all for today. It's already too late. I shall
go home now."

Wiping his sweat off, Peter told Grace.

"Yes, it's too late. You don't have to go home now. We have a spare room. You can stay here."

Grace tried to persuade Peter to stay. At that moment, she was feeling much better. She believed that Peter's massage was really helpful. Therefore, she was thankful for his help.

"Yes, you can stay here tonight. It's too late!" James echoed.

When Peter was doing the massage to Grace, he stood by and watched. He could see that Peter was really good at conducting the treatment. Since Grace was feeling much better and happier, James was also relieved.

In addition, the reason why James appreciated him was that Peter didn't seem too proud of himself even though he was really talented.

"Well... I don't think it's appropriate..." Peter took a look at Audrey who didn't look too happy.

Actually, he was already too tired to return home. He wanted to stay here tonight.

"What do you mean by inappropriate? It's too late, and I won't let you go home alone." Grace stared at Audrey and said, "What are you doing here? Go clean the room! Peter will stay here tonight."

Audrey opened her mouth wide. Obviously, she didn't expect that. However, when she saw the expression on her parents' faces, she said nothing and angrily marched to clean the room. She could do nothing but curse Peter silently.

Half an hour later, Peter ignored Audrey's fury, walked to the bedroom slowly, and had a good sleep.

When Audrey was about to warn Peter not to use the bathroom with no clothes, Peter shut the door and locked himself inside the bedroom.

Chapter 22 Meet Elaine Again

Inside Alfred Club, Alfred was so furious after
receiving the phone call that he threw his phone
onto the wall, shattering it into pieces. He did not
expect that Peter would get away from his well-
planned scheme.

He almost went nuts upon hearing that Captain Niu
and the other policemen were being punished so hard
and that they could even be sent to jail.

Captain Niu was not a very important person for him
but still Alfred had used his money to give him the
position of head of the police. Now, the captain's
career was doomed, and Alfred did not want to
reconcile with this fact.

"I never expected James to do right by Peter. What
is the relationship between them? Peter is not just
an ordinary security guy?"

Alfred was lost in his thoughts. If Peter was just a
nobody, Alfred would chasten him without hesitation.
But now that James was involved, he had to be
careful about it.

Alfred had sent his underlings to figure out the
relationship between Peter and James, and he also
had them investigate Peter's background. He was
waiting for the result of the investigation.

Alfred's other phone rang after one hour. He picked
up the phone with a bleak look.

"I thought Peter had some connections with people in
authority. It turned out that he had just been very

lucky." Alfred hung up the phone coldly and dialed a number.

"Send more staff to wait for Peter at his apartment. I want him to disappear from the world tonight! Once things are done, arrange the staff involved to go abroad. That way, the murder won't be linked to me."

Apparently, Alfred was burning with rage with what had happened tonight. He wanted Peter to die at any cost.

The night had passed quietly, and

Peter woke up at 8 o'clock as usual. He put on his clothes and ran to the toilet. He ran so fast that he did not notice Grace greeting him.

Peter had just been in the toilet for ten seconds when Audrey, who was in her pajamas, also ran to the toilet. She ran so fast that she did not notice Grace trying to inform her of something.

"Oh my god!"

Grace was about to tell Audrey something, but a scream interrupted her.

'Something must be wrong. Audrey should be the one screaming. Why does it sound like Peter?'

Grace was confused.

Peter was taking his number one when the toilet door was opened brutally by someone. Peter screamed out, surprised.

He then looked at Audrey alertly, trying hard to compose his words, "What... what are you going to do?"

The scream sobered Audrey. She was annoyed when she saw the scared look on Peter's face as if she had intended to see him in the toilet.

"I haven't said anything. Why on the earth did you scream? And why are you acting so scared? You bastard!" Audrey shouted out in agitation. She almost hit Peter with her hands.

Peter seemed more afraid, so he lowered his head and said in a low voice, "Now that you've entered and seen me without pants, could you now go out first?"

There was no way Peter would be able to continue peeing under the sight of an angry woman.

"You!" Audrey was so angry that she stomped her feet and slammed the door with a huge bang. "You only have half a minute. Hurry up!"

Peter had no choice, so

He went out in half a minute with a sad look on his face. Grace laughed at Peter's expression.

It was already half past eight after he had breakfast at the Xie family. Peter was suddenly reminded that he left his scooter by the barbecue store, and now, he was not sure whether it was still there.

Without his precious scooter, he had to take the metro. He had no idea that a dozen of people were yawning in front of the apartment he had rented. They had waited a whole night for him to come home because

They were all commanded to beat Peter up to death.

They never expected that Peter would not return home at all. They had been waiting the whole night, but Peter did not appear at all.

With this, they all got frustrated. They had failed their mission, and they even got too tired and drowsy as they waited for nothing.

It was almost nine in the morning. It would not be
suitable for them to wait any longer since many
people were already walking out their apartments.

Alfred did not sleep well last night, either. He was
waiting for some updates. At nine in the morning, he
was informed that Peter did not return to his
apartment at all last night.

He got so furious that he threw his phone,
shattering it into pieces, again.

--

Peter had no idea about all that. Right now, he was
inside the crowded metro.

He had once heard that many beautiful women also
took the metro. It could be a great chance to get
close to these beauties.

As he looked around, he got so disappointed. There
were only men with robust features nearby, no beauty
in sight at all.

Peter was determined to give anybody who would ever
tell him that many beauties gather in the tubes a
slap on the face.

Several stations had passed, and many men had
already gotten on and off the train. Suddenly, one
beauty showed up in his sight.

This beauty had a gorgeous and perfect figure. Her
office uniform fitted her so well.

Peter felt it a pity not being able to see her face
clearly because of the crowding passengers around.
She was definitely a great beauty with a seductive
figure.

He did not want to stay where the robust men were
any more, so he squeezed toward the beauty.

Some of the men also noticed the beauty and wanted to squeeze themselves toward her, too. However, Peter was strong and quick enough to get close to the beauty first.

The other men were obviously pissed at Peter, but they did not dare make any complaints because Peter was six-feet tall and had a strong built.

As Peter got closer to the beauty, he checked her out from top to bottom. When he was about to touch the beauty, a familiar voice interrupted him. He had to draw his hand back.

"Oh, Peter! It's really you! What are you going to do?" Elaine was surprised, but she smiled from her heart. She could not tell what she should feel when she saw Peter drawing back his hand.

"Oh!" Peter let out a sound of surprise and disappointment. What a bad luck! The beauty was Elaine who had once helped him.

'How could you, Peter, take out your hand to touch her! Now, what you did was seen by her!' Peter thought, 'Your good impression in Elaine's mind was totally ruined.'

Fortunately, he was keen enough to have found that there were some dust in Elaine's dress. He pointed that out and said, "Elaine, I saw dust on your dress and wanted to pat it away."

Elaine looked over to where Peter had pointed. There was indeed dust on her dress, but it was close to her thighs. It was nevertheless not suitable for a man to pat a female on the thigh.

Elaine blushed timidly. She felt a little bit disappointed that she had not charmed Peter.

On the other hand, Peter did not know what Elaine really thought about him. He had a special feeling for her and regarded her as his benefactor.

He could act like a jerk and flirt around with Shelly, Lisa, Bella, or Clair, but not Elaine.

"Peter, how was work yesterday in the company? Was everything okay with you? I didn't get any time to see you. I was too busy yesterday, " Elaine asked, hiding her feelings for him.

"Everything went well for me. Don't worry. I'm doing great. Elaine, why did you take the metro? Don't you own a car?" Peter could not figure out why Elaine who earned millions a year took the metro to work. She was just too low key.

Elaine was happy to hear Peter calling her by her name. However, she felt off with his questions.

"I sold my car. Forget about it. It has nothing to do with you. Just take care of yourself and work hard. If you get into any trouble, you can call me. I will support you in any way I can."

"I will. Thank you." Peter felt that Elaine became uncomfortable with his questions, so he asked, "Elaine, why did you sell your car? Tell me. I can do you a favor if you need me to."

Chapter 23 A Call By The President
"Thanks for your concern, but I'm all right, " said Elaine, shaking her head.

She was a little touched by Peter's concern for her, but how could she count on a security guard? He could not help her, for sure. She didn't want Peter to get involved in her own business.

Elaine didn't tell Peter anything, no matter how much he pried. But he still wanted to know, so he had firmly decided that he would investigate what had happened to Elaine. Since she had offered him such a great help, he didn't want her to get hurt.

A lot of the male employees' jaws dropped when they saw Peter and Elaine walking into the company, talking and laughing.

It was the morning rush hour. When their colleagues entering into the company saw their dream girl walking shoulder to shoulder merrily with a security guard, their hearts broke into pieces.

"Peter, you're here. I have brought breakfast for you."

"Hey Peter, Lisa didn't do it sincerely. Look at the breakfast that I prepared for you. I made it on my own."

When Peter's colleagues saw the two beautiful ladies at the receptionist desk run toward Peter, each carrying a breakfast box for him, their hearts got broken, again.

Were security guards that popular these days? They were puzzled and embarrassed because they had no women in their lives.

Elaine was also stunned when she saw this scene. Somehow, she felt a little uncomfortable. She did not expect that such friendly behaviors between Peter and these two girls would foster in such a short period.

"Hey, what are you guys doing here? I have already had breakfast. Enjoy them yourselves, " Peter said as he chuckled, pushing the breakfast boxes back to them.

People standing by were jealous of Peter. How dared he? They really wanted to trample on Peter's annoying face.

"Oh, " Shelly and Lisa said dejectedly in unison and took their breakfast boxes back. It made them feel sad.

They thought that Peter didn't want to accept the food because Elaine was there.

In their minds, they also pondered on the fact that Peter was somebody who had connections with the mayor, so it was no surprise that he wasn't interested in them. Only women with high reputations such as Miss Dai were good enough for him.

Peter's act made Elaine feel good. 'Did Peter refuse their breakfast because he was afraid of making me unhappy? Yes, that must be the case. I knew it. He could not resist my charm.'

Fortunately, Peter had no idea what they were thinking about. Otherwise, he would be very depressed.

He already had his breakfast at the Xie family's house, so he refused the food that the girls were giving him. He didn't think of it too much.

"Lisa, smile a little, okay?"

"Poor Shelly, who had offended you and made you so unhappy early in the morning? Look at your gloomy face. Tell me about it. I promise I will shatter him into pieces!"

After changing into his uniform, Peter wandered around and then went to the receptionist desk to chat with Shelly and Lisa. Strangely, the girls were acting strange today. The both wore long faces and pouted. No matter what he said, they just ignored him.

Ding--

Just as Peter was thinking about why they weren't talking to him, the elevator door opened and an ice-cold voice came out from the inside. "Peter, the president wants to see you!"

Peter looked over his shoulder and suddenly put on a wide grin. "Hey there! What does the president want from me, Miss Yang? Oh, by the way, if she's looking for me, why did she send you here? Where is she?"

Clair's face darkened. She really wanted to punch him to death.

Who did he think he was? The chairman? He wanted Miss Song to call him in person? How cheeky and arrogant!

"Miss Song said if you didn't show up in her office within one minute, then you would be fired!" Clair stepped into the elevator after she dropped a sentence dryly.

"What? Wait!" Peter was startled for a second. Then, he quickly responded as he dashed into the elevator. But it was too late. As he was just about to reach, the elevator had already closed, made a "ding" sound, and went upward.

"How dare you, Miss Yang! I will remember this. Don't ever let me see you again, " Peter said resentfully. He turned around and charged toward the stairs.

In the Secretariat Office, Clair had been wearing a triumphant expression ever since she got back to her office. 'I told you never to show off before me, you hypocrite! Wanna play? Let's play then!'

When she got into the elevator, she had seen that the other elevator was at the 20th floor, and it was still going upward.

That was to say, Peter had no choice but to go up by climbing the stairs if he wanted to get to Miss Song's office within one minute, unless he didn't keep the president's words in mind.

However, could a small security guard challenge a president's authority? Moreover, she was none other than the well-known cold-blooded president.

Peter reached the 38th floor in only 41 seconds. Even though he was strong and energetic, he was still panting when he got there.

He cursed Clair in his mind all along the way, as well as the president.

He really didn't know what was wrong with this moody devil early in the morning and why she had asked for him. He was bewildered every time he faced this moody lady. She could be sweet one second and merciless the next. He didn't want to get fired only because of such a petty thing.

At the 53rd second of the one full minute, Peter showed up in front of Clair who was still in a daze. He looked over at her angrily and deliberately shot a glance at her voluptuous breasts before he snorted and strode toward the president's office.

Peter had walked away when Clair recovered from the surprise. "Asshole!" Clair snapped. She really burst into flames as she thought of the arrogant ways Peter looked at her. "Shame on you! Smelly rascal!"

In the President's Office

As usual, Bella was in a black suit, leaning against the black leather sofa like a lazy female cat.

Her hair was in an up-do, and her makeup was nice and exquisite, which would give people the feeling that she was elegant but distant. Her delicate feet in her black high-heels were placed casually on the coffee table. Clearly, she did not fear damaging her image at all. Her left hand was folded across her chest, while her right hand was slightly lifte with a cup of coffee in her fair and slender fingers. Slowly, she took a small sip and let the coffee cup linger around her sexy, voluminous lips, which would undoubtedly make countless of people crazy for her.

Peter really wanted to turn into that cup of coffee when he saw this.

"Who allowed you to come in? You didn't knock." She couldn't believe that someone had dared enter her office without knocking. She was really furious about it. But she cooled down a little bit when she saw that it was Peter.

"Oops! I'm was in such a hurry that I almost forgot." Quickly, Peter hurriedly explained, "You asked me to show up in your office within one minute, but unluckily the elevator was not on the ground floor at that time, so I had to climb the stairs to get here."

He checked the time as he said those words. "See, I reached your office at the 58th second, and when it came to the 60th second, I came in. I didn't have time to knock."

Since Peter was in a hurry, he didn't close the door when he entered the office, so their conversations were clearly overheard by Clair, who was standing outside the door.

All of a sudden, Clair's face took on a ghastly expression, and she began trembling.

She didn't expect that Peter would tell this to Miss Song. If the president would dwell on it, then she would get...

She didn't dare to think about it.

Even though she was Miss Song's top secretary, she was clear that she would not bat an eye lid if she really wants to fire Clair.

"Within a minute?" Bella was stunned, and a glimpse of coldness flashed in her eyes. "Did Clair tell you that?"

Holy shit!

He didn't realize that he had been fooled by Clair
until Bella asked him those questions. He cursed
Clair in his mind while he said, "Oh no, no, I must
have heard it wrong. Never mind. What's the matter?
What did you ask me here for?"

He closed the door of the president's office as he
said that. When he pushed the door close, he didn't
forget to shoot a nasty glare at Clair.

On the other hand, Clair felt relieved after making
sure that Peter didn't rat her out. At this moment,
she had no mood to care about Peter's nasty eyes,
which looked like shards of glass, wanting to pierce
her. All she thought was whether Miss Song would
look into this matter and replace her with another
person or even fire her.

Bella stretched her hands lazily like a fox,
exposing her sexy curves completely. Then, her
flaming lips moved slightly, following with words
that made Peter's jaw drop.

Chapter 24 Elaine Was In Trouble
"Move in with me!" Bella said straightforwardly.

"Move in with you? Me?" Peter thought hard about it
and was confused at her statement. "I don't think
that is a good idea, " he continued.

"There's no need for you to think about it too much.
I heard about what happened to you yesterday. It
must be Alfred who has given you troubles. He is a

jerk, but he has power and money. If you move in
with me, you will be safer, "

Bella said.

She had asked Peter to come see her after she was
informed of what had happened last night.

Bella knew Alfred well. She knew that he would get
what he wanted by hook or by crook. Now that he was
bent on making Peter suffer, he would not stop.

"If that's what you're worried about, then calm
down. Miss Song, I don't take Alfred seriously. If
he dares show his face to me, I will surely beat him
up! Don't worry about me. But I am afraid that he
will take his revenge on you, "

Peter said that proudly, feeling a bit moved by
Bella's words. He did not expect that the moody
devil cared about him.

"Is that so?" Bella pursed her lips and said
scornfully, "Although you've cured James' wife, it
is not possible for him to always do you favors
without hesitation, or even have your back. Don't be
that na?ve."

Bella apparently knew everything that had happened
to Peter. If Alfred could investigate Peter, so
could she.

Without any pause, Bella spoke again angrily, "And,
you've experienced so much yesterday. Why didn't you
call me for help? Do you hate me that much?"

Her words were more like a complaint. By her tone,
it was like that Peter had betrayed her.

"No, of course not. The matter was solved anyway, so
I did not want to bother you any more. And... I am
not relying on Mr. Xie. I just don't care what
Alfred is plotting against me, "

Peter said that in a tone with a tinge of innocence and depression.

This moody beauty had suddenly turned hostile and started to complain. Peter was not used to that.

"You are right. You have fighting skills and excellent medical know-how. Perhaps, you've got more than I thought. After all, I also did not expect that you had the ability to flirt well with women. You've just worked here for several days, but you've already hit on the receptionists, "

Bella said with jealousy. It sounded like she had been betrayed by Peter.

"I wasn't hitting on them! We are just colleagues, and we just had dinner together. Nothing special about it."

Peter was a little bit fretted. He worried that if Bella went nuts, she would fire Lisa and Shelly. If so, he couldn't do anything about it.

"Take it easy. I won't vent my anger on your girls." Bella rolled her eyes and said in an even poorer tone, "Peter, do you hate me?"

Bella was really curious of Peter. He had mastered great martial arts techniques and professional medical skills. And, he had already been acquainted to James, the mayor of Golden City, within the short time he was living here. Plus, he did not take Alfred, a Golden City celebrity, seriously at all. Peter was really a mysterious man.

If Bella had not figured out that Peter got the job in Silverland Group by coincidence, she would suspect his intentions of working under her.

"No, I don't hate you at all. I like you, from the bottom of my heart, " Peter said hurriedly. He found it so hard to talk with Bella.

"Really? Peter, I think the job of a security guard is far beneath you. I will put you in a new position, " said Bella who seemed satisfied with Peter's words. She blinked her beautiful eyes and smiled.

"There's no need for that. I'm satisfied with my current job." Peter shook his head. After all, he should not receive a reward without working for it.

"You just don't want to leave your little beauties in the reception desk, right?" Bella pursed up her lips and said in coquetry, "Okay, I respect your choice. However, from now on, you are not just a security guard. You are my private driver and bodyguard. You should be at my beck and call 24 hours a day."

Her words were so arrogant!

Peter had no other choice but to nod. "Okay."

"Well, it's settled now. Go to work. And be careful. If Alfred causes any trouble, remember to call me at once."

Bella suddenly stood up and walked toward Peter. She, then, acted like a real girlfriend and fixed the collar of Peter's uniform.

She did it with a charming smile, so nice and so seductive.

If anyone else in Silverland Group saw the scene, they would not believe their eyes. This picture was the last thing they would ever think of.

"Fine!" Peter felt so embarrassed. He quickly nodded and darted out of the room.

Bella smiled at Peter like a beautiful fox when she saw him running away.

"Hmm... All the other men want to chase me, but you don't take me seriously. Peter, you're acting like you're immune to my charms. Just wait! No matter how cold-hearted you are, I will let you throw yourself at my feet someday!"

Peter was sweating as he got out of the president's office. He would rather fight with someone else than confront Bella, the moody devil.

Heedless of Clair, Peter rushed to the elevator and soon arrived at the first floor.

He feared that Bella would suddenly call him back.

Peter was overthinking because Bella did not ask for him the whole day.

Shelly and Lisa finally showed their smiles at Peter after he tried so hard to coax them.

Peter told to himself that women were all like that, moody and so difficult to flatter.

Peter got changed when it was time to get off work. He ran out of the door as fast as he could.

He wanted to follow Elaine to figure out what had happened to her.

Elaine got off work at six and took the metro home.

Peter followed her discreetly in a safe distance.

Elaine seemed absent-minded, worried, helpless, regretful, and miserable. Peter could see that she was in a troubled mood. He was sure that Elaine was going through a tricky situation.

About forty minutes later, Peter followed Elaine to a nice residential area.

When Elaine went near a building, she suddenly stopped and turned back in panic as if she had seen a ghost.

Startled, Peter dodged aside immediately to avoid getting seen by her. A man's voice erupted loudly, "You bitch, how dare you run away! Stop right now!"

An extremely lean man suddenly ran out and seized Elaine's arms. He pulled her back, scolding her, "You bitch, you can run, but you can't hide! You hadn't been home for several days. Tell me if you are cheating on me!"

Chapter 25 Beating The Rascal

"Get your hands off me!" Elaine screamed as she struggled, her face as pale as a piece of paper, her body shaking.

"I am not related to you any more. Whether I have a boy toy or not, it has nothing to do with you. I don't have one, but even if I do, what do you care?"

Pak!

When the skinny, young man heard what Elaine had said, he glared at her and gave her a slap on the face, cussing, "Damn it, bitch! You're that itchy, huh? In just three days, you're already sleeping around? Tell me. Who is your boy toy? Where does he live? I'll chop his balls off!"

Elaine got slapped, and blood spilled instantly from the corner of her mouth, her creamy white face marked with several red fingerprints.

She covered her face with one hand, and tears came out in an instant. She stared at the man and shouted, "Mac Chen, you're a scumbag! You dare beat me? I'll kill you!"

Anger filled her, and she pounced desperately at Mac Chen, scratching at him wildly, her hands turning into claws.

"Oh, you have the guts to fight back? You got a temper now, huh?" Mac Chen was furious when Elaine was attacking him. He was about to slap her again when a seductive voice came, making him stop.

"Mac, honey, don't be so rude to the girl. She's our cash machine. What if you hurt her and we can't get the money? Let's think about business first. I'm waiting for you to buy me that bag. The shop may close soon."

The door of the white BMW car beside them opened, and a coquettish girl stepped out and walked to them while speaking in a coaxing voice, her buttocks swinging side to side. She was so bewitching that people on the street might not be able to move their eyes away from her.

"I'm here to rescue you, sweetie. Otherwise, your fair, tender face will turn as red as an apple. You don't have to thank me. Just give us one or two hundred thousand cash. Is that okay?"

The coquettish girl said very shamelessly, walking to Elaine's side with her slim waist and firm buttocks.

"Lily, why not stay in the car? What if you get a cold or a sunburn outside?"

Mac Chen's attitude toward Lily and toward Elaine were on different sides of the spectrum. After talking to Lily nicely and affectionately, he turned his head and glared at Elaine. "Did you hear her or not? Hurry up, and give me the money. One hundred thousand will do."

Elaine looked at the bitchy girl and the snotty man with anger and twisted her lips. "One hundred thousand? Do you really think I'm a cash machine?

How much money have you taken from me over these years? Count it! You spent my money on a car for another girl and bought things for her. You're a total asshole!

You're no longer my boyfriend. Even if you were, I would still dump you! I'm telling you, the tuition that I owed you in college has already been paid off, and you and I are over. I won't give you any more money!"

Elaine shouted hysterically, regretting that she hadn't seen through the bastard before.

Mac Chen and Elaine were classmates back in college. In her eyes, Mac Chen was a man of both excellent character and outstanding academic performances, and he also had a good family background. Apart from looking ugly, everything else was almost perfect with him.

Mac Chen persistently courted Elaine for two years, and she finally agreed to be his girlfriend. Moreover, as the situation of Elaine's family was not quite good, Mac Chen paid most of her tuition and miscellaneous fees for her as her boyfriend, and he also had bought her a lot of learning materials.

At that time, Elaine naively thought that she had found her own Prince Charming. Every day, her face was filled with happy smiles.

But this didn't last long. After six months of being in a relationship with Mac Chen, things changed.

Mac Chen began to try all kinds of ways to ask her to have sex with him. Elaine, a conservative girl, rejected his moves and told him that she would not have pre-marital sex.

Mac Chen repeatedly tried to persuade her but failed, so eventually he called for a prostitute. Unfortunately, he was caught and thrown into jail.

When Elaine learned about that, she was angry at his behavior, but she also felt guilty. She felt that her conservativeness caused him to suffer and fall low.

So, when Mac Chen first asked her for money two years ago, she did not refuse. But she made it clear that they were no longer boyfriend and girlfriend.

Although Mac Chen agreed to it at that time, his personality had changed for the worse after.

Elaine, a girl who couldn't fight such a rascal, could only put up with him again and again.

"No?" When Mac Chen heard Elaine's words, his look changed immediately, and he kicked her. "You fucking bitch! If it weren't for me, would you be able to finish your college degree and enjoy the good life today? If it weren't for you, bitch, I wouldn't have gotten arrested! Clearly, you need to learn your lesson!"

Such a big brawl, of course, caused a lot of people to gather around and watch them.

It was not the first time that the residents had seen Mac Chen. Although they resented his shameless behaviors, they dared not stand up to oppose him.

They were afraid of offending such a scoundrel for fear that they would not be safe for the rest of their lives.

Although skinny and young, Mac Chen was still a man, so he kicked with such a fast speed that Elaine might not be able to dodge it.

Looking at the indifferent faces around, Elaine could not stop her tears from gushing out. She didn't expect these people to help her out and beat Mac Chen, but as long as they could all reprimand Mac Chen together, he would not dare be so rampant.

When Mac Chen was about to kick Elaine, a fist
suddenly appeared from nowhere, punching Mac. Before
Mac Chen was able to kick Elaine, he had gotten hit
in the face.

Bam!

With blood spilling from his nose, Mac Chen fell to
the ground like a broken kite, screaming tragically.

"Are you all right?" Peter looked at Elaine and felt
a little worried. He could have stopped it earlier,
but in order to find out what was happening, he
waited and held back.

"Waah!" When Elaine saw the familiar face, she was
stunned at first, and then she couldn't help but
burst into tears in Peter's arms.

She was really tired of dealing with Mac Chen, who
was a certified douchebag. How she wished there were
a man who could stand beside her and protect her
from being hurt!

"Peter, go away quickly, you can't fight..." Elaine
only cried for a few seconds before she looked up
rationally with a worried look in her eyes.

She was greatly touched that Peter had showed up and
that he could help her out in such a crucial time,
but she knew that Peter, as merely a security guard,
could not fight Mac Chen at all. She didn't want
Peter to get involved.

"Let me handle it." Just before Elaine finished
speaking, Peter covered her mouth with his hand. The
firm tone of voice made Elaine feel an unexpected
peace of mind.

"Who the fuck are you? You dare to beat me? Damn it,
bitch! You do have a boy toy. No wonder you're
hiding from me all the time lately! You are dead
meat! You dare beat me up. I'll kill you!"

Mac took a breath and jumped up, pointing at Peter and Elaine. Then, he began to cuss and yell. His vicious tone and beastly eyes made people around them shudder.

"Kill me?" Peter glared and bounced up suddenly. He looked extremely ferocious. "Who the fuck are you going to kill? Say that again!"

He said furiously, and his ferocious expression made him look like another man that seemed a hundred times more violent than Mac Chen.

Thank you for reading. Please leave your valuable review. It will help us provide you with more interesting novels. More top billionaire romance novels await you at moboreader.net

Chapter 26 Defeat Mac
Mac looked at Peter, who suddenly seemed to be a totally different man. For a moment, Mac was afraid.

He seemed tough, but he would fold.

'Elaine refused to have sex with me when she's my girlfriend, but she had sex with this man!' Mac thought angrily. As Lily was standing nearby, Mac plucked up his courage and shouted, "I'm gonna kill you. How dare you seduce my girlfried?"

"Your girlfriend? This woman is your friend! I'd rather find a whore than seducing her.".

Peter said, looking at Lily with disgust. He didn't like Lilly because of how she treated Elaine before.

"What are you talking about?!" Lilly yelled, her face red with anger. "You can't talk to me like that! Mac, get rid of him!"

'Saying those things to me is like asking for a death wish! Can't he see my white thighs and firm, full breasts? Only a blind man won't say I'm gorgeous!' thought Lily.

Lily's anger and Peter's arrogance stunned Mac before it infuriated him. Such disrespect, who did this guy think he was? "I will kill you!" Mac shouted, charging at Peter.

People surrounding them began to move away to avoid getting hurt from the skirmish.

Elaine couldn't move. She didn't know what to do.

Pak!

Peter's hand hit Mac squarely on the cheek. Blood filled Mac's mouth and he spat it out with a few broken teeth.

Before Mac could react, Peter grabbed Mac's head and slammed it towards the BMW parked beside him.

"What did you say? You said you wanted to kill me? Who do you want to kill, huh? Not so tough now, are you? Who do you want to kill?" Peter asked, mocking Mac.! ! "No one does that to my woman. I'll teach you a lesson you will never forget. You messed with the wrong guy. You're the first one who challenged me like this in the Golden City."

Blood from Mac's head splattered all over the glass as the car window cracked with the impact.

Onlookers screamed at the shocking sight, while some found themselves wide-eyed and unable to move their legs.

Lilly was very frightened. Her knees gave way and she fell on the ground.

She didn't expect this guy to be so violent.

Mac's remaining courage was drained by Peter's brutality. Frightened and in pain, he knelt with tears falling down his face. "I'm sorry, man. I was wrong. I won't do it again. Please forgive me. I'm sorry."

He's tough but he's also stupid. He messed with the wrong guy. It's okay for him to offend ordinary people, but how could he provoke a big hooligan like Peter?

Absolutely, he's crazy but Peter could be crazier.

Didn't he sense it when Peter started talking? With how he carried himself, it should have been obvious that he wasn't the type Mac should cross.

"Wrong?!" Lifting his eyelid, Peter took out his phone. "So you're admitting your mistakes now, huh, tough guy?

Well, there's someone you need to talk to."

Let's see how confident this guy was.

"No!" Mac sobbed. "I can't!" He said as he cried more bitterly. "Peter I'm really sorry. I'll never do it again. Never! Never again! Forever! Please forgive me, man. Please forgive me, I beg you!"

"You'll never do it again?" Peter slapped him hard. "You bet you won't. You can't do anything again. You can't even make this call! You're fucking useless. You'd better not do this again. If you do, I'm going to be sure I'll punish you, or I'm not Peter."

Peter said as he delivered four more slaps.

He knew how to deal with these kinds of people. You had to be more insane than they were. This was the only way to make them stop messing with you. If you didn't go hard on them, they would keep coming back. He couldn't watch over Elaine 24 hours a day, could he?

Mac didn't scream as he took the hits one after another. All he wanted was for Peter to let him go and to stay away for as long and as far as possible.

"What the fuck is that smell?" Peter turned to Lily. "Did you just pee your pants?" Peter mocked. "Hah! What are you, an old woman?"

Lily flushed, lowered her head, and sobbed. She hoped that the ground would just open and heat her up.

Taking advantage of the situation, Mac got up, grabbed Lilly and ran, without even taking their BMW car.

Peter smiled the moment the two wer out of sight. He looked at the crowd and said, "Okay, everyone, show's over. You can go on your business now unless you want to throw me some money."

Peter was trying to crack a joke, but the onlookers thought he was going to stir up troubles. Immediately, they dispersed.

"That was so scaryâ€¦" they whispered. Peter felt a hint of embarrassment, but he paid it no mind. He walkedup to Elaine. "He won't be messing with you anymore."

"Thank you so much. I really didn't know what to do." She said as she threw herself at Peter. Elaine had been terrified of Mac for such a long time.

"Don't be afraid. I'm here. If that guy bothers you again, just call me. I'd be happy to teach him a lesson again and again, " Peter said patting his chest with confidence.

"Okay, " Elaine replied softly. It felt good to be protected by a man. "I know you haven't eaten yet. Come, let me make some dishes for you."

"Alright, let's go!" Peter was relieved. He actually didn't know what to eat just now.

Elaine got out of her high heels the moment they entered his house, exposing her delicate feet to the smooth floor.

Peter's eyes widened and his heartbeat quickened. He had never seen Elaine act this casually.

Elaine, realizing what happened, blushed. "You can sit anywhere you like. I'll just change my clothes."

She said as she hurriedly ran to the bedroom. Suddenly she realized that she wasn't alone. 'Oh my€¦' she thought.

She was totally exposed. Running with nothing but stockings against the smooth floor, she felt her foot land awkwardly and she slipped, her whole body falling to the ground.

Elaine was dumbfounded. This was absolutely embarrassing.

Before she hit the floor, she felt someone pull her backwards with hands on her chest and inner thighs.

And here was a strong force behind her that pulled her backwards.

Boom!

Her body hit the floor.

"Ahhh!"

She screamed, feeling a sharp pain.

Then, there was silence.

Thank you for reading. Please leave your valuable review. It will help us provide you with more interesting novels. More top billionaire romance novels await you at moboreader.net

Chapter 27 Lady Killers
Elaine's mind went blank.

Peter ran to catch her the moment he saw her
accidentally falling backward.

Elaine tried to move as she was tangled in Peter's
arms, but he was too strong.

"Shouldn't you loosen your grip now?" She said,
annoyed.

Peter loosened his grip at once. It was hard to tell
if he was willing to let her go. He felt her soft
body as she stood up.

Elaine glared at Peter. She couldn't decide whether
she wanted to thank him or scold him, But she also
knew it wasn't his fault. He was only trying to
help. She couldn't find it in herself to thank him
either because she felt like he touched her
inappropriately. She was not an easy woman.

"Uh, Elaine, I think I'd better go. Sorry I can't
stay for dinner." Peter stood up quickly and left in
a flash.

As he was about to go out of the door, he looked
back and said, "Don't worry, I'm not upset. I fully
understand where you're coming from."

Elaine felt embarrassed by what she heard. Thinking
on her feet, she grabbed the first thing she could
from the sofa and threw it at Peter.

Peter caught immediately with his quick reflexes.
"Elaine, if I failed to catch this, it would have
been broken and you'd have had to buy another one. I
will bring this with me and return it tomorrow to
make sure it's safe."

He wasn't done talking when he realized what he was holding â€" a pink piece of lingerie.

Elaine realized that too. She couldn't believe she just threw him a piece of her underwear! This couldn't get more embarrassing! He was actually holding her dirty underwear and was going to return it at work!

Elaine was totally blushed for what just happened.

On the other side, Peter felt weird holding such a sensitive piece of garment, especially Elaine's. He couldn't help looking at the small piece of garment once in a while as he went on his way home.

After grabbing a bite, Peter went to the barbecue store to get his scooter.

"Help!"

Peter suddenly heard a cry as he was passing through a small lane.

'Someone needs my help, ' Peter thought as he tried to follow where the voice came from without hesitation.

"Let go of those girls, or you'll answer to me!" Peter shouted as he rounded up the corner.

He hasn't finished when he froze.

--

"Shout as much as you can, no one will hear you here."

"Stupid fucker! Who do you think you are, trying to molest me! We'll beat the crap out of you! You'll pay for this!"

"Slap, slap, slap, slap."

Gathered around a man were three women with short skirts and heavy makeup. They were throwing him one slap after another.

The man was only wearing his underwear and was kneeling down, screaming, and calling for help. He was clearly the underdog in this situation.

Peter couldn't believe his eyes.

The three women turned to Peter when they heard him speak.

"Iâ€¦ I saw nothing. You can continue what you're doing now. I'm gonna go." Peter said, forcing a smile and quickly running away.

"Hey! Stop!" The woman in the middle called out, while Peter kept running.

"I'm not stupid! I'm not doing as you say, you three bitches are crazy! I don't wanna end up like that man!"

With that, Peter disappeared into the clearing. To his surprise, another set of scantily clad women appeared.

They almost looked naked with what they were wearing. They stood in a line, forming a wall as they moved closer.

Peter was in despair. "Ladies, I was just passing by. Please let me go. I'm a breadwinner in the family. I have elderly parents who need me, and I have a baby to raise."

"Is that so? How about I give you a chance to earn money, then?" The woman in the middle said provocatively, Licking her lips and pulling her collar down. Peter's mouth almost dropped seeing her majestic breasts.

"What do you mean?" Her body was truly distracting, so Peter tried hard to stay calm. "I'm not going to sell my body."

The woman laughed. "Relax. I'm not asking you to have sex with me, or to sell your body."

"Are you sure?" Peter asked, skeptic.

"Of course, " she said as she drew nearer. "All I want is..." Pak! In a flash, she lifted her leg towards Peter's groin.

She knew how to fight! She must know! She's probably even an expert!

There was absolutely no way to anticipate her attack. It was so fast and so strong!

Even an expert wouldn't be able to block that, let alone common people.

No one would have expected that a creature as beautiful as she was capable of such.

Had Peter been hit on the groin, it would have made his capability to procreate close to none.

"Ohhh!" Peter screamed, dodging the attack quickly. He drew his body back and grabbed on to her legs.

He caught it and held it tightly. With his other hand, he made a fist and punched.

"Bang!"

It hit her groin.

"Ouch!" The woman screamed. Her face twisted in pain.

"Aghhh!" Peter also screamed and drew back quickly. "I'm sorry, I didn't intend to hurt you! It was an accident!"

The other five women ignored him and charged.

They turned from sexy to fierce as they all drew knives.

Crash!

Five blades were brought down, stabbing at Peter.

One was to his chest, the other four, to his legs.

He was in big danger! They were all around him.

They must be used to fighting together; their synergy was amazing.

Peter knew he needed to be careful.

He had a feeling they'd be violent, but he didn't expect them to be skilled.

Peter tried to twist his body to set himself free. He made it with a spin kick though it seemed impossible.

After landing on the ground, he gathered all his might and threw a heavy slap at the three women in front of him.

Slap, slap, slap!

The three women fell to the ground and screamed from the pain.

It was unbearable.

Slap, slap!

He did the same thing to the other two and they ended up in the same way as their companions.

In an instant, all six women were beaten up â€" one leaning against the wall, and the other five lying on the ground. They were furious and embarrassed.

"You're lucky I'm rusty. If you met me a few years ago, you'd be dead by now."

"I don't care about what happened and who hired you. I just want you all to leave and I never want to see you again.

I'll let you go now, but if you dare attack me again, you'll get no mercy!"

Peter swore.

He sounded like a king with his authority.

The women trembled in fear.

Peter was gone the moment they were able to gather their senses.

--

'This is the third time you tried to kill me, Alfred, ' Peter muttered to himself, 'No more Mr. Nice Guy. It's time for me to fight back'. Peter rode his scooter, planning his revenge.

Chapter 28 The Chase Along Busy Streets
Wang Village was well-known in the Golden City because of the fact that it accommodated hundreds and thousands of travelers from all over the world.

The prosperity of the village was obvious; but another thing was that it was known for the chaos. Four to five killings occurred every year, on average â€" possibly the sad side effect of its high diversity and population.

Peter had rent a courtyard here where twenty built men tried to ambush him.

Failing at their first attempt, they gathered together, determined to give it another shot.

In a cafe, two heads of staff sat opposite to each other, sipping coffee while waiting for their colleague.

The four main entrance gates of the village were monitored by their colleagues. As soon as Peter arrived, they would have information on those vital checkpoints.

"Matt, it's just eight o'clock and everyone would be busy. Should we get down to business the moment Peter shows up?"

Roman asked as he sipped his coffee. It was pretty late into the night but now wasn't the time to just come up and attack people with so many people around!

"Pak!"

Quickly after Roman finished speaking, Matt knocked at his head and glared at him.

"You stupid fucker! Can't you use your brain? Have you heard of a thing called 'strategy', huh? Do you know what that is? Although we didn't finish school, it doesn't mean we're dumb, eh? We're masterminds, aren't we? The last thing we want is a lot of witnesses when we teach this guy a lesson!"

Roman nodded hard in full agreement. "Oh, oh, great idea, Matt! I agree very much! So uhâ€¦ what's the game plan, let's hear it!"

"Pak!"

Matt gave Roman another hit, shouting, "You stupid pig! You know how the saying goes, 'The divine message is only revealed to the worthy.'"

Roman stopped asking immediately.

Suddenly, Matt's phone beeped. The moment he picked it up, his eyes brightened at the sight of a message.

"The target has appeared! Let's go, and I'll teach you a lesson today about strategy." Matt said excitedly, walking out with a plastic bag in his hand.

As Roman tried to follow, he was stopped by the waiter. "Hi sir, I believe you haven't billed out."

"Oh, I thought my companion paid for it already, " he muttered. There was no trace of his older brother. He had no choice but to settle their bill.

"There are many single men, but no single women. There are people to marry women who are blind or lack noses, but no one pays attention to the men..."

Peter rode his bike on the way home, humming a tune.

Flop!

Suddenly a figure jumped in front of him

From the dark alley. Before he could figure out what it was, a voice came out.

"This is a stick-up!"

Peter was stunned.

Peter had heard about the village's crime rate â€" killings, arson, theft, etc. He wasn't sure if it was true, but now he was convinced.

"Brother, you have the wrong target. I have no money to give you!" Peter was terrified.

Wield!

Light reflected against a shiny metal gun when the stranger revealed what he was holding. With a menacing grin, he slowly approached Peter. "No money, eh? Then maybe I'll just rape you instead!"

Peter felt his genitals grow tense. "No, friend! I have money, I do! I'll give them all to you!" he cried in desperation, Reaching into his pockets immediately.

'I've kept my body pure for twenty-three years. I won't let this goon violate it just like that!'

Peter took out a dozen coins and offered them with a big smile on his face. "These are all I have, brother. They're all yours!"

The stranger was outraged. "Do you take me as a beggar?"

"It's not what it looks like, my friend! You see, it's actually enough to pay for a bowl of delicious beef noodles!" Peter replied innocently.

The man was about to reply, but another man came out from the alley.

"Matt! The target has arrived! Are you sure you want to do this right now?" he said as he revealed himself. "His bike is just as valuable as these coins and it's difficult to lug around and sell!"

"Pak!"

The one called Matt hit his companion forcibly. "Dumbass! Can't you just shut up?"

Roman was usually patient, but this was the last straw. He hit his elder brother with the back of his hand. "I always do as you say! I've always done what

you asked, even when it meant that I had to pay for
what we got in the cafe, but not anymore! The target
has appeared but you're here robbing this useless
son of a bitch! I'm telling the boss about this!"

Peter seized the opportunity to escape while the two
strangers were arguing. He jumped on his bike and
drove away without hesitation.

Realizing the driver's identity, Roman exclaimed,
"Stop him!" "You're so stupid! He's the target!"

"Oh!" "Run!"

The two men went after Peter.

"Help! Help! They want to rob me and kill me! Help!"

Peter screamed, abandoning his bike at the corner
and running as fast as he could. His earsplitting
cry drew the attention from the many passers-by.

There were a lot of these dark alleys in the village
that led straight to the main streets. Peter arrived
at streets quickly.

The sidewalks were filled with foreign vendors and
the inevitable gangsters. Despite Peter's cries for
help, none of them budged.

It was only after they spotted the knives on the
hands of the two brothers coming after him did they
start to panic and move out of the way.

Although they were already pretty accustomed to the
amount of chaos that happened in the village, they
weren't determined to be part of the victims yet.

"Stop him! Stop him!"

Matt roared madly as they chased after Peter, his
blue veins protruding from his neck. How were they
supposed to trap Peter with his stupid brother?

'What a pig!' the on-lookers thought as Matt passed
them by. 'Who is he to give us orders?' No one
meddled.

Peter couldn't help but burst into laughter.
"Hahaha, what, do you think the people in this
village would just do as you say?"

He provoked.

The people around him couldn't help but laugh in
agreement.

Matt grew angrier.

The smile was wiped off from Peter's face when he
realized his predicament.

In front of him were dozens of people holding black
plastic bags in their left hands. Slowly reaching
into the bags as he approached, They took out their
own black metal guns.

"Oh my god." Startled, he started to run towards a
different direction.

The group followed.

Peter changed his direction every few minutes in
hope of losing his pursuers which, from two, Now
grew to twenty armed men.

Their knives and guns reflected the village lights
and the silver moonlight.

The people in the streets were dumbstruck. Rumbles
were things that you'd normally see in movies when
one person crossed gangs! Who would have thought
you'd see it in real life?

"What kind of robbers are you? Do you have to be
that many to successfully rob one guy? Have you
eaten dinner? Why do you run so slowly? How do you
even go on with your profession with conditioning as

weak as that? You should all go home and rest! You
need it!"

Peter mocked them as he evaded, swift as a rabbit.

The young men gasped for breath, furious after
chasing after him along thirty streets.

Peter escaped unscathed out from the village
speedily. A lot of people were able to take videos
of the epic chase and shared it on their own social
media channels.

Thank you for reading. Please leave your valuable
review. It will help us provide you with more
interesting novels. More top billionaire romance
novels await you at moboreader.net

Chapter 29 Like A Toad Dreaming About Eating Swan
Meat
Peter soon arrived at his destination, but continued
to provoke the men running after him."You idiots! I
am home, come in if you dare to. Come! Come!"

Their loud breaths and heavy steps echoed through
the night air.

Their struggle was very visible.

They were so mad at Peter that they had no time to
notice where they were.

"Kill him!" Twenty people with their knives and
guns, charged at the command of their leader.

They were about to finally catch up to him when a
loud sound stupefied them all.

Suddenly, dozens of policemen appeared, the black
muzzles of their guns pointed at them. There were so
many of them that there was no way to flee.

The twenty men looked at each other realizing the amount of trouble they were in. All this time, they've been chasing Peter on his way to the place station!

The policemen were fuming with anger. How dare these troublemakers chase this man down with illegal weapons right to their station! Was this a joke?

This was absolutely insulting!

They would not tolerate this mockery!

Peter laughed loudly.

"You... you tricked us!" The gang leader yelled in rage.

"Shut up!" The policemen were red with anger. "Arrest these troublemakers and put them behind bars! Arrest all of them!"

"Yes, sir!" The officers rushed at the hoodlums at their chief's direct orders.

"Hey, buddy, I'm a victim! I'm innocent! I came here so I could seek your help." Peter pleaded at the two policemen who proceeded to arrest him.

"Bros?"

The two police officers were offended. 'How dare he call us in such a casual way? He should call us Sir, ' the policemen thought.

The head of the police force glared at Peter. "Get him too! He might be one of them. We'll investigate them together!"

"Wait!" Peter quickly took out his phone. "I'm calling Richard Xing! I'll report what you're doing to me!"

Richard Xing?

The two young policemen froze at the mention of
their Director.

"You know our director?"

One of the police officers recognized Peter before
he could answer.

How could it be him?'

He couldn't help shuddering and rushing to his
superior.

The head of the force felt cold when his subordinate
finished whispering something to his ear. He rushed
to Peter's side with a smile.

"Mr. Wang, it's you! Sorry for talking to you like
that! I'm sure you understand, it's been a rough
day. I wouldn't have done that if I knew it was you,
"

He said, putting his hand on his chest to show
sincerity.

'Ah, Peter Wang! He has a strong connection with
Mayor Xie and almost had Director Xing lose his job.
Be sure to remember his face! Don't squint in the
future!' he reminded himself.

When Peter was brought to the South Branch police
station, it angered Director Xie, causing troubles,
not just to the South Branch, but to the Golden City
Bureau as a whole. It was fortunate that Mayor Xie
decided not to press charges, otherwise Director
Xing could have lost his job.

"It's okay, it's okay, " Peter said, putting his
phone back in his pocket. He didn't really have
Richard's number. He was actually just bluffing.

"Please investigate this matter well. I have
children and parents to care for, I can't afford to
be killed and mugged in the streets.

I could've died if I weren't a fast runner. These people look seasoned. I'm pretty sure it's not the first time they tried to do this. I won't be surprised if they've already killed some people."

Peter began to accuse.

The arrested men looked at him angrily when they heard this, but they couldn't do anything to retaliate. Dammit. This was so ironic. It was as if they stole a chicken only to find out that the rice is stale, or kicking a stone away while skinning their ankles.

It was already past ten o'clock when Peter left the police station, taking a cab to the Alfred Club.

He remembered a saying, "Don't let the same thing happen thrice." This was the fourth time; he'd look like a shrinking turtle if he didn't fight back.

Alfred Club, despite not being the top club, was still one of the most high-end ones in the city.

Several luxury cars lined its gates. Mercedes-Benz, BMW, Ferrari, Porsche, and even a Rolls-Rocye Phantom were part of the entourage.

Peter got off a cab at the side of the road.

"Shit. Of all the places rich men blow their cash at, they just have to give it to Alfred." Peter mumbled, determined to break into the door unceremoniously.

"Peter, Peter! Come here!" A voice suddenly called after him. Not far from where he was standing, a beautiful woman in a red shirt and tight-fitting short shorts waved at him.

Her jet black hair fell behind her exposed back. Her pretty face was smooth. She had full breasts and two long white legs that were impossible not to notice in this dark night.

'Who's that?' Peter wondered. 'I'm here to fight, not to go on a date.'

When Peter turned to look, his eyes widened.

What a beauty!

His eyes scanned her beautiful legs and luscious breasts. His mouth dropped.

His eyes climbed up to her face and his mood changed abruptly.

Audrey?

Peter covered his face and turned away.

He couldn't destroy this club in front of the mayor's daughter! He wasn't an idiot!

"Where are you going? Come here, come with me!" Audrey cried running after him and reaching for his arm gently. Her touch sent shivers up Peter's spine.

"Audrey, what's wrong with you?" Peter was puzzled since Audrey always hated him. What was with her today?

Audrey stretched out her hand and covered his mouth. She smelled so good but her tone was firm. "Shut up! Go to the club with me and pretend you're my boyfriend."

"What? Why would I do that? I don't want to be your fake boyfriend, and I don't want to be your option."

'Why am I always the fake boyfriend? First, Bella's, and now Audrey's? When would I be anyone's real boyfriend?' he thought.

"You're like a toad dreaming about eating meat." Audrey said to him in disgust.

"Mwah!"

Peter suddenly pulled her in and kissed her ferociously.

"You!" Audrey was furious and was about to attack when Peter held a hand up against her. "People are watching. You don't wanna be seen hitting your fake boyfriend, now do you?"

Audrey stopped struggling, holding her anger in.

'A toad dreaming to eat swan meat, eh? Well, I'm sorry but I already ate. You have no right to be mad at me', Peter thought.

As they entered, Peter couldn't help but notice that the women were dressed more conservatively than most bars. Their figures were visible, but they were only mildly exposed. They also seemed to be very young, he assumed they were Audrey's classmates.

Chapter 30 What A Loser
Peter subtly admired the glamorous girls. 'They're so beautiful, sexy and fashionable, ' he thought.

"Hey, Audrey, who is he? Aren't you going to introduce the guy to us?" A woman in a black summer top and tight skirt walked over smiling

As she looked at Peter. '180 cm tall, not bad. Butâ€¦ where did he get those clothes?' Peter watched her as she was clearly sizing him up.

Audrey was one of the most beautiful and sophisticated girls in the university. Several boys wanted to date her but all of them failed to catch her eye. It was a shock to Ada Wang that someone like Peter, who didn't even look successful, was the one clutching Audrey against his chest.

"Hey, Ada. This is Peter, my boyfriend, " Audrey said.

Ada Wang was Audrey's roommate, and the boys and girls at the party were indeed her classmates. Audrey seldom attended such parties, but today, Ada Wang didn't take No for an answer.

Audrey preferred to lay low in her university, but her beauty inevitably turned so many heads. Not a lot of people knew about her prominent family background except several governors of the school.

Audrey came from a very powerful family. With her father being the city mayor, she was well-versed with politics and was skilled in equipped with excellent interpersonal skills. When she was told to go to Alfred Club that night, she knew that it was the agenda of one person: Jared Wang.

Jared Wang was known to come from a likewise rich and powerful family. He was extravagant in showing off his wealth, and he wanted Audrey really badly.

The whole time, Audrey was trying to devise a way to avoid Jared Wang at the party. When she saw Peter, the idea to have him pretend to be her boyfriend immediately dawned on her.

Although she hated Peter very much, she had to admit that he was a man of many abilities. He not only had medical prowess, but he was also a very skilled fighter. Despite being attacked by six guys that night, Peter ended up in the police station instead of the hospital.

With him, Audrey felt safe.

Hearing that Peter was Audrey's boyfriend, her classmates were stunned. They couldn't believe it. It felt unfair. Clearly, Audrey deserved someone better. If Audrey were a beautiful flower, Peter was a foul piece of dog poo. 'This is going to be interesting, ' they thought.

"Boyfriend?" Ada Wang repeated, stunned. She shuffled awkwardly before managing to force a smile. "Nice to meet you. I'm Ada Wang, Audrey's roommate, " she said extending a hand.

"Nice to meet you too, " Peter replied, shaking her hand. Right now, he was Audrey's boyfriend so he had to act appropriately.

Ada Wang was a little surprised. She expected Peter to be savage and unrefined. He looked uneducated, after all. Surely he would also be brash. Instead, he was acting like a polite, polished gentleman. He wasn't so bad, after all.

As they were talking, a dashing Maserati stopped at the driveway, turning the heads of the people at the party.

The door opened and a gentleman in his Versace and Rolex ensemble stepped out of the vehicle.

The people started to flock excitedly towards him when they realized who it was.

"It's Jared Wang!"

"Hey man, cool car! When did you buy it?"

"Wow, Jared. You look so handsome!"

Jared Wang basked at their compliments. He greeted his classmates and looked around trying to spot Audrey. His eyes lit up when he caught sight of her! Suddenly his eyes went to the guy she was with and his mood changed.

Everyone knew he hosted this party for Audrey. He spent so much time and money planning this just to get her here.

He carefully selected his clothes and made sure he'd arrive in style with his Maserati. More importantly, he booked the finest club in the city for her!

'How could she have brought a guy here? He looks poor and terrible!'

What pissed him off more was how the guy held Audrey tightly at her waist, and Audrey didn't look a tiny bit annoyed! In fact, they seemed to be having a great time! They were very happy and intimate. They were definitely not just friends.

Jared Wang was very disappointed. He stormed at Audrey, losing his temper.

"Who is he?" he shouted at her. "This is our class party. Why did you bring a stranger here?" Jared Wang was young and impulsive. He didn't have the habit of thinking things through; he just said what he thought and did what he felt like doing. In this case, it was scolding Audrey.

Audrey stared at him blankly. "He's my boyfriend, and he goes where I go. I'm here at the party, so he's here too. We can leave now since I see we're not welcome here."

Actually, she really didn't like the party. Deep inside, she was so happy to finally have an excuse to leave. Audrey saw Jared Wang as someone who was childish and immature. Talking to him was boring.

"What? When did you have a boyfriend? Why didn't you tell me?" Jared Wang shouted at Audrey angrily.

Audrey was outraged. "I don't owe you anything, you brat! My relationship status is none of your business! Clearly, we're not welcome here and we're leaving right now!"

Audrey pulled Peter as she proceeded to walk out.

"Wait, no! Don't do that! Audrey, you just got here. Let's go to the club and have some fun, okay? Don't mind Jared, he's just angry. I'm sure he wants you to stay."

Ada Wang tried to mediate, winking at Jared Wang secretly.

"Audrey, these are your classmates. Don't be difficult, " Peter said.

He didn't want tension between them. After all, Audrey saw them every day, it would be difficult for her if they didn't have a good relationship.

Ada Wang felt relieved that Peter was on their side.

Audrey stopped reluctantly.

However, Jared Wang started throwing a tantrum. "Shut up! She's the reason why I held this party in the first place, but now she has a boyfriend! Fuck this party! Go to the club and have your fucking fun! And you, fucking bitch, stop winking at me! Leave me alone!"

Jared Wang stormed off and climbed back at his Maserati before disappearing completely.

Peter was stunned.

'What a loser, ' Peter thought. 'No wonder he doesn't have a girlfriend.' Peter sighed, shaking his head.

Ada Wang turned red from embarrassment.

The people at the party didn't know what to do now that Jared Wang left.

But for Audrey, she felt so much better. Finally, he left!

"Aww, man, Jared left. We'd better go. We can't afford this place, anyway, " the rest of the class said in disappointment.

They just lost their chance to have fun in the city's finest club. Jared Wang was their golden ticket here.

"No, it's okay! Stay! We can still have fun here!"

Audrey said, slipping the card into Peter's hand secretly.

"Yeah, I have a club card here! Let's all have fun, guys!" Peter said.

"Wow, really? That's amazing!"

"Don't lie to us! This is the Alfred Club, the finest club in the city! It's very difficult to get a card. The cheapest one costs three hundred thousand dollars!"

The classmates couldn't believe Peter could even afford a card at all.

Thank you for reading. Please leave your valuable review. It will help us provide you with more interesting novels. More top billionaire romance novels await you at moboreader.net

Chapter 31 What A Showoff
"Alfred Club? Pshh. I'm a member of the Passion Club! Let's go!" Peter couldn't help bragging in front of the students.

Even though the students weren't very convinced, they still followed his lead because of how he carried himself.

Audrey looked at him in disbelief. 'What a douchebag, ' she thought.

"Sir, please show me your card." The security guard requested.

No one believed that someone who looked like Peter could afford a membership to the prestigious club.

"Here you go." Peter handed his card to the security guard. The officer took his flashlight and inspected it carefully. His face changed when he finally deciphered what it was.

"I'm sorry, sir. This is Alfred Club, not Bayang Beauty Club." The security guard said coldly, almost losing his temper. 'What a foo! Did he think he can fool me with a beauty card?'

"Oh, sorryâ€¦" Peter was so embarrassed. He glanced at Audrey. 'Is she doing this on purpose to make me look stupid?'

Audrey was confused. When she realized what was happening, she quickly scrambled into her bag. "Oh, sorry! I made a mistake!"

She said, handing Peter another card. 'Oh, Peter, you douche. You're so full of yourself but you're nothing without my club card. You won't even be allowed in here if it weren't for me, ' she thought in secret.

The security guard finally allowed them in after seeing the correct card.

Audrey's classmates excitedly entered. With the free-flowing drinks and beautiful lights, they danced the night away and had the time of their lives.

At the club's balcony, Alfred received a message informing him about Peter's presence in the club. He was stunned for three minutes, and then he started laughing loudly.

'Oh, Peter, I've been looking for you everywhere. Who would have thought you'd walk right into my

club? I was furious when my guys failed to kill you.
Now that you're here, I'll be sure to get the job
done, '

Alfred thought to himself. Earlier, he was told that
his men failed to kill Peter, and were even caught
by the authorities.

Going rogue, he decided he'd kill Peter in his club
himself.

This was his turf, and he was certain that nothing
would get in his way this time.

--

Peter didn't know that Alfred had discovered him.
Even if he did, he didn't really care. They went to
the VIP area as soon as they entered.

The room was beautifully decorated. The carpet,
walls, and all the tables were made of gold, making
the room look absolutely exquisite.

The space was about 100 square meters where people
could sing, dance or dine. Six highly-trained and
beautiful waitresses roamed the area delivering top-
quality service to its likewise top-tier patrons.

They all felt like kings.

Pretty soon, Audrey's classmates started to order
drinks and had a good time, even made better with
the excellent service and Peter's graciousness.

Despite the festivities, Audrey couldn't help but
observe Peter. His level of ease piqued her
curiosity.

'He's just a security guard and yet, he blends-in
really well in this high-end place, '

Audrey wondered.

Suddenly, she started to feel so much resentment that she was tempted to throw a bottle at him.

'Why the fuck does he have all those expensive drinks when I'm the one paying the bill? I can't afford all of those even though I'm the mayor's daughter!'

Blissfully unaware of Audrey's concerns, Peter drank to his heart's content with Audrey's classmates.

Peter carried himself really well and was really good at connecting with his new friends. He oozed with charisma, impressing Audrey's classmates very much.

Ada, who was more mature and sophisticated than her peers, was more than impressed â€"she was attracted. Laughing at his jests and making as much eye contact as possible, she was sure that she would throw herself at him if it weren't for her roommate.

Audrey, on the other hand, grew angrier by the minute. 'What a showoff! You'll regret this. Go, drink! Drink more until you die, idiot!'

She cursed, very worried about the bill. 'I can't afford all this, I don't know what to do.'

"What do you do for a living, Peter?" one of Audrey's classmates asked. "You must be so rich and powerful. Why do you wear such simple clothes?"

Sipping on a glass of wine, Peter replied, "I prefer staying low-key. I find it satisfying when I embarrass people who misjudge me because of how I look. Don't you agree? It's calledâ€""

"Something like being a wolf in a sheep's skin. I've seen that a lot in novels, " one of Audrey's classmate cut him off with admiration even before he could find the right words.

Peter laughed, "Yes, that's correct! You're a smart boy, good for you!"

"Bro, you didn't tell us where you work!" The other classmate asked again.

"Silverland Group, " Peter replied uncomfortably knowing that he was only a security guard there.

As he was about to make something up about his official designation, the student exclaimed, "Silverland Group? I've heard of that company! You must be a senior manager or something! You must be earning around ten million dollars a year!"

"Hahahaha, how did you know? You are clever! Okay, cheers!" Peter smiled from ear to ear and took a big gulp of wine.

Audrey's mouth dropped. 'You liar! What a showoff! What a big showoff!'

She wanted to stand up and expose Peter then and there: tell her classmates about his real profession and that the club card was actually hers.

Quickly collecting herself, she decided against it because she already told her classmates that he was her boyfriend.

'Okay, relax. Just hold it in, ' she told herself.

'I have to hold it in if I don't want to be bothered by Jared again, ' she thought.

Audrey's classmates started exchanging goodbyes at 12 o'clock midnight. They would have wanted to stay longer, but they had classes early the next day.

When their bill arrived, the amount shocked Audrey to the core. She couldn't believe her eyes!

'What?!

$830, 000? This is too expensive!

Damn it! I wanna kill Peter!'

Audrey estimated the bill to be $20, 000-$30, 000.
That, she could afford.

But the amount in the bill was just too much! Paying
the bill would put her father on the headlines the
very next day.

If people found out that his daughter spent that
much money in one party, he would surely lose his
job!

Her classmates were just as shocked when they saw
the amount. They've never spent that much money in
one night, their whole lives!

Regular people would need to work for ten or twenty
years to even earn as much. Still, they were at ease
knowing that Peter, one of the top managers of
Silverland Group, could surely afford it.

Audrey knew the truth, though. Peter wasn't a
manager, he was only a security guard. She trembled
and wanted to cry.

'What should I do? If I get my father into trouble,
I would never forgive myself!'

Thank you for reading. Please leave your valuable
review. It will help us provide you with more
interesting novels. More top billionaire romance
novels await you at moboreader.net

Chapter 32 An Intense Battle
Seeing the look on Audrey's face, Peter knew that
she did not have enough money. He could not help but
think to himself, 'Why did she come here with no
money? What a silly girl!'

Peter glanced over the bill. Suddenly, his jaw dropped open. The sight made him want to collapse right then and there.

'Holy shit! There must be something wrong! We only drank a little, but it already costed us $830, 000! That's just too exorbitant!'

Peter wanted to tear down the restaurant. However, he could not. He had bragged to her classmates, so he had to bear the consequences.

After all, men had to reap what they had sown. This was what he had to pay for his whole night of bragging.

At that time, the voice of the restaurant manager came, "$830, 000 in total. Will you pay by credit card or by cash?"

The manager said that with no respect, nor patience. It appeared as though he was looking down on Peter.

'How dare you, a poor guy, fight against Mr. Gao. What a joke! If you fail to pay the bill, you will never be able to leave Alfred Club. You and the two little beauties beside will never leave this place!'

Peter glowered at the manager and shouted at him, "Are you an idiot? How is it possible to bring bills worth thousands on hand? Of course, I'll pay by card! I don't understand how an idiot like you is a manager."

Peter was furious, but he handed his card over, saying to Audrey's classmates, "Well, it isn't that expensive. It costs only $830, 000."

Now that he had bragged so much and the bill had to be paid, he was determined to keep the facade and act like a wealthy man.

The manager didn't expect Peter's words. His mind went blank suddenly. He couldn't find the words to retort him.

Looking at the black and dirty bank card that Peter handed over, he thought to himself, 'This rascal just gave me a card to act like he has the money. If the balance is not sufficient to pay the bill, he will be doomed.'

If Peter had only known what the manager was thinking about, he would surely spit on the latter. Several days ago, Alfred had transferred a million into Peter's bank card, so the balance of that card was for sure sufficient.

The cashier soon inserted the bank card into the credit card terminal. Then, Peter had entered his pin and confirmed the payment.

Audrey's classmates were surprised at how rich Peter was, but Audrey was worried about him. She stared at the cashier, worrying that the card would get declined.

After all, Peter was just a security guard. How could it be possible for him to be able to pay that much? If he really had that much money, there would be no need for him to work as a security guard.

The manager shouted before the cashier spoke, "Card's declined, right?"

Zzt-zzt!

Beep!

The receipt printed out from the card terminal right after the manager shouted out. Peter had received a text message alert from the bank, too.

The cashier did not know what was wrong with the manager, so she said nervously, "Sir, the payment is successful."

She handed the card over to Peter with respect, "Sir, here is your card."

"Thanks." Peter took his card and put it back in his pocket casually.

The manager was so embarrassed and angry that his face got extremely red. He didn't know what he should do at the moment!

Audrey, who was on the other side, was relieved.

"You can't leave!" They were just about to leave when the manager roared out. The club's security team blocked their paths.

Peter sighed and then asked, "What's the matter? I've already paid the bill!"

"We suspect that you have stolen something from this establishment. I hope you would cooperate with our investigation, " the manager said insidiously.

Peter was not a fool. He immediately knew that Alfred had plotted something against him, again.

"How about letting my friends go first? I will stay and help you with your investigation, " Peter said, doing something with his phone before putting it back to his shirt pocket.

Peter interrupted the manager's thoughts, "I was the one who paid the bill. And you're suspecting me of stealing. It will be of no help for them to stay. If you force them to stay, I will call the police and accuse you of assault."

The manager looked to Peter's friends and then nodded. "Okay. Let them leave."

Audrey and her classmates knew that something was wrong. They were just about to ask Peter about what was happening when he said, "I'm fine. Audrey, you and your friends should go first. Wait for my call later."

"Fine. I will wait for your call." Audrey nodded and then went out with her classmates.

She knew that it would do no help if they stayed. Peter would have to take care of them during the fight. Therefore, it was better to leave and let Peter deal with the situation.

Peter got a little bit relieved when he saw Audrey and her friends leave.

The manager spoke with a bleak smirk, "Man, you do know how to care for women. You acted like a real man."

Peter squinted, "It has nothing to do with you whether I act like a real man. I want to talk directly to Alfred Gao. You have bad breath, and I don't want to endure that any longer."

"Screw you!" The manager was insulted with those words, so he raised his fist, about to hit Peter...

Slap!

But Peter was fast, so he slapped the man on the face. "Cut the crap, and don't waste my time. Ask Alfred Gao to come down and see me."

The manager was hit so hard that half of his face became red and swollen. He almost lost his balance even. His face twisted with anger, and then he shouted, "You son of a bitch! How dare you summon Mr. Gao! You've already offended Mr. Gao and beaten me up! You're a dead man now!"

The manager shouted out and waved his hands to signal the club security to come over. They rushed toward Peter immediately.

At the same time, a dozen men with strong, bulky statures came out from a room with long sticks in their hands, running fiercely toward Peter.

"Motherfuckers!" Peter cursed them and squinted. Then, he suddenly seized the manager up and threw him to the dozen of henchmen.

At the same time, he suddenly kicked the abdomen of one of the security guys with his right leg. The security guy screamed out and spat out blood from his mouth, falling down to the ground.

Peter grinned, using both of his hands to grab another two security guys and crashed their heads strongly against each other's.

Bam!

Blood splattered everywhere.

The two security guys fainted to the ground with their heads bleeding heavily.

"Kill him!"

At that time, all of the henchmen with the long sticks shouted out and ran closer to Peter. They all seemed determined to kill Peter with no mercy.

Countless of sticks were waved in the air, making whooshing sounds. The scene was so frightening.

"I haven't had a good fight in so long. Today, I will fight with all my strength!" Peter felt no fear at all. He grinned, a gleam of happiness in his eyes, adrenaline rushing through his veins.

Boom!

He stomped his right feet to the ground, making a huge crack. The marble ground looked like it had been heavily hit by a huge ax.

Peter jumped up with the force he gathered from the ground, and then he suddenly pounced onto the henchmen like a fierce tiger.

Peter's fists started to punch them, like bombs dropping from the air.

Bam! Bam! Bam!

One of the henchmen was punched, and he fell down immediately to the ground. His facial bones disfigured. He was not even able to sound out the pain he had felt.

Peter grabbed the man's long stick and suddenly swept it across and toward the henchmen. The long sticks slipped out from the henchmen's hands with clashing sounds to the ground.

He showed no mercy, hitting on each of the thugs with great strength.

Bam, bam, bam, bam! Four of the henchmen were hit on the head, collapsing to the ground with their foreheads bleeding.

Thank you for reading. Please leave your valuable review. It will help us provide you with more interesting novels. More top billionaire romance novels await you at moboreader.net

Chapter 33 See Alfred Again
In seven or eight seconds, about six or seven young people were knocked down, shocking everyone in the room.

They were totally stunned. It seemed that they did not expect Peter to be so fierce.

But after a short period of stupor, instead of fear, anger arose.

Alfred was looking at all thirty of his hired thugs. If they could not beat Peter up, how could they follow Alfred's instructions? How could they ask him for money?

"Brothers, get up and beat the shit out of him! The one who would succeed will be rewarded with a million bucks in cash!"

The young men all howled and screamed like wolves excited to get down on their prey, and once again, their eyes turned red, blood rushing to their faces.

"Come on, squirts, let me see what you guys have!" Peter shouted at these young people with scorn, and all of them rushed toward him even more crazily.

In an instant, he darted toward one of the young men, gritted his teeth, screamed, and smashed the stick in the young man's hand.

The young man looked at the broken stick in front of him, and his head overflowed with cold sweat. He was about to dodge the hit, but Peter's speed was too fast that he had no chance at all.

With a loud bang, the young man's head was directly hit, and a shower of blood splashed out of his forehead. Then, he fell down to the ground with a soft plop.

"Weren't you just so confident? That's all it takes?" Peter sneered and stretched out his leg.

The young man was kicked away like a sandbag and fell to the front desk, crushing it in half.

Peter no longer paid attention to the young man, but he waved the stick and rushed to the other people, instead.

Bam! One of young men was kicked.

Boom! Another young man was knocked down.

In a few seconds, the young men scrambled toward Peter like packs of wolves, but they all ended up falling to the ground like dead flies.

So far, nearly thirty thugs had been beaten to the ground.

The manager looked at the scene from afar. His legs were like jelly, his face was getting redder and redder, and his eyes were full of rage.

Peter flashed his brilliant white teeth. "These shrimps have been taken cared of. Now, can you call Alfred Gao down?"

"No way! If you dare, go to the third floor and look for him yourself." The manager stomped out and sneaked out using the back door, disappearing without a trace.

"Fuck." Peter was a little upset. Alfred was such an arrogant bastard. Without hesitation, he went straight to the third floor.

Since Alfred dared not come down, Peter decided to go up and confront him, instead.

Peter went to the third floor, but it wasn't easy. Everywhere he passed, it seemed like trouble was waiting for him.

The whole hall on the first floor had become a mess of murmurs â€" unconscious bodies, and broken furniture. It was a horrible sight to see.

Peter soon got to the second floor, but at the stairs on the second floor there stood more than twenty strong, young men waiting for him.

More than twenty people, actually. Obviously, the amount of men here seemed more than those guys on the first floor, and each of them had a sharp machete in his hand.

It seemed that Alfred was not a fool. He had this all planned, sorted, and calculated. And it was smart of him to do so.

"Who are you? Tell me your name."

Just as Peter cursed under his breath, a young man asked aloud.

Peter laughed. Was he stupid? Peter had been fighting for a few hours on the first floor, and they still didn't know who he was.

Peter didn't mean to answer it at all. He raised his stick and smashed it down to the ground, creating a loud sound that echoed through the hall.

"Bring it on!"

The young man only had the time to say three words because his head had already been smashed by Peter's stick.

Another group of young men pretended not to care about Peter's immense strength. They all waved their machetes, whined loudly, and rushed toward Peter.

Peter was infuriated by all of these stubborn people who only had anger and greed in their hearts, even though they knew that they couldn't beat him.

A minute later, all of the young men fell to the ground, unable to get up.

The first floor's done, the second floor's destroyed... Finally, I can get to the third floor, " Peter continued to move up the staircase.

When Peter got to the third floor, the first thing he saw was a spacious hall, which was so much brighter than the one on the first floor.

In the middle of the hall, Alfred sat on a chair that looked like a throne as if he had been expecting Peter.

Behind him, on both sides, were two attractive, young women massaging his shoulders for her, and on both sides of his legs were two equally sexy

creatures rubbing his legs for him, seemingly
enjoying themselves indescribably.

Peter watched the scene, and he was furious.

He was in a fatal fight downstairs, beating people
up, While Alfred was enjoying all along. If this was
acceptable, then nothing was not.

"I didn't expect you to climb all three floors. But
now that you're here, you might as well drink, "

Said Alfred as he looked at Peter with a gentle
smile.

This fellow really loved pretending that he was
better than others, and clearly, he was dying to
kill Peter, even though he had a smiling face.

"Fuck you.

I'm here to beat you up, not drink. Alfred, you've
caused me trouble five times now. If I don't show
the same courtesy, then what good am I."

When Peter finished saying that, he jumped and flew
to Alfred like a whirlwind. His fists were curled
like shells, about to hit Alfred's disgusting face.

'Wait for me to smash your face. Let's see you show
off, then, '

Peter thought proudly.

But before his fist hit the high-profile man's face,
the look in Alfred's eyes changed suddenly.

The two enchanting girls, who had been rubbing
Alfred's legs, suddenly jumped up. Each of them had
a sharp blade in her hand, stabbing Peter in the
abdomen.

Femme Fatale!

Peter smiled faintly, took back his fist, turned his paws into palms, and suddenly stepped back.

The two girls were about to change their tactics, but Peter's speed had accelerated. Before the girls could make another move, Peter grabbed their wrists and gently pinched them. The sharp blades clanged to the ground.

In an instant, the two girls suddenly fell into Peter's arms like beautiful mermaids.

"Haha, thank you for your hugs. Although I know that I'm a handsome hero, now's not really a good time. When I'm done with this, I will fight with you for three days and three nights."

Peter laughed and pinched the two women. Then, they fell to the ground softly, unable to get up.

At last, Alfred could not control his anger. His face became cloudy and cold.

Those hooligans and swordsmen were all defeated by Peter. He was shocked, but he was not worried. But seeing these two girls fall made him panic.

These four girls were his most precious assistants. Whether in handwriting or in gun-shooting, their skills were top-notch.

Each one of the four women was able to sink a gang of fifty to sixty members in blood easily.

Alfred was able to live so well in Golden City because of these four women. One could say that without these four women, Alfred would not be the man he was today.

But now, two of the four girls had been overthrown by Peter in only a few seconds. How could he not panic?

Chapter 34 Trampling Him To Death
"Kill him! Kill him!"

Giving up his gentlemen facade, Alfred yelled.

As soon as he barked out his command, the two girls behind him each took out a silver revolver, suddenly aiming at Peter and firing, not leaving Peter even a second to react.

It was the first time that Peter had lost his calm. He moved so fast that his figure flickered, fury burning inside him.

It was out of his expectations that Alfred's assistants had guns, and their shooting was ruthless and resolute. 'They are fucking killing me!'

"Bang-bang! Bang-bang!" Four gunshots resounded, but the bullets hit nothing.

Opening their eyes in amazement, looking around, the two girls couldn't believe that Peter had disappeared.

"Where is he?" Alfred shrieked. He wasn't a fool to believe that bullets could make a man's body vanish.

"Here I am." A voice called out over their heads. Alfred looked up, only to find Peter plunging down with his arms stretched like a hovering bird.

Alfred panicked. "Kill..."

Before he could finish his sentence, he toppled to the ground as Peter gave him a slap.

The two girls came to themselves eventually. Guns were raised again at Peter but fell off from their hands. They cried out because their wrists were hurt.

"I don't hurt women, but you two are bad, " staring at the two girls, Peter said to them bitterly. Then, he reached out his hand and gave them hard slaps.

Pak! Pak! Pak!

After a few loud sounds, the two girls laid down on the ground ashamed and angry, covering their burning buttocks with their palms, unable to stand up.

Peter kicked away the guns. He smiled at Alfred and said, "Hey, what now? Is that all you've got?"

Alfred touched his face and stood up. With his bloodthirsty eyes glaring at Peter, he said, "Peter, I'll remember this slap. You'll pay 100 times for this."

'The boy still doesn't understand who has the upper hand here.'

Peter curled his lips and gave him another slap.

Both sides of Alfred's face were swollen as he spat out blood with a few of his teeth mixed in. The slap made him whirl three times around before falling to the ground.

Stepping forward, Peter trampled on his face and said in contempt. "You think you have any chance against me? Now, do you believe that I can kill you today if I want to?"

"Ha-ha-ha!" Alfred burst into laughter. "Could you? I dare you to kill me. I'm part of the Gao family, a renowned entrepreneur in Golden City. If you kill me, I swear you won't live to tomorrow, "

Alfred growled, full of madness and hatred in his eyes.

He was Alfred Gao, a bigwig in Golden City. He had never been insulted by having his face trampled on like that.

This was a huge humiliation, a moment that he could never forget!

"You have some character. I like it." Peter smiled. The sole of his foot crushed Alfred's face on the floor, causing shrill cries.

"You are right. I wouldn't dare kill you. But I would dare cripple you." While smiling, Peter stomped heavily on Alfred's leg, mercilessly cracking it, saying, "Remember this. Don't ever bother me any more. Or you'll not only lose a leg. By the way, I have recorded all of these, so you know what I mean."

Then, he left Alfred alone and strutted out the Alfred Club.

Before he left, he said goodbye to the four girls, "Beauties, see you next time. Next time, let's get rough in a different way. I bet you'll get some satisfaction, then. It's getting late, so I'll go first. Bye!"

Upon leaving the club, Peter took a taxi to his apartment and texted Audrey that everything was fine.

Everything that happened tonight really wore him out.

But he didn't care about being exhausted. What he was concerned about was the 830, 000 he had lost. He felt heartbroken as he thought about it.

Taking advantage of a woman was really a loss outweighed the gains. A touch on the waist and a kiss on her forehead cost him 830, 000. Damn it!

Screech!

The sudden break of the taxi almost threw Peter's head onto the windshield.

In front of the car stood a young man covered in blood, blocking their way. And they could see a group of people chasing after him from a distance.

"What do we do now?" The driver was frightened to death by the scene. He had never seen anything like it before.

Peter's head ached upon seeing this, too. What a lucky day! Everything was going so wrong.

"Open the door, and let him in. Then, let's lose the guys behind us." Answering rapidly, Peter opened the door and pulled the young man inside the taxi.

"Are you sure? Who knows what kind of person he is?" The driver still seemed frightened.

"We don't have a better option, so follow my lead. What's more, we witnessed them killing people, so they won't let us go. Let's leave as soon as we can before it's too late."

After he comforted the driver for a while, Peter turned to the young man to check his injuries.

He had no idea what kind of enemy this young man had gotten in a brawl with. He had six ruthless stabs, each of them deep to the bones.

Fortunately, the young man's injuries were not fatal, so his life was not urgently at risk. Well, at least, not for now. He was bleeding heavily. Without any medical attention, he would die sooner or later.

Peter took out his silver needles without hesitation. Then, he tried to stop the young man's bleeding. He would always finish what he started.

If the young man would die in the cab, he might also get involved and be in trouble.

During the treatment, the driver turned the car around, rushing to the opposite direction, leaving the chasing men far behind.

"Thank you. Thank you so much." The young man looked at Peter with gratitude and expressed his appreciation. "My name is Brandon Chu. May I have..."

"Stop!" Peter interrupted, "You are bleeding too much. If you want to save your ass, stop talking. Who you are has nothing to do with me. I'll help you stop bleeding for the moment. Later, I'll dump you into a hospital, and I'd have nothing to do with you any longer."

Peter talked to Brandon as he performed acupuncture.

'This guy is being chased to death on the street. He must be a bad guy if not a gangster.' Peter didn't want to get involved or seek trouble for himself.

Brandon was embarrassed for he had always been extremely arrogant. He would have cursed Peter upfront if he had not been his savior at this moment.

'Fuck! I'm honoring you by showing respect. How dare you ignore me? A lot of people want to associate themselves with me, not only in Golden City, but also in the whole province. And I never give them an ounce of my attention.

Today, I'm taking the initiative to show kindness, but I'm being refused!' Frustration and confusion swept Brandon at the same time.

'But he saved me, so I'll just let it go.' The only thing he could do was to remember Peter's face and look for a chance to return the favor in the future.

The acupuncture was completed soon enough. Peter looked at Brandon and asked, "Do you have any money?"

"Yes, but only a few thousand. I can transfer money through my cards." Brandon was a bit ashamed to answer because usually he didn't bring much cash. A few thousand was not enough for the favor for sure.

"Forget transferring the money. I don't want them. Give your cash to the driver. After all, he's still saving you while you're staining his cab. He might even get in trouble for doing this, " Peter said.

Upon hearing this, the driver almost shed tears of gratitude.

Brandon understood what Peter had meant. He asked the driver for his account number, transferring 50, 000 to him, and then pacified him, "Don't worry, bro. I can guarantee that no one will go after you because of what you did."

Admiration to Peter arose in his mind at the same time. 'This guy saved me, but he's asking for a reward for someone else. I seldom see such a guy.'

He didn't know that Peter was already regretful upon hearing 50, 000 bucks. 'Holy shit! If I had known you were so rich, I would've asked for some. But what's said is said. I can't change anything now.'

Thank you for reading. Please leave your valuable review. It will help us provide you with more interesting novels. More top billionaire romance novels await you at moboreader.net

Chapter 35 False Evidence And Incrimination
Peter asked the cab driver to pull over and sent Brandon in a hospital for treatment before heading straight home.

Shelly approached Peter anxiously the moment he arrived at work the next day. "Oh, Peter, something bad happened. Mr. Zhang came back and asked to see you in his office!"

"Mr. Zhang? Who is he? I don't think I've met him before, " Peter asked, confused.

"Mr. Zhang, whose full name is Jaden Zhang, has worked in our company for a dozen years. He is one of Miss Song's subordinates, but Miss Song won't offend him if not necessary. There are also rumors that he has been supporting Bob."

Shelly whispered quickly.

"He's supporting Bob?" 'This can't be good, ' Peter thought. He would have preferred to decline the meeting, but he knew he had no choice.

He was about to knock when a woman with a voluptuous figure opened the door for him.

"You must be Peter Wang. Mr. Zhang is in a meeting now. Please come in and wait for a moment, " the woman said, giving Peter a subtle but provocative glance.

Peter didn't know what to make of it. 'Is this woman trying to flirt with me at first sight? Am I even that attractive?'

If he weren't in a professional setting, he would have flirted back.

"Thanks, " Peter replied politely as he entered. The woman handed Peter a glass of water before walking out of the office.

Peter was pleasantly surprised. He almost suspected that the woman would seduce him and then accuse him of indecent assault. Apparently, he was wrong.

"Oh god, come on baby..."

Suddenly, a strange voice coming from Jaden's personal computer got Peter's attention.

Confused, Peter walked over to check what was on the computer screen.

His face turned bright red when he caught a glimpse of what was happening.

Jaden Zhang, one of the company's most prominent leaders, was watching pornographic materials in the office! What a pervert! No wonder his secretary acted like a slut.

Peter couldn't take his eyes off the screen for minutes. When he was finally about to go back to his seat, the contents of the screen changed and the office door opened.

"What do you think you're doing?" A middle-aged man in a fine suit walked in, followed by his secretary â€" the one flirting with Peter previously.

"Nothing, sir, " Peter replied.

The middle-aged man looked at Peter unconvinced and quickly walked to also view his screen. "How dare you steal classified information for this company! Who do you work for?"

"What? I wasn't stealing anything!" said Peter, quickly denying the allegations.

Crack!

The man grabbed a flash drive attached to the computer and threw it to the desk. "You can't lie to me. If you did nothing, then how did this flash drive get here?"

Now Peter knew he was in trouble. He was set up!

Shit, the business world was like a battlefield. He should have been more careful!

"Call the police now! I want this man arrested for corporate espionage, " the middle-aged man immediately ordered his secretary, giving Peter no chance to defend himself.

The secretary nodded and did what she was told.

The man was Jaden Zhang, Vice President of the Silverland Group. He had been out for a business trip several days ago. Upon arrival, he was greeted with the news that Bob was beaten up and sent to the hospital.

This infuriated him, especially when he found out that Peter, the guy responsible for Bob's beating, was connected to Bella.

He saw it as an attack from Bella by having one of his henchmen attacked. He then decided to set Peter up to incriminate him as his revenge.

"Mr. Zhang, that flash drive is not mine. I would never steal confidential information from the company, " Peter calmly explained himself.

"Save your words for the police! They'll be the ones who'll decide your fate, " Jaden said, ignoring Peter's explanation.

Jaden saw this as a battle between Bella and himself, Peter as a tool. Jaden wanted to show Bella that she couldn't get away with hurting his henchman that easily.

In the CEO office

Bella immediately stood up the moment the news reached her. "What?! Mr. Zhang caught Peter stealing confidential information?"

"Yes, nearly everyone in the company knows about it now. The police are arriving any minute, " Clair replied.

"This is bullshit. Let's go, " Bella said, marching to Jaden's office.

She knew it was a setup, but what she couldn't understand was why Peter fell into it that easily.

Soon, the top executives of the company were in Jaden's office. Some of them were reprimanding Peter for his crime.

"Never would I have known that a security guard like you would ever steal from our company!"

"I agree! How dare you use your access to the premises to break into Mr. Zhang's computer!"

"He can't deny this forever. He'll definitely spend his life in jail!"

Although Peter could hear what they were saying, he was lost in his own thoughts. No one knew what he was thinking.

The men assumed that his silence was a sign of his guilt so they continued talking down on him.

Elaine looked at poor Peter and couldn't help but ask, "Mr. Zhang, there must be something wrong. How could Peter be a corporate spy? There must have been a misunderstanding."

"Misunderstanding?" Jaden laughed. "Miss Dai, you were the one who hired this security guard, am I right? And now you are defending him. Are you sure you're not hiding something?"

Jaden replied suspiciously, putting some of the blame on her.

Elaine went pale. Suddenly she feared for her career as well, almost losing her balance.

She did not want to be labeled as an accomplice to the crime.

Jaden's words also elicited suspicion from the other members of the leadership team. They looked at Elaine distrustfully, making her feel very uncomfortable.

Seeing what Jaden did to Elaine, Peter spoke up, "Mr. Zhang, how could you just randomly accuse people of such things? I'm fine with you incriminating me, but you don't have to involve other people."

"What did you say? Are you saying that my claims have no grounds?" Jaden was furious. 'This bastard is antagonizing me! I will not let him get away with this!'

"You know what happened today, Mr. Zhang. We both know what happened and we both know there are no pieces of evidence to back up your claims, " Peter said calmly.

"Why, you—""

Jaden got even more infuriated with Peter's calmness. How could he be so composed? He should be worried and sick by now especially with what was coming next! Jaden didn't expect Peter to be so collected, and he didn't like what was happening at all.

Thank you for reading. Please leave your valuable review. It will help us provide you with more interesting novels. More top billionaire romance novels await you at moboreader.net

Chapter 36 Stay Calm
"What are you all doing here? Don't you all have work?" A cold voice sliced through the commotion just as Jaden was fuming. Bella appeared with a still face catching everyone's attention.

The senior managers immediately bowed their heads and moved to both sides to make way for her.

Despite Bella's short stay in the company, she was already able to establish a strong reputation.

Apart from Jaden, no one dared to challenge Bella in Silverland Group, let alone offend or displease her.

Everyone knew of the rivalry between Jaden and Bella. Jaden still harbored ill feelings towards Bella especially after she landed her position as president. Jaden was the main candidate for the post had Bella not been transferred. There had been friction between them ever since.

"What's happening?" Bella demanded, walking to Jaden's side.

"I caught this security guard stealing confidential information from my computer. Miss Song, you need to decide what to do with him, on behalf of the company, "

Jaden advised dutifully, hiding his ulterior motifs. He knew Bella wanted to back Peter up, but he was determined to make the situation difficult for her, not as easy as she wished.

Bella didn't know what to do, cursing inwardly. He was speaking in front of everybody so she couldn't openly defend Peter.

She was sure that if she did that in front of her managers, news of her bias would reach the directors in less than 10 minutes and her position as president would be in jeopardy.

As Bella was trying to find the best way to go about the situation, four policemen suddenly came rushing in.

"Officers, thank God you're here. This man stole confidential information. Please arrest him and find out who he's working for!" Jaden immediately requested, grabbing the opportunity to have Peter detained.

Silverland Group was known as the biggest financial group in the Golden City. The police would surely prioritize this issue and immediately jump at Peter.

But as they came closer, they recognized him right away. "Mr. Wang, is that you?"

The officer-in-charge was Richard Xing, Director of the Southern Regional Bureau. He didn't expect that the spy Jaden reported would turn out to be Peter.

"Mr. Xing, you came right on time. I need your help to prove my innocence, " Peter told Richard calmly.

"Innocence? What else is there to prove?" Jaden said in anger. He didn't expect a mere security guard to even be acquainted with the director of the police force.

"Mr. Xing, as an honorable officer, surely you wouldn't bend the law just because you know the person involved, would you? This man sneaked into my office to steal confidential information. I caught him in action. This is the flash drive he used to store the data. We have witnesses and evidence. You have everything you need to arrest him, right now!"

Richard didn't know what to do. Had he known that the reported person was Peter, he would not have come here. Now what? He was holding a wolf by the ears. How would he find a way around this?

Was it wise to arrest Peter? If the allegations were true, then there would not be any problems. But if they weren't, his position as director would surely be in jeopardy.

If he didn't arrest Peter, he'd surely be under scrutiny for his refusal in front of the senior managers of Silverland Group. Neither side wasn't without risk. Realizing that he was in a severely

precarious situation gave Richard a very bad
headache.

Thankfully, Bella came to the rescue. "You don't
have to arrest him right away, Mr. Xing. Peter is
denying the allegation. We might as well listen to
his side of the story."

"Bella Song, you are obviously covering up for this
culprit. I will file a complaint against you!" Jaden
accused, pointing a finger at Bella.

"How dare you! Who are you to address me as such?
Know your place! As president of this company, I
will not hesitate to put a criminal behind bars; but
also I am not going to allow any of my employees to
be unjustly accused of a crime they did not do."

"If he is a real spy, I won't defend him anymore.
But if the allegations against him are proven wrong,
then mark my words, I WILL find out who is behind
this trickery."

Bella boomed, regaining her control over the
situation.

Peter looked at Bella with appreciation. "Mr. Xing,
I am wronged indeed, " he explained calmly. "First
of all, I have never seen that flash drive before.
You can check it for my fingerprints if you want to.

Second, although there is no camera in this office,
there are cameras in the corridor outside. You can
check the time of when I came in and compare it to
the timestamp on the data in the flash drive so you
can see if I was able to copy all the pieces of
information there, in such a short time.

Third, you can also check his keyboard, mouse, and
even his desk, and see if my fingerprints are on
there.

Fourth, I can admit that I sat on this sofa for a
while. You will surely find my fingerprints on the
armrest and the glass if you want to check it too.

Finally, you can check if his computer is wired to
anything that would allow for remote access. I
believe all these things should be enough to prove
my innocence."

What Peter said left everyone silent.

Both Richard and Jaden clearly did not expect a mere
security guard to be so calm and clear-minded under
a situation as high-pressure as this.

'Is he really just a security guard?'

Jaden felt very uneasy.

Only Bella didn't seem so surprised as she was well
aware of what Peter was capable of.

Richard did not waste time. He immediately called
for his team to check the CCTV footage and the
pieces of evidence Peter suggested.

Jaden's face was white as ash. He knew he lost this
battle and there was no way to salvage the
situation.

Jaden's secretary was sweating so hard that she
couldn't manage to stand up straight. She attempted
to slowly exit the scene, but the police stopped
her.

Two hours later, all the pieces of evidence were
traced back to her. The policemen handcuffed her and
took her to their custody. The storm finally
subsided.

Although he was taken off the hook, Peter could not
help but feel bad that the secretary allowed herself
to be arrested instead of admitting that it was all
the doing of her superior. It seemed that Jaden had
strings that he wasn't aware of.

Back in the President's Office

"You can no longer work at the Security Department. From now on, you'll be transferred to the Logistics Department as my driver. Lisa and Shelly have been performing excellently, so we're going to have them trained to be transferred to the Sales Department, " Bella said, looking at Peter.

The Security Department was managed by Jaden. 80% of the staff there were loyal to him. After what happened that day, Bella was sure that it would be difficult for Peter to integrate himself with the team, so Bella had him transferred.

Peter was against the decision on his new assignment at first, but when he learned that Lisa and Shelly were also going to be transferred, he decided that he also did not intend to stay anymore and finally agreed to the transfer as well. "Can I get a raise?" he couldn't help but ask.

"Yes, you may." Bella nodded.

"Are there many beautiful girls in my new assignment?" he asked.

"Yes, there are, " Bella said, starting to feel irritated.

"Will I be able to touch their thighs?" Peter asked excitedly.

"Go away!" Bella snapped. He was unbearable!

'The son of a bitch is so difficult to change. You give him a hand, he takes an arm.'

Peter arrived at the Logistics Department and found that all the other drivers had gone out to work. He felt bored being all by himself.

As his duty was about to end, he received a text message.

"Don't leave after work. Wait for me at the basement parking."

Peter smiled with glee.

Chapter 37 Seeing An Old Classmate
Peter happily went to the basement parking when his shift ended.

The moment he saw Bella, Peter removed his jacket excitedly. "Bella, boss, I'm coming."

He couldn't wait to see his beautiful boss sitting alone in her red Hummer in the dark garage.

Upon seeing him, Bella flipped her smooth hair and gestured her finger seductively. "Come on, I can't wait for it any longer."

Peter stopped abruptly. "What can I do for you?"

Bella curled up her lips. "You're not a beastâ€¦

You're a coward!"

Peter couldn't take it. With gusto, he banged at the car door and tried to enter forcibly.

If he had a weakness, it would be seduction from an extremely beautiful goddess. He would show her how big of a man he was.

Bang!

Something hit Peter forcibly.

Aghh!

Ahhhhhhh!

"Why did you do that?!" Peter said angrily, clutching at his stomach.

"Get in the car. We're going to a party, " Bella said, suddenly in a serious and authoritative tone once again.

Peter looked at her ambiguous expression. He thought about protesting but eventually decided to give in.

Half an hour later, they arrived at the Bluesea Hotel.

"Wait for me here while I park." Bella said, dropping him off at the hotel entrance.

He immediately noticed the attractive waitresses and their long beautiful legs.

"Peter?" He suddenly heard someone calling, which interrupted his thoughts.

He turned his head and saw a man and a woman looking back at him.

They were both young â€"probably around twenty-four or twenty-five years old.

While you wouldn't say that the man was handsome, he definitely looked good in a suit.

The woman wore a loose top and a fitted cotton skirt. She looked rather average, but the ensemble she wore accentuated her assets well and made heads turn.

The woman looked at Peter suspiciously as she stood close to her companion, holding his arm. She found it odd that her boyfriend would be associated with such a plain-looking man.

"I'm sorry, you are?" Although he looked familiar, Peter couldn't seem to recall who the man was.

"Oh, Peter, it's really you!" The man replied,
amused. "It's me, Beck! We were classmates in high
school. Don't you remember?"

"Oh, Beck!" Peter finally realized.

He had known this man since first grade! Peter
dropped out of school on their second year in high
school, But he could still remember how Beck was
always bullied by their other classmates. Back then,
he was thin and wimpy, but after several years, he
seemed to have grown into this strong and confident
guy.

It was nice to see him again. After he had
experienced many difficult years in his life, his
early memories in school were truly ones that he
treasured.

"It's probably been ten years since we last saw each
other! How are you? What are you doing here? Do you
work here at Bluesea Hotel?"

Beck asked, observing Peter's getup which looked
very plain and simple compared to his.

This didn't come as a surprise especially because he
accompanied Bella but wasn't able to change out of
his work clothes. Anyone would be able to tell that
he was a blue-collar worker based on what he was
wearing.

Peter sighed and shook his head. "No, I don't work
here."

"Oh, where do you work?" Beck asked.

"I work as a security guard in Silverland Group, "
Peter replied. It slipped his mind that he was
recently transferred to the logistics department and
was now a driver.

"Security guard?" Beck exclaimed in surprise. "How
can you be a security guard?" he wondered aloud.

"Come to think of it, you did pretty bad at school, and you seemed to prefer playing with knives and guns. I guess it makes sense for you to work as a security guard."

Growing impatient, Beck's girlfriend started pulling at his arm. "Dear, let's go. We're wasting time chatting with a security guard. I'm hungry, I want to go now."

Beck glared at his girlfriend. "Phoebe, don't talk like that. This is my high school classmate. Back then, Peter was the man no one would dare provoke."

"Ugh, so what, he's a gangster, " Phoebe replied, uninterested. "So what if he was super popular in high school? Who cares if so many ignorant little girls lined up for him back then? Now he's nothing but a stinking security guard."

This time, instead of telling off his girlfriend, Beck looked at Peter and said, "Peter, I think you should quit your job as a security guard. I'll help you. I don't have a very high position, but I'm a manager. I'm pretty sure I can find a better job for you. No woman will take you seriously as a security guard, man. What do you say?"

It made sense for Beck to show off right now. Back then, Peter had been the one that people looked up to in school. At the wave of his hand, crowds of young girls would scream trying to get his attention.

Beck was a nobody that kids pushed around. Girls didn't like him either. Surely it was satisfying for him to see how poor Peter was right now.

Peter had realized that Beck was showing off. He was still caught in a haze reminiscing about the good old days.

"That's really nice of you, friend. But it's okay, I really am fine."

Beck was about to continue talking when his girlfriend cut him off. "Can you stop wasting your time with this security guard? You already offered to find him a new job but he rejected your kindness. Let's go, we're already running late, "

Phoebe complained, pulling him to the entrance.

"Sorry, my girlfriend didn't mean that, " Beck said, but it was obvious he didn't really mean his apology. He clearly looked down on Peter.

Peter wordlessly shook his head.

"You know each other?" Bella asked when she arrived right after the couple entered the restaurant.

She caught a glimpse of them talking but she had no idea what they were talking about.

Peter nodded.

"Let's go inside, " Bella said, grabbing his arm and walking close to him.

The banquet was already filled with guests when they entered.

The Grand Hall was bright and spacious. The ground was covered in a white carpet that made the room look very elegant.

The waitresses looked like fairies in a scenery as they shuttled back and forth in their red dresses.

The sight of the beautiful waitresses quickly erased the earlier conversation from Peter's memory.

Bella whispered something to Peter and left.

Celebrities and high-profile personalities didn't only serve as interesting friends, but presented a big opportunity of social network. Bella would be sure to make the most out of it.

The crowd was very diverse. Generally, the most
well-known were the ones who mingled the most, being
the social butterflies that they were. The ones who
were less prominent were more reserved, clearly
doing their best to broaden their network.

Staying at the corner and munching on what the
buffet offered, Peter marveled at the sights and
sounds around him. He enjoyed looking at all the
people and their body language, their clothes, and
how it all blended with the beautiful setting.

Peter was determined not to waste the opportunity to
bask at the gourmet dishes in the buffet.

As he was enjoying his food, he suddenly heard a
woman crying out, "Frank, stop!" as she hit his
chest.

Chapter 38 Arrogance
"Oh my god!"

Peter exclaimed, touching the woman in panic.

'Wow, that feels great, ' he thought.

However, after he saw who the woman was, his face
changed.

'What the fuck? Why is she here?' he thought.

Realizing that it was Peter, The woman likewise
looked very embarrassed and started to run away.

"Hey, you! Let go of my woman!" a man shouted from
across the room.

SLAP! The man slapped the woman's face and cursed her in rage, "You slut! Where do you think you're going? Your boyfriend sent you here as a gift for me. You have no right to run away! You know I have the money and power to do with you as I please so don't make me angry. You don't want me angry, you understand?"

He said, slapping the woman so hard that she fell to the ground.

Peter looked at the man.

He wore expensive clothes and his sleek hair was as shiny as his shoes. He looked at the woman with arrogance and contempt.

Beck, who was standing behind the man, had his head down and looked terrified.

The girl was Phoebe, Beck's girlfriend!

She knelt on the ground and pleaded, "Frank, please. Please let me go. I'm not that kind of girl."

"You? Are you fucking kidding me?" Frank laughed and slapped her again. "Look at your dress! You look like a slut! Do you think I'm dumb? You'd better come with me or I'll sell you to a brothel."

Phoebe trembled as she looked back at her boyfriend. "Honey, we're engaged. Don't let him do this to me. Please help me!"

She said desperately. "Frankâ€"" Beck tried to say.

"Shut up! Fuck off!" Frank screamed as he kicked his stomach. Beck fell to the ground in pain.

Frank lifted his leg and pressed his shoe on Beck's face. "You said she was all mine. Don't you remember? A deal is a deal. Break your word and I swear you won't go far in this city."

"No, no, Frank, I didn't mean it, I'm sorry!" Beck said immediately. "You can have her for as long as you like. Take her, go ahead! She has nothing to do with me. Please forgive me, Frank!"

"How can you do this to me?" Phoebe cried in despair.

"Good dog." Frank laughed with satisfaction. "Look at your man! What a loser!" he told Phoebe. "You're better off with me, sweetheart. I won't marry you but I won't sell you off like this loser."

"Come, I'll give you a great life if you make me happy, " Frank said, kicking Beck before walking towards Phoebe.

Phoebe looked at Peter with clear desperation. "Please help me. I don't want to go with him. Pleaseâ€¦"

She knew Peter was only a security guard who would most likely be powerless in her situation, but she felt like she had no choice anymore.

Peter was her last hope, even though she knew that it was probably not a good idea for anyone to offend Frank. Peter, of all people, wouldn't risk his life for her, especially after how she treated him in the parking lot.

To her surprise, Peter turned at Frank.

"Stop right there, " he said as he grasped his arm.

Phoebe and Beck were stunned.

'Does this security guard know what he's doing? How could he stand up to a guy like Frank?'

Just as surprised as everyone in the room, Frank turned. "Do I know you? You'd better stay out of this, mate, "

He said calmly. The people at the party were mostly in high society. Peter was the only one who was nameless.

While everyone knew how powerful Frank was, Peter couldn't care less.

Though Frank wasn't the most prominent, he still had a very strong influence in the city and only a small number of people were brave â€"or stupid â€"enough to offend him.

"What are you doing, Peter? Are you insane? You're just a security guard, Frank will kill you! Apologize right now!"

Beck shouted before Peter could respond to Frank's question.

A part of Beck was outraged. He clearly had more resources than Peter, but he was totally deemed powerless by Frank. How could Peter stand up to him like that?

He felt very jealous of Peter's guts. He hoped that Frank would put him in his place once he found out that he had nothing.

Driven by his pride, Beck still wanted to be sure he was a notch above Peter even though his friend was clearly trying to help them.

"Fuck you, Beck! How could you say that!" Phoebe screamed with rage. Why did she even fall in love with this man? If only she knew what kind of a douchebag he was from the beginning!

"Security guard?" Frank smirked in disbelief. "And you dare to challenge me? Hahahahaha! You're dead, you son of a bitch, "

Frank said as he struck to slap Peter.

"Ouch!

Ahhh!

My face!"

To everyone's surprise, it was Frank who was
screaming.

Clutching his face, Frank looked at Peter in
disbelief. "How dare you! Fuck you, you'll regret
thiâ€""

"Pak!" Peter slapped him again.

"Who the fuck do you think you are?" Peter said.

Beck and Phoebe were completely shocked. They didn't
expect Peter to be able to land a hit on Frank like
that.

'You're insane, Peter. You should not have done
that. Frank will not let you go, ' Beck thought.

As for Phoebe, gratitude welled up inside her. She
felt grateful and safe.

"I'm gonna kill you!" Frank screamed. Peter was just
a security guard. How dare he do this to him? This
was embarrassing! He would not let him go!

"Hey! Who are you gonna kill?"

Bella appeared, cold and queen-like.

Frank couldn't believe his eyes. "Bella?"

Everyone in the city knew that Bella was not one you
should trifle with. Even Frank wouldn't dare piss
her off.

"Bella, I'm going to kill that security guard. Does
he have anything to do with you?" Frank said trying
to control his temper.

"Yes, he does. This 'security guard' is my
boyfriend, and it has everything to do with me if

you intend to kill my boyfriend, Frank, " Bella replied.

The eyes of the crowd widened. They couldn't believe what they just heard. 'Is this a joke? Bella and a security guard?

This can't be true!' They looked at Peter with doubt, envy, and admiration all at the same time.

Bella was one of the most beautiful and sought-after women in the Golden City. Men in high society fell at her feet. It was unbelievable that she was dating someone like Peter.

Chapter 39 A Beautiful Fighter
"Boyfriend? Are you kidding? He's just a fucking security guard!" Frank yelled. 'What the fuck? I can't believe this! This security guard bagged Bella Song? That's so unfair!'

Frank felt furious and jealous, as he was also interested in dating Bella!

Bella, however, lost her temper the moment she heard Frank looked down on Peter, and gave him a stinging slap.

"How dare you! Who do you think you are? So what if he's a security guard? I love him and that's none of your business! Besides, he's more of a man than you, you jerk!"

People were stunned with what Bella said. 'What a strong woman!'

Frank glared at her. "Fine! Alfred is going to hear about this!"

SLAP! Bella hit him squarely on the face again.

"Do not say that name in front of me!" she boomed.

Just the sound of his name made her so angry. Did Frank think that she was afraid of him? He couldn't underestimate her like that!

"You!" Frank was enraged. 'This woman can't humiliate me in front of all these people!'

"Do what you want and get out of my sight before I change my mind!" Bella said coldly.

Frank looked at Bella, then at Peter, and stormed off.

He'd surely be a laughing stock if he allowed himself to be pushed around by Bella in front of everyone, longer. He hated Bella and Peter so much and was determined to get his revenge.

The hall was silent.

Bella had always had an elusive reputation, but they didn't know she was so tough.

Beck was also stunned by what happened.

'What the fuck. How did this security guard land someone like Bella?' As with the other men in the room, he was filled with envy and confusion.

Phoebe was teary-eyed, overwhelmed with gratitude for what Peter did.

"Phoebe, let's go, " Beck said, grabbing her and leading her to the exit. Slap!

"Don't touch me!" Phoebe said hatefully. "I never want anything to do with you and I never want to see you again! We're done!"

"Peter, " she said as she walked over to him. "Thank you so much for what you did."

"No need to thank me, " Peter replied, shaking her hand. "I'm just doing my job. I'm a security guard, remember?"

"I'm sorry for what I said before. I was a snob and I was wrong about you, " Phoebe said, her face turning scarlet.

"No problem. Apology accepted. But I do hope that you find a better man, next time, " said Peter.

"Thank you, thank you so much, " Phoebe said, bowing and then turning away to leave.

Peter and Bella followed soon after.

"What you did was really nice, Peter. If I hadn't come, I'm pretty sure she would have fallen in love with you already. Are you sad?"

Bella teased as she walked close to Peter, playfully pinching his waist.

"What makes you say that? I'm not that kind of guy, okay. I didn't want to sleep with her!" he replied. Her pinch was painful! "Oh, come on. I mean it, I don't like her! You're way more beautiful than she is!"

"Really, now? Well, I saw you touch her body a while ago, " she said, pinching harder.

'What? She saw that?'

Peter felt a jolt of panic. Keeping his composure, he replied calmly, "That's not true. I only held her so she wouldn't fall to the ground."

"Okay, fine. I forgive you. But you'd better not touch another woman again, or I'll chop your balls off."

"Yes, my queen."

After giving him a fair warning, Bella left and started socializing with the other party guests.

Peter rubbed his painful waist and walked around until he found a corner where he could sit down. 'What a bitch! That was so painful! Why is she so controlling? I'm just her driver, she has no right to do that to me!'

It was fortunate that because of the size of the hall, a commotion as small as what happened earlier didn't cause much of a disturbance.

No one recognized Peter on the other side of the hall.

Unknown to Peter, though, was that it was rare for people in these kinds of gatherings to sit down.

So being the only one seated made people look at him, puzzled. He was clearly out of place.

Peter, on the other hand, was still very angry with Bella for what she did, and he needed to let it out really badly. He went to the buffet table and started to eat as much food as he could.

Suddenly, Peter caught a glimpse of something shiny from the corner of his eye.

Quickly checking to see what it was, he found a fork on the table, Right where he was sitting!

'Damn it! Who did this? That almost got me killed!'

Before Peter could say anything, he spotted a swift movement at his periphery â€" an attack!

"Fuck!"

Peter exclaimed, barely avoiding the attack.

Finally seeing the source of the blows, Peter found himself gazing at a breathtakingly beautiful girl with perfect features. He was stunned.

She looked like an angel, except that her eyes were cold and showed little emotion, just like a robot.

She wore a white T-shirt and a pair of jeans that fit tightly around her two long legs. Peter almost lost his mind.

The girl, on the other hand, looked at Peter, somewhat surprised at his quick reflexes.

"Are you insane? Why did you do that?" Peter yelled at her. If she weren't this beautiful, he would have already kicked her ass.

The girl frowned as she prepared to deliver another kick to Peter's head.

'Fuck, crazy bitch!'

Peter grabbed her leg the moment it swung toward him.

The force was so strong that it pushed him to step back.

'Oh, wow. She can fight!'

Peter didn't expect that! This was the first time Peter met someone who could fight like this in the Golden City.

Equally shocked, the girl didn't expect Peter to be a challenging opponent! Angrily, she swung with her right hand attempted to hit his head.

The punch was strong

And it hit him cleanly.

"You're insane!" Peter cursed, pushed the girl to the sofa, and started to walk away.

"I have to get away from this place!"

He thought, irritated at tonight's turn of events.

"Stop!" The girl lunged forward, stood in front of Peter, and held a gun to his head.

Peter's expression changed abruptly.

Chapter 40 Felix Yang
"Are you crazy?" Peter screamed as he charged towards the girl like a cheetah.

Moving was difficult after all the food he ate, but the adrenaline of having a gun pointed to his head got the better of him.

Surprised by his sudden move, the girl attempted to pull the trigger, But Peter was too fast. Before she could do anything, he used his hand to slash the weapon out of her by hitting her wrist.

Pak!

Before she knew it, the gun fell to the ground. On reflex, she backed up quickly and lifted her knee, throwing Peter a kick!

"You're insane!" Peter said angrily as he deflected the woman's kick and counterattacked with a strong shove.

Unable to avoid it, she fell to the sofa, infuriated.

As she was about to push herself up, she heard a slam and a burning pain swept through her body.

In a flash, Peter disappeared.

"Asshole!" she cursed, and then she saw a bright flash of light.

"Woah! Who is that guy beating up that beautiful woman?"

"I can't believe he hit the director! My goodness!"

"This world is crazy!"

Onlookers were dumbfounded with what they saw.

Indifferent to their reactions, Peter slapped the woman and immediately made his escape.

He'd be dead if he stayed longer.

He wasn't a fool. That was no ordinary woman. She fought too well and it was clear that she was known to the people at the party.

He didn't want any more trouble, and he didn't want to get Bella into trouble simply by being associated with him.

Before he reached the exit, a group of young men arrived, catching the attention of the people at the party.

The young men had an air of arrogance. Clearly, they were of strong influence and possibly from a prominent background.

The guy at the center was about 1.8 meters tall. He wore a white sleek suit and was extremely handsome. The women swooned.

"Oh my, he's so hot!"

"Is that Felix Yang?"

"It's him! The legendary Felix Yang. Oh, he's so dreamy!"

Admirers started to scream and those who knew who he was looked at him with astonishment. It seemed that it wasn't usual for him to grace such events with his presence.

Peter inspected Felix Yang's companions and felt a rush of panic when he realized that Frank was one of them. Perhaps Felix Yang was here to take revenge for his friend's injuries.

Frank knew who Bella was but he did not hesitate to fight Peter. Felix Yang could be worse because unlike Frank, he wasn't afraid of Bella.

"That's him!" Even before Peter thought of hiding, Frank, with his swollen face, jumped out and pointed at Peter.

In an instant, Felix Yang and all the people in the crowd had their eyes on Peter.

The people who witnessed the skirmish that night felt worried about what would happen next.

In their eyes, the toad who ate swan meat might be kicked out of the bucket this time. Once Felix Yang was involved, even Bella couldn't protect Peter.

"You beat up Frank?" Felix Yang asked in a chilly voice as he walked up to Peter.

"Go away. I don't want to fight, I have better things to do, " Peter said grudgingly and intended to leave. He had no intention to fight with these guys.

Since he was discovered, there was no need to hide.

The girl with the gun scared Peter more than these guys did.

Felix Yang stood in front of Peter, blocking his way. "You hit my man, don't you think you owe me an explanation?"

In Felix Yang's eyes, Peter was afraid of him and wanted to leave this instant. Peter was only a security guard. He only survived the skirmish with Frank because Bella got between them. How could he possibly stand a chance against this group?

"What explanation do you want?" Peter asked patiently.

"Frank is one of my dogs. You know how the saying goes, 'when you hit a dog, you answer to its owner'. I'm not going to let you do that to my dog. Don't worry, what I want is simple. I just want you to kneel, bow your head to the ground three times, and slap yourself three times, and we'll forget this ever happened, "

Felix Yang said calmly.

"You're crazy, " Peter said angrily. "Get out of the way or I'll beat both you and your dog."

Bang!

The whole room was stunned.

'Wow, this guy is insane! Did he really think he could do whatever he wanted just because he had Bella?

How could he talk to Felix Yang like that? Does he have a death wish?

Any sane person who cared for his life would know when to shut up. This guy looks like he's asking for it!'

The same thoughts echoed in everyone's head.

"You are a funny guy, Peter Wang. No one has ever talked to me like that! Very interesting!" Felix Yang replied sarcastically.

"Can you stop showing off? Let's fight if you want to fight. If not, then I'd suggest you get out of the way, "

Peter said while also checking his periphery for the bitch with the gun.

"Alright, I've had enough." Felix Yang's eyes darkened. "Kill him!"

At his leader's command, a tall and muscular goon behind him charged at Peter.

The bodyguard, without any hesitation, slammed toward Peter, eyes full of disdain.

His arm was large as an adult's calf, and his fist was as heavy as an iron ball. Everyone held their breath while some closed their eyes. They couldn't bear to watch.

Wasting no time, Peter balled up his own fist and threw it at the beast in front of him.

Phew!

The sound of wind resounded as his fist hit the bodyguard's directly.

'This guy is clearly insane, '

Everyone thought.

Crrkk!

A crisp sound of a broken bone echoed in the room.

Frank laughed hysterically. "You idiot! Mr. Yang's bodyguard is a soldier from the special forces! You're nothing but a security guard, you're no match for him! See, now your arm is broken!"

"Ahhhhhh!" someone screamed.

"You deserve it!" Frank said in triumph before he
turned pale with what unfolded in front of him. He
was stunned as if he saw a ghost.

The big burly bodyguard fell to the ground clutching
at his arm, filling the room with an ear-splitting
cry of pain.

Everyone was dumbfounded.

Chapter 41 Brandon The Tough Guy
Felix's face felt hot as if he'd been slapped
severely.

Not only did he fail to do what was asked of him, he
also made such a big fool of himself in front of the
Golden City's elites.

He would have felt better losing to him if Peter had
a prominent status; instead, he was a useless
security guard who happened to have an influential
girlfriend. Losing to him in a fight was extremely
embarrassing.

"You're a tough guy, aren't you? Boys! Get him!"
Felix was so angry that he didn't even bother
containing it. With no restraint, he waved and
ordered his men to take Peter on.

In an attempt to save face in the eyes of Golden
City's celebrities, he was determined to defeat
Peter no matter what.

Following Felix's orders, four men in suits jumped out of the crowd and rushed towards Peter.

They all looked like experienced fighters. Their reflexes were fast and their forms were on point even in a messy skirmish â€" a result that only extensive training could bring.

"Who dares to hurt my brother?" Just as they were about to charge and as Peter prepared to fight, a loud voice echoed through the hall

Along with a loud slam and a rush of people coming in.

"Hey! I'm standing right here!" the man said kicking over a table. "I want to see who dares to touch my brother!" The man strode towards them, standing tall and proud. He had an air of superiority that was hard not to notice.

Everyone looked at him puzzled.

Despite his authoritative demeanor, no one knew who he was. It was only by the way that he spoke did they concur that he must be someone of influence.

Peter felt very curious at his unexpected appearance.

Felix looked at him intently. Clearly, he knew who the man was, and he was not pleased.

Frank was looking forward to seeing Peter down and defeated. He was eager to get his revenge through his four bodyguards. What happened next was truly unexpected.

"Who are you? How dare you talk to Felix like that! Do you want to die?" he shouted at the man. 'Who does this stranger think he is?' he thought to himself.

He was clearly a nobody since no one in this party seemed to know him. Frank knew every influential person in the Golden City, including the most elusive ones. Even if not everyone knew him, he made sure that he was familiar with every person who mattered. He was sure that he should be able to recognize him if he were someone of importance.

When the young man saw Frank, he rushed over and kicked him.

Frank didn't see it coming. What kind of lunatic would do that at the blink of an eye? Before he could react, he had his face to the ground. The young man stepped on his face and looked at him with disdain.

"You don't get to talk to me like that, Frank. Who do you think you are?"

Frank turned red and tried to get up, but the man's foot pressed down on him harder. He felt even more embarrassed when he saw that the man knew who he was.

"Brandon Chu, that's enough." Felix said through gritted teeth. He was very angry.

"Too much?" Brandon Chu grinned and stepped forward. "Felix Yang, you're about to beat my brother up. Do you expect me to just stand and watch?"

"This guy is your brother?" Felix couldn't believe it. "He's your brother? All I knew was that he's a security guard in Silvermand Group, and that he's with Bella Song. How was I supposed to know that a useless man like him is your brother?"

Felix was very angry. He and Brandon Chu had had friction for the longest time. He felt sure that Brandon Chu only wanted to embarrass him in public.

He wanted to punch him so badly for intruding in his affairs in front of all these people, but he knew it would be a bad idea. The people didn't know who Brandon Chu was, but he did.

"He's a security guard? And he's with Bella Song? And he's… useless?" Brandon Chu paused and laughed out loud. Turning to Peter, he said, "Brother, you are unbelievable! I can't believe you're with Bella Song! I've heard about her, she's famous in the Golden City. You lucky bastard, I'm proud of you!"

Before Peter could respond, he turned back at Felix.

"I saw my brother today and I'm in a good mood. I don't feel like beating you up now. Get out of my sight and bring him with you, before I change my mind. The next time I hear about you wanting to hurt my brother, I'll be sure to get to you first."

"Are you sure about this Brandon? You'd rather help this security guard and go against me?" Felix asked against gritted teeth. He obviously had no intention of leaving yet.

Pak!

He got a loud slap in response.

Brandon Chu glared at him. "Are you going out, or do I need to pull you out of here myself?"

Felix covered his face out of frustration. He looked at Brandon Chu wordlessly and turned to leave.

He has already embarrassed himself enough. Staying would only make matters worse. Who could have thought Brandon Chu would do this to him?

No one would have predicted what happened, especially Frank, whose face right now was difficult to decipher.

He didn't expect that Felix would be the one leaving in defeat. As for the rest of the crowd, despite their confusion about Brandon Chu's identity, they were all pretty sure they wanted to be on his good side.

Indifferent to the reaction of everyone around him, Brandon Chu turned to Peter, seemingly pleased.

"It's great to finally find you, brother. I knew you'd come here. By the way, what's your name?"

The people watching were all dumbfounded when they heard this.

'What is happening? He's been saying that Peter was his brother but he doesn't know his name?'

Felix heard it too as he was almost out the door. He was so surprised that he almost fell to the ground.

What a disgrace!

He felt so confused!

"I'm Peter Wang, " he said. Brandon Chu was such a big help, and it would have been rude not to answer.

"Peter Wang! That's a good name!" Brandon exclaimed, making the people around him even more puzzled than they already were.

Peter rolled his eyes and thought, 'Is this fellow laughing at his name?'

"Peter, who is this beautiful lady? Aren't you going to introduce me?" Just as Peter was already considering to slap Brandon Chu, Bella walked over with a big smile across her face.

She saw what happened. In truth, Bella was in panic when she saw Felix appeared.

She was fully aware of Felix's reputation and she knew that it was a bad idea to offend him.

All the while, she was trying to think of how she could help Peter. It was lucky that Brandon Chu appeared.

His strong entrance shocked her, but even more so, Peter was associated with such a powerful personality.

"You must be my brother's girlfriend. I've heard many rumors about your beauty, and now I see that they were all true. I'm Brandon Chu, Peter's brother."

Brandon Chu said, greeting Bella with a big, warm smile.

"It's amazing how my security guard brother landed a girl like you, " he added.

'Why is this guy so friendly?' Peter thought.

"Hi, Brandon. It's great to meet you." Bella replied with a giggle and sat down with both of them.

As Peter sat, he felt someone's cold glare, not far away from him. Turning his head, he saw who it was. He broke into cold sweat.

Chapter 42 Don't Provoke Her

A woman of indescribable beauty appeared before him, But at the moment, Peter could not appreciate the sight of her. 'This is too strange, why is this crazy woman here?'

He felt relieved that, at least, she wasn't armed.

Brandon noticed Peter's face going pale and followed the direction of where he was looking. It looked like he saw a ghost!

"Do you know that crazy woman?" Peter asked.

"Crazy woman?" Brandon jumped in surprise. "Keep it down and don't let her hear us, otherwise we're dead meat!"

"We'd better get out of here! Hurry! Don't say I didn't warn you: do not provoke her!"

After saying that, Brandon left like a mouse that caught sight of a cat.

Peter decided it was best not to ask any more questions. He pulled Bella to leave as well.

He knew it would be a bad idea to stay longer when he saw the woman. It was just too dangerous! Who knew what she'd do next? What if she suddenly decided to shoot him again!

Realizing that something was wrong, Bella also looked at the beautiful woman and wordlessly allowed Peter to pull her away.

She was startled!

Who was that? Even Bella felt jealous when she saw her. Even tough guy Brandon, who didn't give a shit about Felix, was scared of her!

"Who the hell is that woman? Do you know her?" Peter asked after they left the hotel. He was very curious about her identity.

"I only know that she's the current police chief of Golden City Police, but that's about everything I know about her."

"I also know that she's a person you do not want to mess with, so don't try her!" "Peter, I'm telling you, do not provoke her! We'll both die if you do!'

Brandon said once again.

"Police chief?" Peter couldn't believe it. "That can't be true! How can such a person be the police chief? The city will be in chaos!"

Peter was very confused. 'A woman that took out a gun on a whim is the police chief? This cannot end well.'

He felt very worried about the security of Golden City.

"Yes, well, there's really nothing we can do. Forget her! Just don't get in her way. Anyway, it's been a while. Why don't we go to a bar and catch up?"

Brandon said, changing the topic.

His sheepish grin was a giveaway his other motive about going to the bar.

Peter was about to say yes but he felt a pang of pain on his waist. Bella rejected Brandon's invitation for Peter. "It's getting late, Brandon. Forget about the bar, let's go home and rest. We can catch up tomorrow."

"Oh, right! My brother has a beautiful girlfriend like you. No one in the bar could possibly match that! Besides, he's only devoted to you. My brother is not a playboy."

Peter wanted to kick Brandon's ass. Why was he talking so much bullshit?

Peter and Bella parted ways with Brandon and got in the Hummer.

As soon as they entered the car, Peter proposed with a grin, "Miss Song, look, it's been a long night. Why don't we find a place to unwind?"

"Great idea." Bella smiled. Her flushed cheeks from the alcohol made her look cuter. "But before going somewhere else, I want to ask you something, dear, " Bella said raising a crooked finger at Peter.

Peter's heart beat faster. He swallowed hard. "What is it?"

"Who is Brandon Chu?" she asked, looking at him with charming eyes.

She couldn't help but wonder about Peter and how he seemed to attract trouble one after another within only a few days. There must be more to him than what he seemed.

"I don't know, " Peter answered honestly.

"Damn it!" Bella curled up her fingers and pouted her lips grudgingly like a spoiled brat. "We already have this relationship, can't you tell me everything?"

"I really don't know, " Peter said, frustrated, thinking, 'I'm telling the truth, why doesn't she believe me?' But then he grinned again. ??"It doesn't matter. Let's just focus on finding a place where we can go right now so we can finally have a great night."

"Get out of my car!" Bella yelled, suddenly looking furious.

"Huh? Why?" Peter asked, confused. "Why don't you believe me? You can't just get rid of me without a plan, flying by the seat of your pants! I really don't know who he is!"

"Flying by the seat of my pants? How dare you!" Bella raised her leg and pulled one of her shoes off, wanting to hit Peter on reflex. 'Who does he think he is?'

"Oh yeah, I forgot you're not wearing pants! Anyway, it's not nice to raise your legs when you're wearing a skirt, too! Wow, how ladylike, that's so attractive!"

Peter said sarcastically. Before Bella could do anything else, he opened the door and got out of the car.

"Bastard!" Bella shouted after him, angry and embarrassed.

Many people lay sleepless that night, bothered by its events.

Peter's name spread all over Golden City, and he became instantly notorious to the city's rich bachelors.

Think of it: a mere security guard managed to gain the favor of one of the city's most sought-after women, Bella Song. He'd definitely be impossible to ignore.

Moreover, he bested Frank and Felix both in courting Bella and in fighting. Surely he would be the talk of the town.

Peter became a legend to the rich young men, overnight. Everyone was curious about the ordinary man who bagged this extraordinary goddess. Did he have three heads and six arms? How did he beat up so many strong men?

Alfred went into a fit in the hospital upon hearing the news, breaking everything in his way.

It was common knowledge in the Golden City that Alfred and Bella were once engaged. It felt like a huge slap in the face when he found out that Bella was flaunting her new security guard lover all over the city.

Now, Alfred was known as the loser â€" the city elite's most famous cuckold.

"Just you wait, Peter Wang and Bella Song. I am going to kill you both! I won't stop until you're both dead!" His resentful words echoed throughout the whole hospital ward.

"Mr. Gao, it seems you need some help." Three young men entered.

"Fuck off!" he shouted at his unexpected guests. ?'Not even knocking? Who the fuck are these assholes?' Realizing who they were, he stopped abruptly.

He knew these men.

One was Frank, and next to him was Felix.

Both of them were respectfully tailing an obviously powerful young man. He stood tall and walked with his chin up, proud as a king.

"Who are you? If you've come to remind me of what a loser I am, please leave, " Alfred said, trying to control his anger.

"It doesn't matter who I am. What matters is that we have a common enemy, " the young man said, looking at Alfred.

"Peter Wang?" Alfred asked, grinding his teeth with fury.

Chapter 43 Being Despicable Is Being Unbeatable
"Daaaad! It's for you!" Peter woke up from his ringtone abruptly, ending his dream. 'This sucks!' was the first thought in his head.

"Who is this?" Peter answered impatiently.

"Peter, my mom is very ill. Please come to the hospital and treat her. NOW!" The anxious voice from the other end of the line immediately sobered Peter up.

Not bothering to change or shower, Peter rushed to the hospital.

The girl who called was Audrey. He couldn't understand why Grace's illness was still recurrent even after he had treated her several times. The treatments should have been enough to cure her totally.

Peter pushed his thoughts aside. They wouldn't help for now. The most important thing was that he got to see Grace as soon as possible.

"There you are. Go to my mom, now!" Audrey said, greeting Peter immediately at the hospital entrance. Her eyes were red and swollen. It looked like she had been crying.

"What happened?" Peter asked as they were running towards the ward.

"Yesterday, my auntie visited, bringing along a practitioner of traditional Chinese medicine. She suggested that mom would get treatment from that person, and my mom felt too shy to say no.

The person did acupuncture on mom several times. We didn't pay much attention to it because it seemed harmless; but today, her illness seems to have gotten worse!"

Audrey narrated.

Finally arriving at the floor of Grace's ward, They navigated through a crowd, all looking anxious. It was impossible to tell if they were sincere or not.

Accompanying James were a man and a woman. He was clearly in a bad mood, but he maintained a respectful demeanor.

"Dad, Peter is here, " Audrey told James loudly as they approached.

James walked towards Peter. "You're finally here!" he said, relieved. "We're all counting on you. Please save Grace."

"Let me see her first." Peter rushed towards the ward, wasting no time.

Vicky, the woman beside James stopped him abruptly. "James, who is he? My sister is being treated by Doctor Wu and Director Wang. They shouldn't be disturbed!"

She was about forty and had a voluptuous figure. She looked really good for her age. However, her intrusive tone made Peter feel uncomfortable.

"Auntie, this is the doctor who treated mom last time. He can help!" Audrey answered quickly.

"Doctor? How can he cure my sister?" Vicky looked at Peter, unconvinced. "Are you sure he's a doctor, Audrey? He looks too young to be one."

Before Audrey could answer, Vicky shouted at Peter, "Which hospital do you work for?"

"I don't work for any hospital, but I can cure her, " Peter replied, scrunching his eyebrows.

"How can you cure my sister without even being a doctor?" Vicky asked, skeptic. "You want my sister to die, don't you? How could you let a random guy come in and treat her?" she accused James. "Don't pretend like you care! I can see through you, you hypocrite!"

"Auntie, Peter can really..." Audrey tried to say something but she was stopped by her aunt. "Shut up,

Audrey! You're a university student! You should know a scam when you see one!"

"And you, fraud!" she said, addressing Peter, "How dare you prey on a sick woman like my sister. I should be calling the police now and have you arrested!"

"Stop it!" James couldn't take it anymore. "Just stop it. I know you look down on me, but please don't insult anyone else."

"Insult? Well, I'm just insulting you! Who do you think you are? I'm not like other people who fear you, James! It's just too obvious that this guy is not qualified to give out treatments! He's a quack doctor! He will not be able to treat my sister!"

James stayed calm despite his rising anger at his sister-in-law making a commotion out of nothing.

Audrey, though, didn't care much about what other people thought. "Auntie, how could you be so shameless? Mom is in a comma now because of the quack doctor YOU brought. How can you blame my dad for what YOU did?"

Pak!

Vicky slapped Audrey furiously. "Quack doctor? How dare you address Doctor Wu as a quack one? Are you saying I intentionally hurt my own sister?"

Audrey was about to answer when the door of the ward opened suddenly and out came two men.

Vicky quickly approached them. "Doctor Wu, how is my sister? Are there improvements?"

Doctor Wu was about sixty years old and had a long grizzled beard. He had an air of calm wisdom and superiority, similar to Chinese ancient gods.

"I'm sorry. I did everything I could. I should have been able to cure her, but she seems to have received too many wrong treatments before. Now her illness is worse and there is no way for me to salvage the situation anymore, " he replied with a heavy sigh.

Vicky's face turned cold.

Audrey almost burst in fury. 'Who does this Doctor Wu think he is? Bastard! How dare he!'

In her fury, she drove a kick towards the old man, but Peter stopped her before her foot could land on her target.

Peter was about to enter the ward after calming Audrey down.

He wanted to beat the quack doctor himself and tie Audrey's auntie up, but he knew that he had to focus on Grace first.

Someone stopped him again as he was about to enter the room.

This time, it was Doctor Wu.

"You can't go in there, young man. The patient needs to rest and cannot be disturbed."

"I know some good treatments that could address her symptoms. I want to give it a shot, maybe I can cure her, " Peter replied.

"Doctor Wu, this is the quack doctor who gave the wrong treatments to my sister! He's the reason why she's very sick now. I'll call the police and have him arrested!" Audrey's aunt took out her phone and started to dial.

Doctor Wu's grasp at Peter grew tighter when he heard Vicky's words. "You! If it weren't for you, we would have cured Mrs. Xie! I will not allow you to do any more harm!"

"You old bastard!" Peter screamed, fed up with all the false accusations. "You're the quack doctor here! Everything you did was wrong, and that's the reason why Mrs. Xie is in the worst situation now. You're despicable! Shame on you! Get out of my way!"

"How dare you! You can't talk to me like that!" Mr. Wu was infuriated. "Even I can't cure her, what can you do..."

"So what now?" Peter boomed. "If you can cure her, be my guest. If not, don't waste my time. Every second counts and the longer we take fighting, the fewer chances we have for saving Mrs. Xie, "

Peter said, shoving Mr. Wu aside and entering the ward. "Do not let anybody disturb me in the next two hours!" he told James as he was rushing in.

Doctor Wu followed, wanting to fight Peter, but James closed the door before him, guarding it with cold finality.

Doctor Wu couldn't be angrier. "What the hell are you doing? You trust this guy more than me?"

Thank you for reading. Please leave your valuable review. It will help us provide you with more interesting novels. More top billionaire romance novels await you at moboreader.net

Chapter 44 Shameless Quack
"Doctor Wu, I didn't mean that I don't believe you, but you said you couldn't cure Grace, so I want to give others a chance, " James explained politely.

Doctor Wu trembled in anger but decided to stay silent. Since he had already done everything he could, it made sense to give way to others.

"Fine, I'll wait here. Let's see if he is really as good as he boasts, " Doctor Wu murmured and sat at the corner.

Audrey's aunt calmed down and likewise sat with a livid look.

Despite the fact that she was mean to James especially regarding this matter, she still cared about her sister and would take every chance to make her better.

Director Wang followed Doctor Wu out the room and waited quietly.

As the head of the First People's Hospital of Golden City, he was well-aware of Grace's illness and was already convinced that there was nothing they could do.

All the guests in the hall waited patiently. So solemn was the atmosphere that every breath could almost be heard.

Most of them thought the same thing: Peter perhaps couldn't do anything successfully, for he was too young.

â€"â€"

Peter entered the ward and rushed to Grace's side.

Both her breathing and her heartbeak were weak. Although she was in a coma, it was evident that she was really suffering.

Forcing himself to stay calm and focused, Peter took out his acupuncture pins and started to begin the treatment.

Her situation was really severe. It would have been too late to save her had he arrived 10 minutes later.

Meanwhile, Peter was infuriated by the quack doctor, Doctor Wu. How despicable could a person be to danger sick patients?

What the most crucial was to move the sin to a scapegoat by blaming someone else for his ineffective methods. How could such a person even become a doctor?

In one glance, Peter knew that Grace's current condition was caused by the quack doctor's false diagnosis.

An hour later, the ward remained still and there seemed to be no signs of Peter coming out anytime soon.

James' visitors had no choice but to keep waiting despite their legs tired from standing.

'Just get out already if there's nothing you can do anyway. Waiting here sucks.'

Of course, no one dared say this out loud. After all, they were aware that James thought very highly of Peter.

"Its been an hour already!" Doctor Wu exclaimed impatiently. "For all we know, the guy has already escaped through the window! Policemen are already waiting for him outside!"

The authorities alerted by Vicky's previous call had already arrived but dared not barge in due to James' instructions. Doctor Wu's speculation was reasonable given that the ward was only on the third floor.

James felt nervous and also frustrated that he might be right. Still, he decided to not let his emotions get ahead of him.

He had faith that Peter wouldn't do such a thing even if he failed to cure the patient.

Audrey, on the other hand, wanted to curse the old quack doctor. Thinking that it might disturb Peter, she thought it would be best to restrain herself.

Vicky wanted to speak, but seeing James' face, she didn't want to make matters worse.

Ignored, Doctor Wu went back to his corner, closed his eyes and just kept silent as anger welled up inside him. 'Okay, fine. Let him do what he wants to do. And then what will you do after he realized she's incurable?'

He was convinced that Peter wouldn't be able to right his wrong.

Another hour passed, and the visitors' legs were tired as ever. One wouldn't be able to guess how many times they cursed Peter.

James and Audrey were just as uneasy.

Peter only used an hour to treat Grace last time, but now it had been two hours and there has not been an update.

Was it already so hopeless? Was Peter already at his wits end?

Despite his silence, Doctor Wu was starting to feel quite pleased with Peter's apparent defeat.

"I can't take this anymore!" Vicky exclaimed. "I have waited long enough! I'm checking to see whether the bastard has escaped or not!"

Boom!

Just as she finished talking, the door of the ward suddenly opened. Out came Peter, clearly exhausted.

"How is she?" James grabbed him and asked anxiously.

Peter looked at him and let out a long sigh,
pointing to the inside of the room. James rushed in.
"Graceâ€¦"

Tears falling down her eyes, Audrey followed in.
"Momâ€¦"

Vicky entered too, ignoring Peter. "Sisterâ€¦"

Doctor Wu stood up and boomed with laughter. "See?
What did I tell you? Did you cure her? You worthless
piece of scum!"

"Officers, arrest this man! He's a scammer
pretending to be a doctor! Arrest him right now!"

"You're a fraud!" he said, addressing Peter. "You're
clearly unqualified and waste such a long time! You
should be sent to prison!

You're a fool for messing with the mayor's family.
How stupid can you be?"

"You're the one who deserves to be shot!" Peter spat
at him. "I wonder how many people you've tricked to
be this confident in dealing with the mayor?

Do you know how many people die and how many
families are destroyed because of the things that
you do? Even death would be too kind of a punishment
for you!"

The crowd didn't seem to believe Peter. They glared
at him and started to curse.

The two hours that they waited were all in vain
because of his trickery.

Peter was stunned.

'What the hell? I just have cured Grace! What are
they saying?'

He didn't know that his body language had been
misinterpreted!

He took a breath because he was exhausted. He pointed inside to invite them to see Grace for themselves. They must had thought that the treatments he did weren't successful and that he invited them to say goodbye to Grace, themselves.

Hearing Doctor Wu's accusations, the policemen started to approach Peter.

"Arrest the quack!" James finally commanded. "This person is unqualified to be a doctor! Bring him in to have his crimes investigated!"

The policemen started to rush towards Peter in response to the mayor's direct orders.

Doctor Wu jumped with joy. "Look at you now, you arrogant fool! How dare you accuse me of being a quack and a scammer! You can't use me as an excuse for your failure! What do you have to say about yourself now, huh?"

"Wait! You have it all wrong!" Peter cried.

The policemen ignored his protests and proceeded to cuff him.

"Wait, what's wrong with you?" James interrupted, "Why are you arresting him?"

He clearly wanted them to arrest the quack doctor. Why were these idiots arresting Peter?

Confused, one policeman asked, "We're arresting the quack doctor, Peter Wang? Wasn't the instruction that you wanted us to do?"

"No!" James replied angrily. "How could Peter be a quack doctor? He just have cured Grace!" "Arrest Doctor Wu, you idiots! He's the quack doctor!"

Realizing their mistake, the policemen quickly turned to Doctor Wu and proceeded with the arrest.

Chapter 45 Jack Was Humiliated

Doctor Wu was about to resist his arrest when he saw something by the door of the ward that shocked him to his core.

Supported by her daughter, Grace was walking slowly towards them. Doctor Wu couldn't say a word.

He looked at Vicky in hopes of support, but she ignored him completely.

Doctor Wu's face turned pale. He knew his career was over.

"Thank you very much, Peter. You saved me again!" Grace said with overflowing gratitude. She would have died if Peter didn't come to help her.

"You're welcome, " Peter replied.

"Peterâ€¦ I owe you an apology, " Vicky said, embarrassed for how she acted. She didn't expect that Peter truly could cure her sister.

"I'm glad you're feeling better, Auntie. Forgive me for leaving, but I have to go to work. Please make sure to get some rest." Peter told Grace before leaving, ignoring Vicky.

Although he understood that Vicky was very anxious earlier, he still couldn't manage to forgive her just yet.

Embarrassed, Vicky turned red and decided to keep quiet.

As Peter was about to leave, Director Wang stepped in front of him. "Sir, excuse me. I'm the director of the Golden City First People's Hospital. Would you like to consider being a physician here? I assure you that the compensation would be very satisfying!"

He said excitedly. Golden City was a second-tier city, and the First People's Hospital wasn't known in the country.

Having Peter around might help give the hospital a great reputation.

Grace had seen many doctors to have her disease cured, both locally and abroad. She had met with the most prominent doctors in the industry, and yet, they all said that her disease was incurable. Peter was the only one who cured her illness! He must be a really good physician!

"I'm sorry, Director Wang, but I have to decline. I'm neither a doctor nor do I want to be one. I really appreciate your offer, though. Forgive me but I must go, " Peter replied and left the hospital immediately.

Director Wang stood dumbfounded and took a while before he recovered.

He later found out after investigating that Peter was only a security guard. He didn't expect Peter to say no to such a lucrative compensation. He was so sure his offer was attractive.

After leaving the hospital, Peter hailed a cab and went on his way to Silverland Group. Entering the building, he was greeted with a sight that made him really angry.

Twenty security guards stood along the hall while in front of them, Bob was beating one up.

"You are too weak to be the security guard for the reception hall, Jack! Will you be able to intervene if someone breaks into the company? Huh?

You're a fucking loser! Fuck you! Stand up and fight me! If you lose, you're fired! Stand up! Stand up now, you son of a bitch!"

Bob shouted, kicking Jack very hard.

Jack was trembling on the ground with a bloody nose and swollen face. He looked really terrible.

His face red and his hands clenched, he did his best to stand up but failed.

The other security guards watched silently, not daring to say a word.

Suddenly, Bob noticed Peter and shouted, "Peter! As an employee of this company, do you remember its policies? Your shift starts at nine o'clock in the morning. Look at your watch! What time is it? You're late!

You're useless and you don't respect our code of discipline. Because of that, you're fired! Get out and do not show your face here tomorrow!"

He roared. He would have wanted to kick Peter too if he could.

"I'm sorry, Bob, but you have no right to fire me, " Peter said coolly.

"What are you talking about? What do you mean I have no right to fire you? You're insane! You got lucky last time, but now, you were late for two hours. Even Miss Song can't protect you!"

Bob was furious, especially when he remembered what he went through in the hospital because of Peter.

"I'm sorry to disappoint you, Bob, but you can't fire me because I don't work under the security department. You're not aware of that?" Peter asked.

"You've been transferred? Why don't I know that?" Bob replied even angrier because of Peter's composure.

"You were in the hospital. Of course, you didn't know. Besides, Miss Song did the transfer. Does she need to report to you? You're not her boss, are you? Speaking of the hospital, how do you feel? Do you miss it?"

Peter said.

Finally, Bob couldn't keep his cool anymore. "Are you challenging me to a fight, huh? Okay, fight me! Come on, coward!"

"Bob, don't take it the wrong way! I'm a civilized man! I don't solve my problems by fighting. I can't even harm a dog!

I do care about you! I called 120 for you when you fought with Eric and Director Kang. It would have been worse if I hadn't called.

Besides, has Eric and Director Kang left the hospital? I haven't seen them around! Also, I have good news for you, Bob. I didn't realize it, but I got to record your fight! Let's enjoy it, shall we?"

Peter said happily and took out his phone.

Losing his temper, Bob hit Peter's head forcefully.

"Fuck you, bastard! How dare you! I'm gonna kill you!

Are you mocking me?"

Bob was planning to provoke Peter and have him beaten up by the security guards around him when he attacked him first.

Unfortunately, he was the one who lost his temper first because of what Peter said. Totally losing sight of his plan, all he wanted to do now was to kick Peter's ass.

"What's the matter, Bob?" Because of Peter's quick reaction, Bob missed his head by an inch and hit his chest.

Peter screamed and fell to the ground, blood gushing out from his mouth.

"You started this, Bob. I'm gonna kill you!" Peter was infuriated. He stood up quickly and ran to bob without hesitation.

Now that he successfully provoked Bob and he delivered the first attack, Peter could do as he wished without getting into trouble.

Although Bob wasn't at a very high position in the company, Peter still decided that it was best to play smart, especially after his bad encounter with the Deputy General Manager of the company, Jaden.

Peter hit himself against Bob's body roughly.

The reason why Bob humiliated Jack was because of Peter. Now, Peter was determined to teach him a lesson.

Thank you for reading. Please leave your valuable review. It will help us provide you with more interesting novels. More top billionaire romance novels await you at moboreader.net

Chapter 46 What A Powerful Woman
Peter pounced at Bob and gave him another kick without hesitation.

Unable to block his attack, Bob fell to the floor, screaming.

Ignoring his cries of agony, Peter continued kicking him forcibly.

"You're a fucking loser! Why did you hit me? You think you're so great, huh? Why don't you try to stand up now, huh? You're too weak to be the head of security here. You don't deserve to be head! Why are you even still here? You don't deserve to be head of security!"

Peter cursed as he delivered one hit after another.

Bob tumbled on the ground badly after being beaten up.

The security guards were stunned and watched silently as their commanding officer was given the beating of his life.

They knew Peter was strong and skilled, but they didn't know that he was strong enough to do this to Bob.

They didn't realize how powerful Peter was until today.

Bob was known to be a good fighter. What was happening now was truly unimaginable to them. 'Oh my god!' they thought, 'he is really powerful!'

Hearing Peter's words as he beat up Bob felt oddly familiar, 'Oh, that's right! That was what Bob has been telling Jack when he was beating him up.'

Lying on his stomach with his hands clenched, Bob turned red, but from humiliation instead of just pain.

He was in a rage. He wanted to kill Peter right now but he couldn't.

Watching from the side, Jack felt very grateful to Peter.

He knew Peter did this for him. He was punishing Bob for what he did to him.

"Hey, loser! Stand up! Why don't stand up?" Peter shouted as he kicked his belly.

Bob said nothing, failing to stand up after trying to do so.

"You'd better be sure to kill me, Peter. You'll regret it when I kick your ass in revenge. I will kill you and all the people you know!"

Bob swore.

"How dare you threaten me!" Peter cursed as he gave him another hard kick. Taking out his phone, he called the police.

"Hello, sir! I'm an employee of Silverland Group. Someone here just threatened to kill me, my family and friends!

I'm so scared, sir.

Please, I need protection!"

Bob's eyes grew wide with shock from what Peter said. 'This bastard! I'm the victim here! What the hell is he saying?'

"What are you doing here? You should be working! Peter, stop right now! Violence to co-workers are in direct violation of our office policy. What do you think you're doing?"

Jaden suddenly appeared on the hall and started reprimanding Peter when he saw what was happening.

"Oh, Mr. Zhang! I was wronged!" Peter looked like he was about to cry even though he was very pleased with himself deep inside.

"I'm so glad you're here, sir. I really need your help. I was two hours late because I had to do something for Miss Song. When Bob here found out, he punched me so hard! I was scared so I fought back really gently.

Not only that, he also threatened to kill me and all the people I know, sir. And sir, you know you're one of the people I know and respect dearly. So he's actually threatening you too! He needs to be punished for threatening you, sir!"

The security guards did their best to contain their laughter when they heard Peter.

'How shameless!'

Bob was so angry that he couldn't say a word.

'Fuck! Fuck you, Peter! Shame on you! Gently? I'm dying, motherfucker, what do you mean you hit me gently? You did this on purpose!'

Bob now really wanted to kill Peter after witnessing his dramatic act and pointing out that Bob was also threatening Jaden. If he had a gun, he would have already pulled the trigger with no hesitation.

Jaden quivered with anger. "I don't care what happened here. I'm going to call the police!"

"You don't need to do that." Peter showed him his phone. "I already called the police."

Stunned, Jaden looked at Peter angrily and wordlessly walked away.

He couldn't stand Peter anymore.

The police arrived a little while later

And Peter was stunned by what he saw.

The head officer was breathtakingly beautiful!
Everything about her looked perfect!

Her uniform showed her beautiful figure. She didn't
look like a policeman, but an international model!
She carried herself with dignity and authority while
also looking very sexy and attractive.

It was difficult to find a word to describe her
beauty. The only thing that was somewhat wrong with
her was her eyes.

They looked so cold and showed very little emotion.

Peter's mouth fell, totally not expecting her
presence.

'I heard she's the director of the police station.
Why is she here? This isn't even a big case!'

Something seemed very wrong.

The beautiful cop got everyone's attention,
including Jaden who was equally stunned.

They instantly came to their senses the moment they
saw her cold eyes.

"Someone called the police?" she asked as she walked
up to them. While her voice gave them tingles, her
cold eyes set them straight right away.

"I did!" Peter answered. Now was not the time to try
to figure out why she was here. "I called the police
because this man threatened to kill me and all the
people I know."

Peter pointed at Bob.

"These security guards are my witnesses.

If you still don't believe me, I recorded it too!

If you still think this isn't enough evidence, you
can check the CCTV cameras. You can find that he hit

me first. If I weren't skilled, I would have been dead!"

Peter said, sounding aggrieved. Bob passed out. He couldn't take it anymore!

"You, check the CCTV cameras. You, make the police record. The rest of you, take these two men down to the station." The beautiful cop gave orders without hesitation.

"Officer, don't listen to this man!" Jaden protested.

Bob was his henchman. If Bob was taken to the police station, he would be exposed and it might cost him his position!

Bella wouldn't pass up the chance to take advantage of the accident and fire Bob.

Unconvinced, the female cop pointed at Jaden. "Take him down the station, too, " she commanded at her men.

"How dare you! I am the deputy general manager of Silverland Group! You can't just arrest me! I want to speak to your director!"

To his surprise, she smiled with disdain. "I am the director."

Thank you for reading. Please leave your valuable review. It will help us provide you with more interesting novels. More top billionaire romance novels await you at moboreader.net

Chapter 47 Amelia Mo
Peter, Bob, and Jaden were soon taken to the police station.

In the car, Peter felt it difficult to stay calm.

It was his second time to be taken to the police station.

The last time he was really wronged. Today, he only came along to answer questions. He was taken to the city police station before, but now he'd be taken to the one for the whole municipality.

'At least I get a level up!' Peter thought.

They arrived at the municipal station half an hour later. Instead of being taken to an interrogation room, they took him somewhere looking like a training room.

Bang!

The female director entered the room, shut the door behind her and locked it.

Peter was alarmed.

"Madam, I might have been taken to the wrong place. I'm here to answer questions, right?" Peter asked weakly, secretly glancing at the her statuesque figure.

"Fight me. If you win, I'll set you free!" she said in a cold voice as she clenched her fists tightly.

Peter found himself in a dilemma. "I... I'm sorry, ma'am, but I don't feel this is appropriate. I'm an ordinary citizen..."

Pak!

The sight of a gun at the hands of the director cut him off.

He knew he had no choice. "What if I lose?"

"If you lose, you'd still get to leave… but you'll be in an emergency stretcher to the hospital, " she replied impatiently.

Thump!

Peter knelt down and put his hands up. "I give up! I admit my defeat! Please ask someone to put me in an emergency stretcher and carry me to the hospital!"

The director grew angry.

Tired of nonsense, she ran toward Peter, determined to stop talking and fight.

"You broke your promise! I lost the fight, I should be taken away in a stretcher!" Peter complained. 'This woman is insane! She seemed to have already forgotten what she just said!'

Peter jumped up and ran away to avoid her.

Crash!

Peter took the first chair he could grab and threw it at her. His opponent responded with a kick and the chair shattered into pieces.

"Why did you do that? The chair is a property of the municipality! You need to have this replaced, you know!"

Peter shouted, this time throwing a desk.

Crack!

Another strong kick from the woman broke the desk to pieces.

"Madam, please stop! I apologize for what I did last night, okay?"

Peter shouted, dragging a punching bag and throwing it at her.

Furious, she punched it hard and tore it into shreds.

Splash!

The sand from the punching bag poured out like heavy rain from the sky, covering her in dust. Poor lady!

She got sand all over her face and at some parts of her body! She shifted uncomfortably and slightly embarrassed.

"You're a jerk! I'll kill you!" she said in her fury. Unwilling to go on with the chase, she took out her gun and was about to shoot when Peter pleaded.

"Madam, please. Please put the gun away. I'm unarmed but I will do everything I can to fight back if you continue to threaten me with that gun!"

Peter charged at her screaming and grabbed the gun from her hands before she could shoot.

With all his strength, he put one hand on her waist and another at her legs, and lifted her upside-down.

Splash!

The sand in her body went down to her collar and poured out to the ground.

"Bastard!" Red with anger and embarrassment, she clenched her fist ready to punch Peter's crotch.

Quickly intervening, he strongly threw her to the desk and said angrily, "You're unbelievable! You'd be able to buy a new one if you broke your gun, but what am I to do if you break MY male 'gun'?"

She grew angrier when she heard his words but thought it best not to fight anymore.

Peter looked at her with relief.

'At least now she'll keep her distance. She knows I can fight and would think twice before fighting me next time.'

His thought was interrupted by a sharp pain in his arms â€" she bit him!

Peter screamed in agony.

He felt worse when he saw his arm!

His bones were almost visible from the bleeding in the teeth marks!

Peter glared at her with anger but reminded himself that she was the boss here. This was her turf.

"So did I win or did I lose? What do you say?" he asked weakly.

"My name is Amelia Mo, " she replied, not answering Peter's question.

"Amelia Mo? That name sounds so gentle and female. You should live up to it, right?"

He regretted saying it the moment it came out of his mouth and felt very embarrassed. "I should leave whether I win or lose, right? I guess I'll go now. Goodbye."

'I have to leave as soon as possible. This woman is insane!'

"You're not allowed to leave!" Amelia Mo spoke again without moving.

"I've defeated you. You should keep your word, " Peter said, walking towards the door. 'You can no longer boss me around the moment I go out of the police station, ' he thought.

"Fine, " Amelia Mo replied coldly.

"Step out of this room and I'll accuse you of attempted rape.

You have teeth marks on your arm. That's evidence.

I'll post this on the internet and ruin your reputation for sure.

You could still find a job in other cities, but definitely not in the Golden City or the whole Ling Province. You'll be so tainted, no one would want to hire you, "

Amelia Mo said coldly and firmly.

Peter stopped, sweating.

'This woman is vicious. She feels no mercy at all! She's a bitch! A devil! She's Satan herself, For sure!

Bella is an angel compared to this woman!'

Peter thought.

Now Peter understood Brandon's warning about this woman. She truly was evil. It made sense that Brandon didn't want to go anywhere near her.

She was more than evil, she was Satan!

"I don't believe in reason, " Amelia Mo said arrogantly. "You just need to have lunch with me. That's not difficult, right?"

"Lunch?" Peter couldn't believe what he was hearing. 'She did all this just so I'd go out for lunch with her?'

He was totally confused. How could this insane woman be the director of the municipal police station? She's insane! It's unreasonable for her to hold such a high position!

"That's all I want, " Amelia Mo said with finality.

"Okay then!" Peter conceded. He knew things couldn't be that simple but he agreed anyway.

Amelia Mo got changed and soon took Peter out of the police station.

The other policemen sat in disbelief as they saw Amelia Mo go out with a man and ride her private car together.

'Is it the end of the world or are we just imagining this? Madam Mo, who always seems to look down on men, is going out on a date?'

The policemen thought, trying to remember Peter's face. Maybe he's going to be her boyfriend?

The Rose Restaurant was a famous dating place for couples in the Golden City.

Still very confused, Peter followed Amelia Mo to a private room.

They were alone in the room — no crazy fiance or suitors.

Peter thought that he'd have to act like her boyfriend just to discourage other rich men from hitting on her.

'She did all that just to have a lunch date with me? I guess I was too paranoid, '

Peter thought, still unsure about what will happen next.

Thank you for reading. Please leave your valuable review. It will help us provide you with more interesting novels. More top billionaire romance novels await you at moboreader.net

Chapter 48 The Brutal Young Man

Peter ate the meal very carefully and with serious trepidation.

He kept glancing at the door of the private dining room he was eating in, time and again, scared, that it would be kicked open at any moment and someone would show up.

On the contrary, Amelia enjoyed her meal with great comfort and ease. She savored every bite as though it was her last.

The meal lasted for more than an hour before it was finally over.

And nothing dramatic had happened yet, which gave a sense of relief to Peter.

As soon as they left the Rose Restaurant, Peter tossed a question toward Amelia, "Miss Mo, the dinner has ended. Can I leave now?"

Amelia was just about to answer when suddenly her phone rang. She hung up, grabbed Peter and said, "Do not leave right now. The traces of a major criminal have been found. You should just come with me."

"I am not a policeman, you see?!" Peter thought to himself, 'Is it really so difficult to get rid of this crazy woman?'

Peter was in the middle of his thoughts just when Amelia announced, "It is the duty of every citizen to cooperate with the police in handling cases!" Further, coming up with lame excuses, she tried to manipulate Peter. "Are you so hardheaded that you will let a weak woman fight with armed criminals all alone? What if I get injured? Are you so hardhearted?"

Peter had no words to say. But he rather thought to himself, 'This is not the way to cooperate with the cops just in order to handle a case. They cannot

just pick a random guy up from the streets and
expect him to arrest criminals on their behalf, can
they?

What's more, you are a weak woman? If you are a weak
woman, 80% of the men in the world would be lame
sheep.'

Peter just thought about these in his mind, of
course, as he dared not say them out loud.

Twenty minutes had passed when Amelia finally
decided to take Peter to the Harvey Grand Hotel.

"Hello, I'd like to take a honeymoon suite on the
eighth floor, near room number 802." Amelia walked
straight to the front desk and announced.

By now, Peter had no clue what was happening. He was
taken aback and so out of shear fear that he asked
Amelia, "Why are we checking in to a hoenymoon
suite, is it really necessary?"

"Can you please keep your mouth shut! Who do you
think has the final say here, you or me?" Amelia
coldly condemned what Peter had to say, took out her
card and handed it to the girl at the front desk.

Being talked back, Peter felt quite adusted, but had
to shut up obediently.

Amelia swiftly completed all the necessary
formalities required for checking in and walked
towards the elevator.

Peter had no other option but to follow her lead.

The two girls at the front desk looked at them
strangely.

"How eligible is this man that he manages to have
date such a gorgeous lady? That woman is so
beautiful and elegant."

"Well, he must be a boy toy at first glance. Who knows how he'll be abused by the woman. Don't you see, he dare not even take a deep breath?"

"Yes, the boy toy is very pitiful. But it's worthwhile to hook up with such a beautiful woman, even if he's just a boy toy."

Peter overheard their conversation and wanted to turn around to argue with the two girls at the front desk, but he controlled himself not to.

'Who is a boy toy? Have you ever seen such a handsome boy toy? I'm just cooperating with the police in handling some case, understand? God! Why do they have such weird thoughts while being so beautiful?' Peter thought to himself.

Soon, Peter followed Amelia into the honeymoon suite. As soon as Peter entered the room, Amelia almost immediately closed the door.

Peter could not understand what was happening. "Miss Mo, what are you going to do now? Why are we here if not to arrest the criminals? Why the hell are we checking into honeymoon suite and closing the door behind us? I'm telling you, I'm not a saucy man."

"You're not a saucy man? Are you saying I am a saucy woman?" Amelia looked at Peter, her tone as fierce as ever, "Don't think too much. We just checked in to keep a watch on the criminals."

"Can we not just walk into their room and arrest them?" Peter was all sorts puzzled, "Besides, we should keep a lookout over them stealthily with the door open, shouldn't we? How can you surveille on them with the door closed?"

"Are you crazy?" Amelia reasoned with him, "Since they are criminals, they are bound to be extremely vicious and have weapons on hand. What if we run into danger if we rush in?

And since they're criminals, they must be on their guard, of course. Well, imagine a scenario when a man and woman check in to a hotel and take the honeymoon suite. Would they leave the door to their wide open for the world to see their business or would they close it? By leaving the door open, all we will do is raising the suspicion of the criminals, is that what you're trying to do? Why on earth are you being so incompetent?"

"All right. Fine." Although, it made sense to Peter, he still couldn't help but ask Amelia, "When you already have a gun, what are you waiting for? Why don't you just walk into their room and shoot?"

"I'm a police woman, not a criminal. How can I just shoot randomly? Do you have no brain?" Amelia scolded him with a scornful look.

"I..." By this time Peter just wanted to slap Amelia on the face, instead he chose to keep quiet.

'She always takes out the gun and points it at me as if I were a criminal. Now when she actually comes across real criminals, she has the audacity to tell me that the police can't and doesn't shoot randomly. Who is she kidding?'

"I'm going to take a quick nap, until then, keep a close watch at the door, " Amelia instructed Peter, and then lay down comfortably on the big bed.

Peter didn't utter a word, rather thought to himself, 'Well, who is the police now, hmm? Suddenly, why am I getting the sub-ordinate vibes?'

Peter was in no mood to stay close to Amelia so he just picked up a chair, placed it near the door and quietly observed what was happening outside.

At this point, Peter had no clue that three men had just entered the Harvey Grand Hotel. A young man, along with two well-built men, who looked like his body guards, walked in and toward the front desk.

The young man appeared to be the same person who was present in Alfred's ward last night, and even Felix paid great respect to him.

"Which room was taken by the couple that just walked in?", the young man asked the girls at the front desk, in a loud hostile voice.

"Sorry, we can't share any customer's information without their consent." The girl at the front desk apologized and smiled, keeping it professional.

The young man slyly grinned

And suddenly grabbed the girl by her hair and pressed her head against the table forcefully. "Do not doubt it, I'll find someone to rape you tonight?"

The girl turned pale, her heart throbbed, and tears rolled down her cheeks.

The security guards saw this and rushed in, but they were stopped by the two bodyguards.

When the security guards saw a black book in the hand of one of the body guards, the expression on their faces immediately changed. They then complied with the body guards and backed down.

"They... they're in the honeymoon suite, room number 803." The other girl at the front desk shouted out loud, as she trembled with her pale face.

"Very good." The young man smiled and slowly slapped the delicate face of the girl, twice, before loosening his grip over her.

The girls looked at him with fear in their eyes.

To everyone's surprise, the young man didn't come looking for Peter, rather turned around and left the hotel. On his way out, he took out his mobile phone and dialed a number.

As soon as his call was answered, his expression changed from that of being the king to being a slave.

"What's the matter?" A heavy voice asked from the other end of the line.

"Sir, there is something that you should know. Miss Mo... em... Miss Mo, has been out with another man since the afternoon. Right now they are...."

The young man was sweating like a pig, scared to death, struggled to complete his sentence.

"What have they done? If you can't speak in one go, from the next time, your tongue won't be needed anymore." The voice on the other end of the line sounded angry and discontent.

"They... they've checked into a hotel, a honeymoon suite." The young man spoke, as he shivered.

The man on the other end of the line was dead silent.

The young man, even worse than before, trembled more intensely and couldn't breathe.

Chapter 49 The Worst Is Coming
Peter felt uncomfortable. "Why is it taking the police such a long time to arrive? It has been ten minutes, " he asked.

With criminals at large, Amelia should have already gotten here in advance while the rest of the squad would follow.

"What are you worried about? This isn't new to me. You should just stay put, we can handle it, " Amelia said impatiently, reacting to his suggestion.

Peter was stunned. "You can't catch them on your own so I'll give you a hand, " he said through gritted teeth

As he opened the door and walked out of the room.

He decided that it was better to help catch the culprits rather than stay with Amelia for another minute.

"What are you planning to do? Come back here!" Amelia bounded up and seemed angry.

Ignoring her, Peter rushed to room 802 and kicked it.

The door swung open.

Peter froze in shock.

Looking back at him was a foreign woman with blonde hair and blue eyes. Peter seemed to have walked in on them as they were making hot, intoxicated love.

Lost in the moment, they clearly did not expect to be caught. They both looked at Peter, equally shocked.

"I'm sorry, wrong door." Peter quickly collected himself, forced a smile and turned to leave.

Just as he was backing up, the woman stood up and started to charge at him, Exposing her full, naked body. It was enough to overwhelm anyone.

As she approached, she took a silver object from her hair and forcibly stabbed at Peter.

Peter quickly focused in on the object that she was holding, grabbed at her wrist, and slammed her to the ground.

The woman was shocked. She didn't expect Peter to react very quickly to her unexpected attack.

Before she could realize what was happening, she was already down on the ground.

Bang!

"Ughhhâ€¦" she groaned painfully, hitting the ground with a loud thud.

Peter raised his eyebrows. He really didnn't feel comfortable hitting women.

Recoiling immediately, the woman started to try standing up to attack Peter again.

Peter pressed a foot against her body to keep her down. "Please, I don't want to do this! Please don't force me to hurt you, I don't like hitting women!"

He said as he was now charging at the man

Who, at this time, already managed to put on pants and pull a gun from under the pillow.

Unable to aim at his current intoxicated state, he only managed to shoot at Peter's direction.

Bang!

Bang!

Bang!

Bang!

Four loud shots in a row!

Three bullet holes decorated the wall and the chandelier shattered all over the floor, broken in pieces.

The man's face grew dark when he realized that none of his shots hit his intended target. Raising his gun, he proceeded to pull the trigger. But alas! He had lost his chance.

Peter rushed in front of him and punched him squarely on his face.

Seeing this, the man quickly raised his gun to hit Peter instead.

Bang!

A thud.

The man's eyes widened. The gun he was holding was bent by the shackles! Then, a crack and a sharp pain at his elbow €"his arm was shattered.

"Ahhhhhhhh!" he screamed in pain

And received another blow to his nose.

Crack!

His nasal cavity broke under the force of Peter's fist, instantly. Blood spurted out of his pale face.

"I'm sorry. I said I don't like hitting women, but you're clearly not a woman."

Peter smiled as he pressed his foot against the man's body, totally preventing him from making any more moves.

It was hard to believe that these events only took a few seconds to happen.

Seeing what Peter had done to her friend, the woman sneakily tiptoed towards Peter to attack him from behind.

"What's happening here? Who are these people?" Just then, Amelia arrived.

"Aren't they the criminals you want to catch? Well, I've taken care of them for you. Now you can do your job."

Peter felt odd. 'Is there something wrong with Amelia?' he thought. These were notorious criminals. They had been trying to catch them for a while now. Why did it seem like she wasn't familiar with them?

Remembering his desire to stay from Amelia, he decided not to bother with his thoughts and walk away instead.

Amelia squinted at him for a long time wordlessly. By the time she could collect herself, Peter had already disappeared.

She kicked the man and the woman one after the other, took out her gun, and dialed the number of her police squad.

â€"â€"

At Silverland Group

Bella was extremely excited at the big gift that Peter seemed to have sent her.

Hearing about Bob's arrest, she launched the 'Thunder Action' for the very first time.

First, the authorities took him in their custody because of the evidence provided by Peter. Then, they had him permanently removed from his post at Silverland Group for threatening the staff.

Even Jaden wasn't able to do anything because of Bella's quick decisive actions. Powerless, he helplessly watched as Bob got fired from the company.

The news of the head of Security Department quick
dismissal shocked the whole Silverland Group.
Bella's iron-clad leadership became truly visible to
her people and she immediately got promoted.

At the Vice President's office

Jaden was fuming with rage.

Bob was instrumental to him, especially in getting
rid of obstacles when he carried out his plans. What
would he to do now that Bob was out of the company?

This didn't only make him powerless, it also tainted
his reputation as well.

Losing his main resource in controlling the company,
he was afraid that it wouldn't be long until he'd be
fired too.

"Peter Wang! "Bella Song!" Jade cried out through
gritted teeth. He had made up his mind and proceeded
to make a call.

"Mr. Dreamer. My name is Jaden Zhang from Silverland
Group. I need your help, " Jaden said respecfully.

"You know my conditions. Are you sure about this?"
The man at the other end of the line spoke through a
machine that distorted his voice. It was impossible
to distinguish who it was.

"Yes. I have thought it through, " James confirmed.

"Okay. I will send someone to help you in three
days." Then, he hung up.

Jaden put down the phone slowly with bitterness in
his eyes. "You'll regret what you did to me. I'm
going to make your life a living hell, Peter Wang
and Bella Song."

At the same time in the police station, Frank
appeared before Bob.

Chapter 50 A Storm Of Jealousy

After leaving the hotel, Peter ran back to his office.

As soon as he reached the office, he tumbled into Shelly and Lisa, who were just about to leave for lunch.

They were both wearing the office uniform â€" a formal suit with a black vest and a white t-shirt, paired up with black pants.

Under those tight black pants, Peter could see the silhouette of their perfect thighs.

Both of their faces evidently brightened up on seeing Peter. They were both blushing, as they greeted Peter.

Shelly being the blunt one, as always, straight up said, "Peter, I haven't seen you in a couple of days! I missed you so much!"

Peter glanced at both of them and then replied to Shelly, "Woah, Shelly! You stole my words, we definitely have some telepathy going on here."

Then he reached out his finger and scratched Lisa's cute little nose, teasing, "Lisa, did you miss me?"

In her own revolting ways, Lisa announced, "I didn't miss you at all, Peter!"

Lisa was not as blunt and straight forward as Shelly. As soon as she uttered those words, she started turning red and looking away in embarrassment.

"Don't listen to her Peter. She's completely smitten by you. Also, I heard her calling out your name in her sleep last night." Shelly had begun to robe Lisa of her innocent image, already!

"She's just blabbering random stuff, don't take it seriously", Said Lisa, reaching out to Shelly to pinch her, while still feeling extremely embarrassed.

"Look at her Peter, so annoyed! She's turning red in anger."

Chuckling, Shelly moved away and near Peter so as to avoid all the pinching, and continued teasing Lisa.

"You literally provoked me into this!"

"How? What is wrong with me calling out Peter's name in my sleep? You called out his name in the shower, last night!"

"You said you would keep this between us. I'll hit you hard, you whore!"

Shelly's face became red, and waving her arms, she jumped out at Lisa.

She quickly raised her hands in the direction of Lisa to playfully hit her, for saying what she did.

Peter glanced at the two women, fighting playfully. He was shocked, yet happy to see them fighting for him.

He was one charming gentleman.

Seeing that the fight was getting intense, Peter intervened in order to stop things before they got ugly. "What are you both beautiful ladies fighting for? I can take on both of you at the same time, don't worry!"

"You are such a jerk, you!"

Both, Lisa and Shelly, rolled their eyes at him.

Other employees, passing by and leaving for lunch, saw this scene and felt envious of Peter.

A few employees wondered how Peter got so lucky that those two women were literally throwing themselves on him.

"Peter, did you have lunch?" Shelly casually asked Peter.

Peter himself was starving, so he proposed that they all eat together. "No, let's eat together. My treat!"

"You're kidding, right? It should be our treat to you not the other way around. Without your support and help, we'd still be stuck at the front desk."

"Absolutely, it should be our treat, not yours!"

"So, how's it going in the sales department? Have you got accustomed to your work there yet? I hope your superiors aren't bothering you?

If anything of the sort happens, just let me know and I'd be there for your rescue."

"Not as of yet. But if anything of the sort happens, we will definitely call out for your help!"

"All right. Don't forget!"

"Leave such kinds of work for me only. Only if I save you, can I ask you guys to surrender your bodies to me."

"You are a mean man. I won't speak with you."

All three of them shared a laugh and soon left The Silverland Group.

The entire scene had taken place just outside the
CEO's office.

Bella stood right in front of the windows and
observed the entire things, the fight, the flirting
and the laughs.

Bella had been grateful to Peter for all his help in
the 'Bob Case'. But after witnessing the whole scene
between the three, Bella was raged. All the
gratitude she felt towards Peter, disappeared in the
blink of an eye.

"Such a bunch of useless bastards! We pay them for
their work, not for their dates here. Absolutely
shameless!"

Bella was worked up and probably even jealous. She
had even considered firing both, Lisa and Shelly, to
keep them away from Peter.

Peter had no clue that Bella had witnessed the whole
scenario first hand. He'd left and already reached a
decent restaurant for lunch with the two ladies,
Shelly and Lisa.

Soon after placing their order, Peter began to
boast.

Time and again, he'd tease both the ladies and leave
them blushing and giggling. They occassionally
spoke, only to recite single phrases or words like
"You are a bad man", "Repugnant", "I will not speak
to you".

Their laughter spread throughout the room which had
a romantic aura.

Right at the entrance of the restaurant, on a
minibus, seven young people could be seen, with
tattoos engraved on their bodies and cigarettes in
their hands.

The insides of the minibus were full of smoke.

A relatively thin guy ran across the road, opened the car door and got in.

He looked at restaurant with resentment, and then turned towards a long haired man.

"Tommy, that is the man, sitting right there with those two women, who'd pretended to be an underworld don and, grabbed my woman and car."

This young man, speaking, was no one else but the slouch named Mac, who had earlier entangled with Elaine.

Initially when Peter hit Mac, he got scared to death and never thought about taking any sort of revenge.

But that morning, he received a mysterious phone call informing him that Peter was just a mere security guard, not some underworld thug.

After getting to know this, Peter immediately launched a search for Peter.

He spared some cash and hired a private detective to do this for him.

Barely in two hours, this detective had found out who Peter really was. A security guard, not some underworld kingpin.

Initially, Mac had let go of the whole idea of seeking revenge but as soon as he found out that Peter was just a security guard, he got really furious. He had even set a group of people to wait for him outisde the Silverland Group and ambush him.

"You are cent percent sure it was him?"

Tommy asked.

It wasn't long before Peter came into the restaurant, accompanied by two beautiful women. It wasn't really difficult for Tommy to remember him.

"Yeah, I'm pretty sure!"

Mac said, "This bastard pretended to be an underworld biggie, He took away not only my woman but my car as well. I could recognize his ashes as well, let alone his face."

Mac's hatred for Peter was increasing exponentially.

Elaine was his walking ATM machine, and now Peter had hold of her. How couldn't he possibbly hate him?

Moreover, Peter not only robbed his cash machine, but also grabbed his car, which directly caused that his new girlfriend Lily dumped him.

From being a rich, handsome and successfulman who had at all to being a man who had nothing, it was quite obvious for Mac to hate Peter in his heart.

"How do you really wish to take revenge from him?"

Tommy asked while taking a puff from a cigarette.

"I want to scrap his legs!", said Mac without a hint of hesitation.

"For that the price would be 100, 000, and you'd have to you pay a deposit of 50, 000 upfront."

Tommy explained.

"All right."

Without giving it any thought, Mac transferred the money to Tommy, via his phone.

As soon as Tommy received the money, he looked at one of the boys from his gang and instructed him, "You go in first and spot where the target is."

"Okay!"

The young lad replied and got off the car to go inside the restaurant and check.

He returned after ten minutes.

Tommy was informed that Peter was sitting in a private room with the two ladies, all the people present were divided into three groups and entered the restaurant.

Needless to say Tommy was very familiar with these kind of scenarios.

He knew it very well that if a group of seven people would enter any place together, it would make people suspicious and hence, he had asked everyone to dispersed in different directions.

All seven of them, divided in three groups, ran towards to the room in which Peter was present.

Chapter 51 Buy One Get One Free
"Oh, stop it, Peter, you naughty boy!" Shelly said in giggles. "I'll soon tell Elaine if you keep doing this!"

Her cheeks flushed. She couldn't bear Peter's flirtatious words!

Neither of them realized that disaster was coming.

"Tell Elaine?" Peter was confused. "What's with Elaine? She's not my girlfriend. Shelly, we're both single. Why can't we be open to the idea of dating?"

"Peter, you're crazy! I'm a university graduate! A
pretty university graduate!" she said winking.
"Besides, what about Lisa? She'll be heartbroken!"

She told Peter.

"No one will be heartbroken, " Peter grinned. "Isn't
it 'buy one, get one free'?"

Shelly and Lisa hit Peter lightly with their fists,
giggling uncontrollably.

Peter jokingly feigned a scream of pain.

"Hmm, Peter? Is it true, what you said? Don't you
really have a girlfriend?" Shelly couldn't help
asking after they all calmed down.

Both Lisa and Shelly looked at Peter, eager for an
answer.

While they both knew that Peter was out of their
league, they still couldn't help but hope for he'd
say yes.

"Yeah, it's true." Peter nodded. "Nowadays, finding
a girlfriend is like finding a second-hand car. You
have to be meticulous."

"What do you mean?" they asked, confused.

"Society is a big hotchpotch." Peter sighed.
"Actually, buying a second-hand car is horrible.
Previous owners still keep the keys and drive the
car from time to time. They run the oils while you
should repair from the damages they're responsible
for."

Shelly and Lisa couldn't understand his comparison.

When his message finally dawned on Shelly, she beat
his chest gently. "Oh Peter, you're so mean. You
can't compare women to used cars. It's actually the
men who are more difficult to understand."

"Who told you this?" Peter started, "I don't know about other men, but I'm loyal when it comes to love."

"You? You said you wanted us both just now, didn't you?" Shelly rolled her eyes.

"I was just kidding, but I am really faithful." Peter began to explain, "I just really like beautiful women. Is that so bad?"

"Hahaha, Peter, you douche!" Shelly and Lisa rocked with laughter poking at Peter.

Crunch.

Suddenly, the door of the room opened. Tommy entered, followed by seven people before he closed the door behind him.

Shelly and Lisa quickly stopped their laughter, leaning towards Peter, which made them feel less afraid.

Peter blinked. "Brother, are you lost? You seem to have entered the wrong room."

"Didn't we used to be classmates, Peter?" Tommy sat down and looked at Peter with narrowed eyes.

"Don't you remember me? You seem to have lived a happy life with these two beautiful women in your arms. Who are these angels? Won't you introduce them to an old friend?"

He said as he picked up a pair of new chopsticks, behaving like at-home and ready to eat.

His men reached for their weapons and stared at Peter and the two girls. One wrong move â€" a scream, a cry for help â€" and the men would act immediately.

Peter heard his words, knowing that Tommy came here for him, obviously, So he decided to feign fear.

Shrinking back he began to concede to offering the two girls. "Brother, if you like them, I can give them to you. Please justâ€¦ let me go?"

"Good job! You are learning fast." Tommy paused, then laughed.

"Someone paid me 100, 000 dollars for your legs, but it seems to work that you can afford to pay double. I'm sure we can work with that.

Because you're so kind as to offer these two beautiful ladies, I'll give you a 100, 000-dollar discount. Now, you just need to pay me 100, 000 dollars to live."

"Thank you, Tommy. I can give you the money now." Peter nodded right away, fearing that Tommy would change his mind. "Thank you for the good deal, my friend. If you don't mind me asking, can you tell me who paid you 100, 000 for my legs?"

"Well, I am under strict orders of confidentiality. But for you, I don't mind crossing the line. Have you heard of Mac Chen?" Tommy replied.

"It's that bastard!" Peter's eyes narrowed with anger. Mac hadn't learned his lesson. Peter decided to go harder on him so he'd surely learn and stop going after Elaine.

"Transfer the money right away and run. These two ladies and I need to talk about our future together, " he said before he turned to the two girls. "Beautiful ladies, what are your names?"

As usual, Lisa was always afraid to speak. Shelly was more daring and gave Tommy a charming smile. "Hi Tommy, I'm Shelly."

"Shelly?" Tommy muttered unconsciously.

"Good boy! You're smart! Here, have some boiled meat!"

Shelly laughed as he mouthed her name. Quickly, she
bent forward and grabbed the dish beside her that
held boiled meat and hurled it at him."

Clatter!

The scalding hot dish spilled all over Tommy's face.
Tommy screamed hysterically as boiled chilly oil
rolled down his face.

Covering his face with his hands, he felt like he'd
go blind! The pain was unbearable.

Taking after Shelly, Lisa grabbed the dish nearest
to her and struck the young man beside her.

Clatter!

The plate smashed against his head and he started to
bleed.

Compared to Tommy, the young man was fortunate
because there was no hot broth that burned his face.

"I like this!" Peter couldn't help exclaiming after
seeing the two's quick wit and action. He grabbed
the glass and bowl and threw them to the other men
as well.

Thump! Thump! Two young men covered their heads and
fell down.

With Peter, Lisa and Shelly working together, they
took four men down including Tommy.

The remaining three men changed their look, pulling
out three knives as they started to approach Peter.

It wasn't usual for men to touch women in these
scenarios. They were only used to threaten men as
leverage if he was difficult to handle.

They clearly had no clue about Peter's fighting
prowess so they didn't think it was necessary to
hold the ladies as hostage.

"What do you want?" Peter shouted as he tipped the table over.

The three men stepped back for fear of being soiled with the disgusting leftovers.

Peter and the two ladies stood up and lifted their stools above their heads, ready to strike should the men come nearer.

In a flash, two of them were knocked back and one ended up with a bleeding skull.

"You guys are great!!! What fast learners! If you keep learning from me, you'll both be masters in no time!"

Peter exclaimed feeling more drawn to the two.

They weren't only naughty and sexy, they were complete badasses too when it mattered the most. Rare gems they were, indeed.

Chapter 52 You Are My Boss
Despite Peter's instructions, Shelly and Lisa kicked the two men forcibly.

It seemed that they both had violent tendencies. Their eyes beamed with satisfaction as they delivered their attack.

The men who were both trying to stand up fell back to the ground.

"Son of a bitch! I'm gonna kill you, you assholes!" The others shouted in rage, positioning to pounce at them.

They quickly failed and fell down again as Peter quickly moved and kicked him at the belly. Two guys fell down clutching their stomachs as their faces twisted in pain.

They felt like their guts would explode.

After seeing what happened to their partners, the other guys decided to give up their plans of fighting Peter.

Seeing how strong he was, it was a bad idea to fight against him.

Tommy, who finally came to his sense, pointed at Shelly. "You ugly bitch, I'm gonna kill you!"

He shouted as he picked up a piece of the broken bowl and ran towards her.

He was infuriated.

No one dared stand up against him before, and now he was fooled and beaten by such a weak woman!

Tommy looked horrible with the blisters on his burnt face. He looked like an angry demon!

Scared, Shelly hid behind Peter.

He looked so scary that she couldn't find it in herself to do anything.

Suddenly, a chair came right at him and hit Tommy in the face.

Peter did this!

Tommy fell to the ground and screamed.

As Peter was about to kick Tommy hard, a waitress entered, Stunned with what she saw.

Tables were turned over, chairs were broken, and guys groaned in pain on the ground. The room was in chaos! It was horrible to look at!

Realizing the situation, the waitress grabbed her phone and started to dial the police. Peter stopped her, smiling.

"Hi, beauty We're friends. No need to call the police. These men are drunk. They did this. We'll make sure that the damages are paid for."

The waitress looked at Peter, clearly unconvinced.

"Yeah, we're friends, " Tommy agreed with Peter. "Don't worry. We'll compensate for the cost."

They had no intention of being arrested. They only wanted to kill Peter!

They had done a lot of illegal things. It would be difficult for them to get out of jail if they got caught now!

"You may leave the room now. We'll settle the bill in a little while, " Peter said. As soon as the waitress left the room, he marched right at Tommy.

"How do you want to go about this, Tommy?" he asked raising one of the cups in threat.

Tommy went into a cold sweat as fear splashed across his face.

Realizing that he couldn't beat a man as strong and as skilled as Peter, He replied immediately, "I'll pay for all the damages."

Picking up a steel fork and bending it with his hands, Peter asked once again, "I don't understand. Come again?!"

Completely scared because of what Peter did, Tommy added immediately, "Apart from the damages, I'll give you 100, 000 dollars to compensate for the hassle!"

"100, 000 dollars?" Peter curled his lips. "You barged in on our lovely conversation, flirted with my girlfriends and threatened us. You should pay us for the mental damage that caused too! Since you also got us scared, you have to pay for our hospital bills for when we have ourselves checked up, in addition to the salary for the days we'll have to miss at work."

Tommy's mouth dropped in shock.

'Son of a bitch! For shame!

We've almost been beaten to death, and we didn't ask you for anything!'

Despite how he felt deep down, he dared not lose his cool. "I'll pay you 200, 000 dollars!"

"200, 000 dollars?" Peter frowned.

"Please take it! You're the boss. I beg you!" Tommy knelt down and cried. "200, 000 dollars is all I have. I can't afford any more than that. Please take it!"

He felt so desperate because he just wiped his savings clean.

"Don't do that!" Peter backed up. "Don't kneel! I'm not your dad! You're too ugly to be my son! For god's sake, I'll take your money. Leave now!"

Tommy stood up with tears in his eyes and transferred the money to Peter at once, With a heavy heart.

"Enjoy your dinner, everybody. We're leaving now. See you all next time!" Peter said happily as he walked out of the room with the two girls. Receiving the money left him in high spirits.

When the waitress stopped them, he pointed at the room and said, "They're paying."

Tommy almost passed out. 200, 000 dollars was all he had, and now he had nothing!

He pushed himself up and kicked two of the guys on the ground. "Stand up, you son of a bitch! Get Mac's ass here! He owes me 200, 000 dollars!"

"Yes, sir." The two men immediately got up and rushed out to look for Mac.

Waiting by the door of the restaurant, Mac saw Peter walking out with his lady friends unscathed.

"Why are you here? Didn't anyone talk to you?" said Mac.

"No. Who wants to talk to me?" asked Peter.

Mac's face went red from his anger. "I need to make a call. Wait here."

"Okay, I'll be here, " said Peter.

Suddenly, Mac saw the two guys coming out of the restaurant

And his eyes lit up in recognition. "Stop right there! I'm calling Tommy!"

Ignoring his orders, One of the guys punched him hard on the face.

"Fuck you, son of a bitch. Put that phone away and follow me. Tommy is waiting for you inside."

The two guys grabbed Mac's arms and turned to Peter. "Sorry for the hassle. Please do take care. Goodbye, " they said before leaving.

Mac's face went pale at what he saw.

He knew something was wrong. Tommy and his men would never let him go that easily.

'What a poor boy!'

Peter and the girls soon arrived at the office. Shelly and Lisa made their way to the Sales Department while Peter rushed to the Logistics Department.

Logistics Department and Human Resources department were on the same floor.

He spotted Elaine as he came out of the elevator.

"Follow me, " she said in a low voice as her cheeks turned red at the sight of Peter. She looked around to check if anyone was there and then they went to her office.

She looked weary about being watched.

Despite his confusion, Peter decided to follow the drill and move quietly as well.

In the CEO office, Bella burst in anger as she watched them from the CCTV cameras.

Thank you for reading. Please leave your valuable review. It will help us provide you with more interesting novels. More top billionaire romance novels await you at moboreader.net

Chapter 53 The Joy In Helping Others
"Elaine, if you need my help â€" physically or mentally, just tell me. I'll surely do everything I can to help you. You won't even need to thank me. I love helping others, "

Peter assured her as he snuck into her office. He couldn't help but admire Elaine's beautiful body.

The office was a little stuffy. She wore a slim-fitting shirt with the top buttons unfastened, her coat hung on a rack beside her table.

The skirt she wore seemed a little bit too tight for her ample buttocks. On her long legs, she wore silk socks and high heels.

Elaine turned red at Peter's words.

"You're such a jerk, " she retorted shyly.

"Woah, how did you get to know my nickname?" Peter replied in jest.

"Bastard!" she shouted.

"That's the name of my cousin, " Peter kept joking.

"Go die, " Elaine replied, losing her patience.

Immediately wanting to take it back, she bowed her head in embarrassment. "I need my stuff back."

Her words were hardly audible.

Elaine couldn't explain how she felt when she saw Peter. The idea that Peter held her underwear still bothered her a lot.

She was actually trying to figure out a way to ask for it back when Peter suddenly appeared.

Feigning ignorance, Peter asked, "What are you talking about?"

After everything they've been through â€" helping her get rid of Mac and touching her body when he caught her from an accidental fall, Peter felt comfortable showing Elaine his true colors.

Elaine stamped her foot in frustration, not knowing whether Peter was telling the truth or still goofing around. "Give the thing back to me!"

"Oh, dear!" Peter shouted out, "Why did you stamp your foot so heavily while you're wearing such high heels! You worry me! Will you pay for the tiles if you accidentally break them because of that?"

Elaine was starting to feel warm with the concern he showed but quickly turned angry when she realized that Peter was still goofing around. "You're such a jerk! Give me back the thing! ASAP!"

"What?" Peter asked pretending to be confused. It was an unusual sight for him to see this gentle woman raise her voice. "What did you lend me? I'm sorry, I can't seem to remember."

'Stupid Peter pretending not to know! He's just waiting for me to say it out loud in front of him!'

She felt so frustrated and desperate to convey her message.

What she did next was a proof that even the gentlest person can transform, given the right triggers.

In her anger and embarrassment, she took off one of her heels and threw it at Peter.

"Oh Elaine, you were always so gentle! Don't be violent! You're the goddess of Silverland Group â€" always so calm and composed. How could you do that? Are you trying to abuse me?"

Peter caught her shoe with one hand, while the other reached into his pocket, where he took out

A female undergarment wrapped in a plastic bag!

"I was planning to keep this as a souvenir. But now I guess my plan has to change.

Here you go, Elaine. I washed it for you, so you can wear it whenever you want, "

He said as he gently put it and the shoe on the table.

"I need to go back to work now. Take it easy. I'll close the door as soon as I leave so that no one will see you changing your underwear, "

Peter finished and dashed away.

Elaine was fuming.

She was totally embarrassed!

Peter had a really special gift of infuriating even the gentlest people.

He then proceeded to the drivers' office. He hadn't had the chance to introduce himself to his new colleagues, so he needed to meet them finally.

On his way there, he noticed Clair standing at the corridor.

First, shock, then anger.

The memory of her setting him was still clear as day.

"Miss Yang! It's you! What are you doing here? Ohh I'm really scared now, " Peter said sarcastically.

"The last time you gave me a task, I felt totally exhausted. Are you going to continue asking me to do such things? Do you want me to die?"

Some staff that were passing by the same corridor overheard him talk.

They turned eyes at Clair, shocked.

'Who is this employee and why does he seem to have a special relationship with Clair?

Clair is the senior secretary in our company. Yet from the way she blushed with his words, it's easy to tell there's something going on between them!'

Clair's mouth fell at Peter's words. She almost freaked out.

'I didn't know he felt that way about climbing stairs.'

Coming to her senses, she glowered at Peter. "Don't you dare imply confusing innuendos! I just asked you to climb the stairs to get to the 38th floor. Stop confusing people. I apologize for that, okay?"

Clair clarified calmly.

She played tricks on Peter last time but he didn't tell Bella about it. She got a good impression of him because of that.

'Shit!'

Disappointed that there wasn't new interesting gossip, the staff around them rolled their eyes.

"Confusing innuendos?" "I mind my own business but you play tricks on me!" Peter shouted.

Clair did not know what to do. She realized it was impossible to argue with him in a reasonable way. She stamped her foot to let her anger out. "Peter, Miss Song needs you in her office."

"Me again? What for?" Peter was confused.

Clair put her lips near Peter's ears. "I don't know either, but she doesn't seem to be in a good mood. I'd be scared if I were you."

Peter was surprised, Not because of the thought that Bella would be hard on him, but because of Clair actually warning him.

He shot her a confused look trying to figure out why she had to say that.

"Why are you looking at me like that?" Clair said angrily. "I'm trying to be nice here!"

Peter showed up at Bella's office a little while later. Clair didn't put any obstacle in his way this time.

"Peter, why can't you just behave as a good employee of our company? Why didn't you show up to your duty morning? Where have you been?"

Bella asked as Peter stepped into the office.

"Miss Song, don't misunderstand, I did all that for you!" Peter shouted.

"Last time you told me that you're upset that Jaden had control of the security department, so I wanted to help you with that.

This morning I found out that Bob would be back on duty. I deliberately came two hours late to give him an excuse to scold me.

Now, he's fired for fighting. Isn't it great news for us? Miss Song, I'm working so hard for you, putting all my hours on the job. Perhaps you could give me some encouragement... something like a bonus?"

Chapter 54 Beset With Suspicions
Bella gazed at Peter, silent for a long time.

She had to admit that this guy really had a glib tongue.

He could make something illogical sound like it made sense, so much as if he even deserved credit for it.

A man with his talent was truly a rare find!

Bella wasn't easily swayed, though. She quickly put the topic aside knowing that this was the best way to maneuver the conversation. "Don't worry about the bonus. Do well in what I am about to ask of you and everything is negotiable."

Realizing that Bella was up to something, Peter quickly retracted his request. "No, never mind, forget it. I don't want to get into any more trouble."

As she guessed, he refused. Instead of being disappointed, she proceeded to discuss a grievance.

"The past two days, I'm afraid that Shelly and Lisa have not been performing well in the Sales Department. I would very much like to transfer them, but unfortunately, all other positions are already occupied. I no longer have anywhere to assign them.

As for Elaine, there also seems to be some problems with her lately. I'm having doubts if she's still qualified to be a Human Resource Manager."

"Hold it!" Peter interrupted, "Miss Song, are you threatening me? Why are you meddling with the lives of other innocent employees to get back at me? Isn't that unfair?"

"No, it's not." Bella looked at him innocently. "I really do think that they are underperforming."

"Stop it!" Peter said desperately. "Fine, I'll do it! Are you happy now?"

"Well, okay if you say so. Once you get this done, we'll talk about the three of them later." Bella smiled, sly as a fox.

"What do you want me to do?" Peter asked crossly.

"Well, our company is recently negotiated for a large order worth twenty million dollars. It was all settled! We were going to sign the contract tonight, but we suddenly received a call that the cooperating party is canceling their order without giving a reason at all."

"I suspect that Rowen Group is behind this, and they are threatening our business partner, as it's an open secret that the Rowen Group uses their connections with gangs for foul play."

"We're not really afraid of the Rowen Group, but the last thing I want is to be left in the dark while someone sabotages our company. Peter, the business is really important to me. I want you to do whatever you can to make sure this contract is signed."

Bella frowned as she spoke, looking distressed.

"Miss Song, are you kidding me?" Peter quickly protested, jumping to his feet. "I am an ordinary man, I don't have any business background. How do you expect me to dictate terms to a huge company with underground connections?"

"I'm just a woman, Peter. I don't know what to do. Can you help me, please?"

Bella said as she looked at Peter with her big eyes, with a voice so sweet that it was impossible to refuse.

Moved with sympathy, he finally decided to help her out.

"Fine. Give me the information and I'll see what I can do. But if I get it done, be sure to give me a bonus."

"That's so kind of you!" Bella jumped happily, and dashed to Peter's side, stood on her tiptoe and gave him a kiss on the cheek. "This is a small bonus for you in advance. If you work it out, you'll not only get a big bonus, but also... all of me, if you want."

She shook Peter's arms sheepishly like a little girl.

The affair really upset her. As she said, she wasn't afraid of the Rowan Group. Rather, she was afraid of being caught flat-footed while someone was plotting against them.

No matter how powerful and dominant she seemed to the employees of Silverland Group, she really was just a woman at heart.

No one dared to mess with her, back when Alfred Gao was on her side, even if their relationship was fake. Now, almost all of Golden City's elite knew that they were done. It was an opportune time for her enemies to make their move.

Seeing Bella's helpless expression, Peter felt an urge to hold her in his arms and comfort her with his care.

Deep down, he knew that Bella was in a very difficult situation. Underneath her strong facade was a layer of sorrow and bitterness. No one understood her.

"I will do everything I can, I promise. Now give me the information, " said Peter, resisting the impulse to embrace Bella.

"Yeah." Bella nodded, her eyes filled with grateful tears.

She knew she was taking advantage of Peter's incredible strength and previous background, and she was aware that Peter also knew he was being used by her as well. On the other hand, Peter couldn't really blame her for doing what she could to keep her company afloat. He also appreciated her gratefulness.

Peter left Silverland Group after going over the pieces of information handed to him.

The big customer was a Southerner named Carey Wang, a hotshot worth hundreds of millions of dollars. He was currently staying at the Harvey Grand Hotel.

The president of Rowen Group, Rowen Bian, 53 years old, was a native of the Golden City with a complicated background. It was said that even James Xie, the mayor, consulted him for major decisions. Rowen Bian was a real guy who ran the city.

Just as Peter headed out, an unknown number started calling his mobile phone.

"Hello! Who is this?" Peter answered.

"This is Amelia Mo, " said Amelia from the other end of the line. "The two men we caught at noon are killers under the gang Dark Hand. They came to Golden City to kill Bella Song, for a reward of ten million dollars. I know you have a good relationship with Bella Song, so I called to inform you."

Amelia said, her voice indifferent as always.

"What? Someone offered a reward of ten million dollars to kill Bella?" Peter was confused.

He expected Bella's head to be worth a lot, but ten million dollars was too much! She was only a president of a company. Sure, Silverland Group was big, but she didn't even come from a prominent background. It didn't seem to make sense.

Not to underestimate her, but Peter knew how these things usually went.

Something that bothered him more than the bounty, though, was Dark Hand.

They weren't the most powerful organization, but they were still very difficult to deal with.

They would stop at nothing until their job was done when they had a target. This meant that even after getting rid of two killers, Bella would still be in danger. The organization would send as many assassins as needed just to make sure she went down.

Moreover, revenge would surely be delivered if even one of their men was killed. They also didn't take deals lightly. Even employers could still be killed should they failed to fulfill their end of the bargain.

Dark Hand would not stop until their target was killed.

This was why people who were in their circle dare not offend them or their members. They usually worked so cleanly that it could not be traced back to them.

"Where are the two killers?" Peter asked.

"Dead, " Amelia replied.

"Dead?" His head ached. Peter had a terrible feeling about this. "Wait for me at the police station. I'll be right there."

He arrived half an hour later.

Dread flashed across his face the moment he saw the two bodies sprawled on the ground. His worst fear was realized.

Thank you for reading. Please leave your valuable review. It will help us provide you with more interesting novels. More top billionaire romance novels await you at moboreader.net

Chapter 55 The Mysterious Murderer
The throats of both two killers were slit and they
were killed to death without any pains.

Peter was flabbergasted, looking at the two dead
bodies. He was wondering who could have dared to do
such a heinous crime inside a police station.

"Who had the guts to kill them?" Peter said with a
frown.

Amelia stood there, silent and embarrassed. "I feel
terrible, but even I don't know who did this."

After a long pause, she continued, "As a matter of
fact, we know nothing about the murder. Nothing at
all!"

Peter was taken aback after hearing this. "Are you
fucking kidding me? It's a damn police station!
People got murdered here. I totally understand that
you missed out on the murderer, maybe because he was
highly skilled, but how can you not know anything
about the whole scene?"

"I'm only stating the facts here. We really do not
know anything about the murderer. The murderer seems
to be extremely skilled; he didn't leave any clues
behind. Hence, we can't backtrace him. Also, I think
a hacker was involved. As our security system has
been hacked into and thus, we can't check the
monitoring records."

Peter felt as if he might have been involved in a
consipary, somehow.

About one thing they were pretty sure: the two
killers had not been murdered by Dark Hand. They
might be strong and powerful, but they wouldn't dare
to meddle in the affairs of the H country. Moreover,

Golden City was a very small place, which didn't deserve their attention or power.

If the murderer was among the policemen, it would be tricky and scary. Maybe spies were present everywhere.

Alternatively, if the murder was not hiding in the police station, it might come from some powerful association.

As it was way too difficult to murder someone in the police station even if one could follow the guidance offered by the hacker appropriately.

In a nutshell, all assumptions pointed towards the murderer coming from an extremely powerful and strong background.

Peter couldn't really figure out who had done this. 'Could it be possible that anyone knew I am here? Or maybe I'm not their target. I'm just thinking too much!'

"Well, you take your time. I have to leave, if you don't have any issues with that." Peter didn't waste anymore time there and left as quickly as possible.

He'd decided to act according to the situation. Although, Peter would prefer living a normal life, he would demonstrate his courage and power in an event where someone would threaten his life.

After leaving the police station, Peter went straight to Harvey Grand Hotel.

After reaching the hotel, he went straight to Carey. If Carey had been threatened by Rowen Group, he'd have to act violently.

This was the second time in a day that Peter had come to the hotel.

On entering hotel, he saw a familiar image.

It was a sexy woman! Men could melt on seeing how attractive and tempting she looked.

This woman hadn't spotted Peter yet and soon entered the elevator.

Peter kept staring at her until she disappeared.

"Hello, nice to see you again, sir. How can I help you?" A melodioust voice hit Peter's ears.

The receptionist couldn't stop thinking about that morning, as she saw Peter.

Amelia had checked into a honeymoon suite with Peter that morning, while he looked all petrified. Therefore, she thought he was a toy boy.

However, many cops had been coming and going in order to catch the killers, therefore, the receptionist assumed that Peter was a cop too.

She felt embarrassed because of all that she had been thinking about Peter.

"Sir?" Peter was utterly surprised and wondered why would she address him as "Sir".

"Well, I apologize, I shouldn't be addressing you like that." She winked at Peter as she said this, thinking Peter wouldn't want others to know who he was. She further believed that Peter was visiting the hotel for some investigation and she had an obligation to keep that a secret.

Eventually, Peter understood what she was doing and decided not to clarify it to her.

In the meantime he was wondering how could he get to know in which room as Carey stayed. It'd be pretty difficult to persuade the receptionist to leak that kind of information and to let him go to the room.

Well, now that she thought he was a cop, it should be very easy!

"Hi, can you please tell me the room number in which that woman, who just went inside the elevator, is staying?" Peter asked her very professionally.

"Room number 809, " she replied. As the receptionist thought Peter was a cop, she gave him the information without thinking twice about it.

"Okay, thank you. Also, there's a guy named Carey Wang who is staying here. Can you please tell me his room number as well?" Peter continued to question her.

"Mr. Wang is staying in room number 806, " she replied almost instantly.

"All right. Thanks. That'd be all. So, since you've helped me with these room numbers, I will forgive you for what you've said earlier!"

Peter looked at her and smirked. He checked her out from top to bottom and then went to the elevator.

The receptionist couldn't get what had just hapened. Her jaw dropped as soon as she realized.

''Oh, my god! He heard what I said in the morning! That's pretty embarrassing. Looking at his dirty smile, he must have thought I am a slut!'

Finally when he arrived at the 8th floor, he figured out who the woman was.

He was met with disappointment. He then walked to Carey's room, directly.

Peter didn't knock at the door or broke inside. He just stood outside the room door and tried to listen what was going on inside.

He tried to figure out if he could hear any sex noises. Also, he didn't want to barge in while Carey was having sex.

Suddenly, the door of the room next door opened up, just when Peter was about to hear what was happening inside Carey's room. Peter was terrified and was just about to walk away, When suddenly someone called him from behind. "Hey, bro! What are you doing here? Well, didn't you have work? Good for you! I would have called you if I knew you were free!"

Regardless of how Peter felt about this situation, Brandon dragged him to his room.

"Fuck off, will you! I'm not gay!" Peter shouted on him and quickly got rid of his hold.

He didn't understand how and why did he met Brandon here!

On entering the room which Brandon had dragged him to, Peter got shell shocked.

He couldn't believe what he saw. Two sexy women were laying on the bed, half naked! To add cherry on the cake, one of them dressed up as a nurse while the other as a stewardess.

'What a playboy!' Peter thought to himself.

Now, it was clear as to what was Brandon doing there.

"This is my elder brother, Peter Wang. He's also my best friend. We can share anything and everything with each other except our wives! So, my brother, would you like to share these two beautiful women with me?"

Brandon asked Peter, while giving him a dirty look.

"Well, you continue to play by yourself! It's not a really good time for me." Peter was stunned.

"Change your clothes and meet me in the bathroom, I'll wait there. Brandon, I really need your help." After saying this, Peter went inside the bathroom.

"Don't be a mood-killer! Didn't you hear what my brother said? Go and change your clothes, " He instructed the two girls.

Peter stepped outside the bathroom, ten minutes later.

The two girls were fully dressed by this time.

However, Peter admitted to himself that Brandon had a good taste in terms of girls.

The two girls were extremely pretty with perfect bodies. They looked young, and they must be in school still.

Well, Brandon came from a rich and powerful family. He wouldn't sleep with ugly girls, ever!

"Well, tell me what can I help you with? I'd do anything for you! Also, till the time I'm in Golden City, I can solve all problems and everyone shall respect me except for Amelia Mo, "

Brandon said.

"Well, that sounds comforting!" Peter continued, "I really need your help. It's actually very simple. All you have to do is walk into the room opposite to this one, where we are standing, kick the door and come back."

Brandon was surprised on hearing what Peter said.

Thank you for reading. Please leave your valuable review. It will help us provide you with more interesting novels. More top billionaire romance novels await you at moboreader.net

Chapter 56 Brandon's Prestige

"Brother, is the person staying in that room bothering you in any way?"

Brandon couldn't help but ask Peter, in order to understand what was happening.

"No, not really"

Peter shook his head as he replied.

"Then, do you dislike him for any reason?"

Brandon raised another question.

"Neither is true. I don't know him at all, for that matter"

Peter shook his head yet again.

"Then why do you want me to go and kick on the door of his room?" Brandon asked Peter with a lot of annoyance in his tone.

"I want to discuss business with him."

Peter replied, in a heavy voice.

"What the fuck?!"

Brandon couldn't help but swear.

'Is there anyone in this world who discusses business like this?

Is that how people are behaving in the society, or he is the only one gone bonkers?' Brandon thought.

"Ah, well, It'd be to explain the situation to you for a while.

Just answer my question, Will you help me with this or not? If not, I shall go ahead by myself."

Peter seemed to be a little impatient at that moment.

Brandon bit his lips and agreed to go. "Fine, I'll go with you!"

Soon, Brandon walked out of the room.

The two girls laying in the bed were stunned after witnessing the whole scene.

As soon as Brandon reached Carey's room, he took a deep breath, collected his forces, and kicked the door with all that he could.

A loud thud was heard.

Brandon winced with pain of his leg because of kicking the door too hard but even post this, the door only trembled, it didn't open.

Peter's eyes widened and he was speechless as he saw Brandon miserably fail at opening the door. "Brandon, can you even do it? Any chance you are already high by the wine you had? What a shame! You can't even open a single door!?"

Brandon was agitated; he kicked the door yet again.

With a loud bang, this time.

The door shook but didn't open.

After failing for the second time, Brandon thought he'd be a loser if he wouldn't be able to open even a single door. Ignoring the pain of his leg, he kicked the door again with all the strength that was left in him.

He was shocked and couldn't believe that he was unable to even open a door.

With a loud thud!

Bang!

This time, it didn't disappoint Brandon. However, to everyone's utter surprise, the room was empty.

"Nobody? Really?"

Brandon felt stupid. All that kicking for what? To find the room empty?!

After realizing that the room was empty, Peter was stunned. He didn't know what to do. After thinking for a few minutes, he called Carey over the phone.

Initially, he was afraid that people from The Rowen Group would be all around Carey, hence he chose to break the door rather than calling him. But now he was out of options. He had to call Carey in order to find him.

A beep was heard over the phone.

"This is Carey Wang. Who's on that side, please?"

The phone rang three times and was then picked up. A man who's voice sounded like that of a middle-aged person could be heard from the other end.

"Hello. I'm Peter Wang, the manager of Silverland Group. I would like to meet you now."

Peter lied about his position and jumped straight to the important part.

"Oh okay. Well, right now, I'm at the Golden Eagle, you can come over here if you'd like to see me."

The way he spoke, sounded fishy.

"All right."

Peter frowned and then hung up.

He could figure out from the phone call that Carey had been threatened.

"Brother, are you headed to the Golden Eagle, now?"

Brandon asked Peter with concern in his tone.

"Yeah, I'm going there. You stay here and deal with the things I'm leaving behind."

Peter nodded as he pointed towards the broken door.

"Wait, I'll come with you! I haven't gone out to relax for a long time.

The door is not a big deal. I can get that sorted with one phone call, "

Said Brandon. He then turned to the two ladies in the bed and instructed them, "Get ready, you're coming with us!"

Peter agreed to everything Brandon had said, As Brandon might help him solve his problems.

Brandon then made a phone call to take care of the broken door. Later, all four of them walked towards the elevator.

While walking, Peter suddenly frowned and acted differently. He abruptly turned around and kicked the door of one of the rooms.

His sudden action shocked all the other three people walking with him.

Did this guy have a thing for kicking doors? Why didn't he kick the previous door as well?

With a loud thud, the door opened with just one kick, which formed a stark contrast with Brandon's previous three kicks.

As soon as the door opened, they could see a woman kneeling down on the ground with most of her clothes looking messy and torn. Right in front of her, sat a young man in a chair who was pulling her hair with one of his hands while slapping her with another.

The sound of slapping was very loud and clear.

"I was wrong. I was very wrong. I wouldn't dare to do it again. Please spare me."

The woman begged, with teardrops rolling out of her eyes.

She struggled and begged to be set free. The whole was very awkward to watch.

"Wrong?

You bitch, do you have any clue how much shame did you throw my way and make me suffer?" The man looked furious.

"Even killing you wouldn't do justice to my hatred for you. I'll not only rape you, I'd make sure you'd be known to be the cheapest woman in the entire Golden City!"

The man told her, while slapping her face.

He was treating her like an animal, not a human.

Right when he was vigorously slapping her, he heard the sound of the door being opened. He was angry and agitated. He immediately turned around and shouted, "Who the fuck has the audacity to kick my room? Do you want to die?"

As he roared in anger, he gazed at the door with his red horrendous eyes, as if he'd eat whoever walked through that door. However, when he figured out who actually was at the door, his expressions changed drastically.

"Peter Wang?!"

The man gnashed his teeth, with anger and disgust filled in his eyes.

"Frank, I thought that you were just a beast yesterday, but today, after seeing what you were doing, you don't even deserve to be a beast!"

Peter said out loud, looking straight into Peter's eyes.

The man was no one else but Frank. And the woman who Frank was beating, looked familiar as well. It was Beck's girlfriend, Phoebe or maybe it was time to say, ex-girlfriend.

Initially, Peter assumed that Phoebe had no self respect, as she was there to make an appointment with Frank, so, he sighed.

He never imagined for things to be like what they were at that moment. Obviously, Phoebe would definitely had been threatened by Frank, otherwise why would she walk inside that room and face all that abuse?

"Peter One! Get one thing straight. Now, she is my woman. I can treat her however the fuck I want to, you better stay out of it. Besides, whether I am a beast or worse, is none of your business to decide."

Frank clenched his fist and resisted punching Peter in the face.

He hated Peter extremely now. If he could overpower Peter, he would have already rushed into punching him.

"You piece of shit! You are such an arrogant man! My brother will handle you!"

Brandon rushed into the room after hearing these words. "So, you think you can fight me? Come, I will give you a chance. Go on call for help before I crush you under my feet."

Brandon arrogantly bellowed at the man, which perfectly performed his essence of rascal!

Frank was really furious and screamed at Brandon saying, "Brandon Chu, I know that you are a part of the Chu family in Golden City.

Though I can't afford to provoke you, there sure are people who can, you better beware and not act cocky!"

With a bang!

As soon as Frank finished his sentence, Brandon kicked him and laughed wildly. "What can you really do even if I act aggressive? Bite me! Fuck! Even after knowing that you can't afford to provoke me, you still dared to shout at me! Do you wish to die from my hands?"

Brandon continued to laugh loudly along with stamping Frank on his body. "Do you not know who I am?

You shouldn't dare to threaten me, I can literally stamp you to death!"

Frank was screaming out of pain but couldn't speak anything as he was hurting. But on the inside he was an angry mess. If he could, he would burn down everything that lay in front of him.